Gardening Under Glass

Gardening Under Glass

Edited by R.H. Menage

BLACK CAT

ACKNOWLEDGEMENTS
A–Z Collection 76, 83, 84–5, 87, 88, 89, 122, 124
B. Alfieri 11, 18, 36, 74, 83, 97, 124
Heather Angel 106, 112, 113
Ardea Photographics 83, 86
Barnaby's 10
Pat Brindley 53, 62, 63, 67, 69, 70, 90, 96, 98, 99, 100, 103, 109, 122
Camera Press 6–7
R. J. Corbin 37, 42, 43, 59, 60, 61, 68, 75, 90, 104, 105, 110, 111
Crown Copyright 112, 114
Samuel Dobie & Son Ltd 11
Electricity Council, The 46, 48, 49, 50
Brian Furner 21, 102
Stephen Gardiner 116, 117
Glasshouse Crops Research Institute 114
Halls Homes and Greenhouses Ltd 22–23
J. Hamilton 16, 17, 18, 20, 102
Angelo Hornak 115, 116
Humex Ltd 32
ICI 12
IGDA 78–81
Richard Leale 55, 58
Tania Midgley title page
Mid-West Photographic Agency 82
Murphy Chemicals Ltd 113
Oxford Scientific Films 113
Ray Procter 92
F.M. Proctor 48, 50
Rex Rathmore 114
Richards of Darlington 118
Wilma Ritterschausen 85
Harry Smith 9, 19, 33, 62, 63, 64, 65, 66, 67, 71, 76, 77, 91, 92, 94, 95, 96, 97, 101, 107, 108, 109, 124, 125, 126
Peter Stiles 70
University of Reading 45
Michael Warren 72
Elizabeth Whiting 118, 119

This edition published in 1988 by Black Cat, an imprint of Macdonald & Co (Publishers) Ltd, Greater London House, Hampstead Road, London NW1

a member of Maxwell Pergamon Publishing Corporation plc

ISBN 0-7481-0080-6
Printed by Resopal, Portugal

CONTENTS

INTRODUCTION

If, not so long ago, someone had predicted that greenhouse gardening would become one of the top hobbies, it would have been met with as much scorn as the idea of man on the moon once was – yet this is just what has happened.

The vagaries of the weather have finally impressed upon the home gardener the many advantages of using protected cultivation, whether a small cloche, frame, or full size greenhouse. Each can have its own individual and special applications.

Although in the past wise gardeners may have employed cloches or a frame or two, and perhaps have yearned for a greenhouse, a structure of any considerable size was not very easily acquired. This was owing to the unavailability of suitable designs, erection difficulties, and especially to financial problems. Today, with the mass production of simply erected, prefabricated greenhouses and the introduction of plastics, and with firms springing up everywhere to supply them at reasonable cost, a greenhouse in every home garden will soon be accepted as part of the routine of life – along with the television, refrigerator, and car.

The rise of greenhouse gardening as a hobby is not really difficult to understand. A gardener entering the world of the greenhouse encounters a land of enchantment, fascination, and delight. The Victorians appreciated this fully and those who could afford them would not be without their conservatories, which were sometimes very spacious and grand indeed. For them, fuel costs, its supply, and enough servants to look after the work, were no problem, and most prominent households had their 'tropical paradise'. The years following the Victorian age saw a decline in greenhouse gardening, and it was for a long time still regarded as an expensive, rather 'highbrow' hobby. However, the more recent 'boom' has again made the idea of a conservatory feasible – this time for most people. It's now more modest in most cases, and takes the form of a sun lounge, garden room, or home extension, as well as the more conventional glass, lean-to greenhouse. These structures often tend to become the favourite parts of the home because of the restful and relaxing effect an environment of plants and greenery can have.

By keeping a greenhouse frost free or slightly heated in winter you can enjoy growing plants from almost the world over. You can look forward to as much colour in winter as in summer, and you can have a wealth of pot plants and cut flowers for the home. Aesthetic considerations aside, there are many culinary pleasures too: fresh salads the year round, luscious fruits such as grapes, melons, figs, and nectarines, and earlier or better vegetable plants for the kitchen garden. If you think heating may overburden your budget, there are numerous uses for an unheated greenhouse. It can be regarded as a covered garden in which to grow to perfection, unblemished by the weather, most outdoor hardy plants.

A greenhouse, frame, or cloches, can greatly influence household costs. Both food and decorative plants for rooms or garden are hardly cheap. Any structure enabling you to grow your own, soon pays for itself.

A greenhouse or a few frames can make an enormous difference to your outdoor garden. You can enjoy the new varieties and seed novelties introduced each year, and protect and save your more tender garden plants over winter. Today, a frame or small greenhouse used for bedding plant production only, will quickly recover its cost. Many superb house plants, and pot plants for gifts, can be raised for a matter of pence, yet they are extremely expensive to buy in florists.

An often overlooked aspect of greenhouse gardening is its value as an ideal hobby for the disabled, infirm, or not-so-young. It is frequently pleasant to have weather protection for ourselves as well as our plants. Flower show enthusiasts and floral art lovers will also find the greenhouse has much to offer.

In this book we have tried to collect together practical information derived from past experience as well as from modern trends, discoveries, and inventions. This should help beginners to start right as well as being of interest to 'old hands'. We have also tried to sweep away some cobwebs in the form of incorrect or outdated customs. Green shading which is quite wrong, and growing in unhygienic hit-or-miss potting composts using unsterilized animal manures, are just two examples of practices still difficult to persuade gardeners to abandon. In other ways as well, modern research and development, and the work of plant breeders, has made growing much easier for the greenhouse gardener and we have tried to emphasize these. The FI hybrids or new selections of many plants are much stronger and more vigorous than old varieties, and there are also better and universally safer pesticides. A combination of where the advantages of two of these benefits can be seized, for example, is in the case of cucumbers and tomatoes. Both can now be grown very successfully together in the same greenhouse. Foliar feeding using vitamins and plant hormones, and systemic pesticides, which can attack pests from inside the plant's tissues, are two more very useful modern aids.

Cloche and frame gardening is a little 'art' of its own, one that can be fun as well as useful, embracing the production of flowers the year round as well as edible crops. The subject is well covered by this volume, although often omitted in books on general greenhouse gardening.

We also look into the future by including sections on the use of artificial light. There is much yet to be discovered in this field and it gives the ordinary home grower a chance to research and perhaps add to scientific knowledge of how plants react to light. The subject is really in its infancy, and as well as having applications under glass it is possible to apply the techniques to growing rooms or chambers, and places where natural light cannot normally penetrate. Another special section deals with conservatories and garden rooms now rapidly becoming eagerly sought after as features of modern homes. Fancy shapes are rarely desirable for the utilitarian greenhouse and it is wise to stick to conventional squares and rectangles. The conservatory or garden room, however, lends itself to many exciting possible architectural designs which could be exploited more frequently.

You don't have to be an experienced outdoor gardener to embark on greenhouse gardening. Remember that greenhouses can be erected on paving or asphalt, in yards, and even on flat roofs and balconies, where there may be no soil for miles. A greenhouse with no ground soil is, in some ways, an advantage – it eliminates the temptation to use it! Except where the greenhouse is portable as already mentioned, the ground soil in a permanent greenhouse can lead to trouble if grown in. Its use is a common beginner's mistake. The lure of the ground soil is of course greater if you have been used to outdoor gardening. Under cover, soil may give good results the first year and then soon deteriorate. This is called 'soil sickness': a vague term denoting a build up of unbalanced fertilizer salts, waste products from plants and other chemical substances, and possibly pests and disease organisms. Outdoors a plot intensively cultivated can get 'sick' too, hence the practice of rotation, but the effect is delayed by washing out by rains, the action of frost and the sterilizing effect of ultra violet light from the sun (which does not penetrate glass), and natural pest and disease predators. In any case, far more reliable and certain results are obtained by growing in containers of one or other of the specially designed potting composts, and sowing seeds in proper seed composts.

Dirty water such as collected from gutters or stored in filthy open tanks and butts, must not be used for irrigation – this is a frequent common mistake! What is the point of employing clean sterilized seed and potting composts if you do. Clean tap water is much safer even if it is limey. Dirty rainwater can be a 'soup' of infection.

A frequent mistake is to buy a greenhouse that ultimately proves too small. The more capacious the greenhouse the easier it is to maintain a steady environment. In a tiny greenhouse, for example, the temperature can fluctuate alarmingly with changes in the sun's power during the day. Plants rarely enjoy this. Reasonable room also makes working easier and more comfortable, and there is more scope for growing and arranging plants.

A final hint, left last so that it remains well remembered, is to pay great care to summer shading and ventilation. Study this section of this book well. Far too many beginners lose a whole greenhouse of plants in a matter of hours because shading is overlooked and vents are left closed on a sunny day. When this happens the temperature absolutely rockets up, and even tropical plants can get boiled or baked to death.

This book should give the beginner an excellent introduction to the possibilities and scope of greenhouse gardening as well as useful practical basic advice. It is especially hoped that the book will inspire the desire to adventure further and perhaps to specialize as well.

Ronald Menage

FRAMES AND CLOCHES

CHOOSING FRAMES AND CLOCHES

A large glass-to-ground frame, with aluminium-alloy framework, being used to house trays of seedlings and plants waiting to be transplanted

A frame – or two – costs little to buy, or make yourself, and can be fitted into most gardens. Nearly everything you grow in a greenhouse can also be grown in frames, allowing for the restrictions in height and size.
Even if you have a greenhouse, frames can take over much of the work to leave more space for decorative plants and those demanding full greenhouse height.

First you must decide whether to buy a ready-made frame or make one yourself from a frame kit of glass-to-ground design with timber or metal sections. An all-glass frame is suitable unless you want extra warmth for propagation, or for growing cucumbers or melons.

Lids, known as 'lights', can be bought separately and you can place these over your own timber or brick-built sides, or even set one over a pit dug in the ground, adding to it as required. The lights can be easily stored away in the summer, when not in use.

Modern frames are often fitted with sliding glass sides, to give access or for added ventilation, and lights that slide aside as well as lift up so that they can be removed completely for easy working.

Choice of material

Aluminium alloy framework has many advantages: it is long-lasting, requires no maintenance and, being lightweight, is ideal for moving about. If you prefer timber, choose wood that is noted for its weather resistance, because frame sides are likely to come into contact with damp soil for long periods. Avoid soft woods treated with creosote as the vapour continues to be harmful to plants for some time. Green Cuprinol is suitable, but before using any other preservative check the maker's literature to be sure that it is safe for plants.

Plastic, instead of glass, for garden frames is light, easily portable and obviously advisable where small children are using the garden. From a gardener's point of view, however, glass has many advantages (see the section on choosing a greenhouse on page 22). You must use glass if the frame is to be heated, and would be advised to do so in windy areas as plastic can blow away.

Siting the frame

If you use a frame as an adjunct to your greenhouse (and it has vertical sides), you can push the frame close up to one side. This helps to reduce warmth loss from both the greenhouse and the frame.

If using a frame for greenhouse and pot plants, put it in a shady place – against the north side of your greenhouse is ideal. But most vegetable crops, and those alpines which you may be housing

Above left: timber-sided frame, with glass lights, shelters bedding plants prior to planting out. Above: rows of barn cloches protect lettuce that are almost ready for cropping

in frames when not in flower, prefer a bright, open position.

With many frames it is often convenient to set them back-to-back, or alongside each other in rows. To obtain more height, stand your frame on a base of bricks or concrete blocks, or place it over a pit (providing you make sure that water does not collect in it).

Electric soil-warming cables

Frames do not have to be 'cold'; you can heat a large one with a small paraffin lamp provided you take great care to see that there is always ventilation. But installing electric soil-warming cables is by far the best method. Lay them in loops across the floor of the frame, making sure that they do not touch each other. Place a little sand on top and keep it moist: this will hold the cables in place and conduct the warmth more uniformly. Use only about 2–3cm (1 in) of sand, then a thermostat can be installed above the sand level to control the frame's temperature.

If you need extra warmth (as for pot plants) run cables round the frame sides as well. With glass-sided frames, fasten the cables to wooden battens with cleats and thrust the battens into the ground.

If you are growing plants to be rooted into a deep layer of compost (such as salad crops, cucumbers and melons) site the warming cables near the bottom of the compost. In this case a thermostat of the rod type should be thrust into the compost. Temperature can also be controlled manually or by a time switch. The considerable bulk of compost will hold warmth over the periods when the electricity is off.

Wattage depends on the size and purpose of your frame; decide after you have consulted the suppliers of such equipment.

You can use small heated frames inside the greenhouse for high-temperature propagation, or for housing a small collection of low-growing tropical plants. An aluminium framework, glass sides and top, and 2–3cm (1 in) or so of sand over the cable, are recommended. The wattage required is usually about 20W per 1000 sq cm (20W per sq ft) of frame floor, and a thermostat is essential.

Frame cultivation

If possible, avoid using soil. Instead, line a trough or pit with polythene sheeting, slitted here and there for drainage, and fill it with a proprietary potting compost. You can grow excellent, high-quality salad and other crops with little risk from pests or diseases.

Where you are moving pots or other containers in and out, firm the floor and cover it with polythene, over which is spread coarse sand or shingle. If you keep this damp, it will moisten the air in the frame; the polythene will help to keep out soil pests.

Grow house plants, and pot plants like cineraria, calceolaria, primula and cyclamen, in frames until the decorative stage when they are ready to transfer to the house, conservatory or greenhouse. Use frames to raise bedding plants and for many forms of propagation from cutting and seed. You will also find them especially useful for crops like lettuce, radish, beet and carrots that you want in the kitchen even before winter is over.

Keep plants like dormant fuchsias, chrysanthemums and pelargoniums (that are used for summer garden or greenhouse decoration) in frames during the winter when they often look far from attractive. Store dormant tubers and bulbs there to leave the greenhouse less cluttered. Some crops, like strawberries and violets, lend themselves particularly to frame culture.

Keep glass frames (and cloches) as clean as possible to admit maximum light and discourage plant pests and diseases. Remove any mud splashes by careful use of a hose, if necessary.

CLOCHES

Early cloches were of glass and often held together by clumsy wires that were difficult to manipulate. Modern designs are simpler and often make use of plastics, which are very suitable for this purpose as cloches are frequently used only for weather protection, high temperatures being rarely necessary.

Select your type

There are tent, barn and T-shaped cloches, and a flat-topped 'utility' one. These are usually held together by special metal or plastic clips. Some cloches can be opened for ventilation or for watering, others have perforated tops to allow the rain to enter. Plastic ones with a cellular structure give greater warmth retention.

You can make simple and effective tunnels, ideal for protecting rows of vegetables, by sandwiching lengths of polythene between wire arches at intervals along the row, or by aligning ordinary cloches end-to-end. Anchor your plastic ones carefully in windy areas as they can easily blow away; use stones, bricks, wooden or metal pegs, or some special cloche fitments.

Cloches are most useful from autumn to late spring for providing protection from excessive wet and cold. Set them in place to dry and warm the soil before you dig and fertilize it, in preparation for sowing or planting.

Top: tunnel cloches of polythene sheeting are versatile. They can be cut to any length, depending on whether you want to cover one plant or a whole row. Above: corrugated plastic cloches are used here to cover strawberry plants; being lightweight these cloches need to be anchored against the wind with wire hoops. End pieces can be added to give the plants greater protection

Cloche cultivation

Use individual cloches for protecting isolated tender plants (such as fuchsia) in beds and borders, and protect groups of hardy and half-hardy annuals until they become established. You can also root cuttings directly into the ground of a nursery bed if you use cloches to cover them.

Many flowers grown for cutting benefit from cloche protection, especially low-growing bulbs in pots or bowls. Other favourite cloche flower crops are anemones, hellebore (Christmas rose), lily of the valley, violet and polyanthus. You can harden off bedding plants under cloches if frame space is not available. Also use them to protect sweet peas in the early stages.

In the vegetable garden, cloches give you year-round cropping. If you plan carefully you can move them from one crop to another as needed, thus putting a limited number to maximum use.

Working with cloches

You do not need to remove cloches for watering; the water that drains off them will seep into the soil provided that it has been well prepared. It should be porous and moisture-retaining, but well-drained. Work in plenty of humus-forming material, like peat or rotted garden compost. To avoid the wind rushing through your cloche tunnels, block the ends. This also applies to individual cloches used as miniature greenhouses to cover single, or small groups of, plants. When the weather permits ventilation, move the cloches along to leave a small gap between each one and remove the ends of tunnels.

Leave plenty of room between rows for comfortable access and keep the soil along the sides of the cloche rows well hoed to allow water retention. Soluble fertilizers can also be applied along the outside edges of the cloches.

Store glass cloches, and plastic tent and barn types, on their ends and stacked inside each other. For this purpose put down some clean boards (or lay a section of concrete) in a corner of the vegetable plot, and cover it with roofing felt for glass cloches.

HOW TO MAKE A COLD FRAME

The cold frame, measuring 1350 by 915 mm (4 ft 5 in by 3 ft), is big enough to satisfy the most enthusiastic gardener. Our instructions can easily be adapted to different dimensions according to the size you want in your garden

If you haven't yet reached the greenhouse stage with your gardening, what better than a cold frame to give you a taste for growing your own vegetables and flowers from seed? And if you have a greenhouse, how are you going to cope with all those seedlings in it waiting to be hardened off if you don't have a cold frame? In any case, you will be needing as much space as possible in the greenhouse for your growing plants as spring merges into summer.
Like most good things in life, a well-made frame is not cheap, so you can save money by making it yourself.

Tools

steel measuring tape
set square and pencil
panel saw
tenon saw
hammer
bradawl
medium screwdriver
hand or electric drill with 4mm ($\frac{3}{16}$ in) and 3mm ($\frac{1}{8}$ in) bits
plane

Materials

timber (as cutting list)
110g ($\frac{1}{4}$lb) 25mm (1 in) plated panel pins (general nailing)
110g ($\frac{1}{4}$ lb) 40mm ($1\frac{1}{2}$ in) plated panel pins (general nailing)
twelve 40mm ($1\frac{1}{2}$ in) No.8 countersunk brass or plated wood screws (top frame)
twenty-two 30mm ($1\frac{1}{4}$ in) No.8 countersunk brass or plated wood screws (joint reinforcing)
eight 50mm (2 in) No.10 roundhead brass or plated wood screws (final assembly)
2 handles (top frame)
2 sheets horticultural glass 610mm (24 in) square
2 sheets horticultural glass 610 × 305mm (24 × 12 in)
waterproof wood glue
1 litre (2 pints) horticultural wood preservative

TIMBER CUTTING LIST

PART	QTY	NAME	SECTION	LENGTH
A	2	edge stop	25x15mm (1x½ in)	615mm (24½ in)
B	2	top frame rear	50x30mm (2x1¼ in)	1320mm (52 in)
C	3	top frame ends; centre strut	50x30mm (2x1¼ in)	915mm (36 in)
D	4	glass ledge	25x15mm (1x½ in)	810mm (32 in)
E	1	rear panel top	19x150mm (¾x6 in)	1325mm (52¼ in)
F	4	front and rear panels	19x150mm (¾x6 in)	1325mm (52¼ in)
G	4	side panels	19x150mm (¾x6 in)	865mm (34 in)
H	2	side panels top	19x150mm (¾x6 in)	865mm (34 in)
I	3	vertical battens	30x30mm (1¼x1¼ in)	380mm (15 in)
J	2	vertical battens	50x30mm (2x1¼ in)	265mm (10½ in)
K	2	runners	30x30mm (1¼x1¼ in)	785mm (31 in)
L	2	vertical battens	50x30mm (2x1¼ in)	380mm (15 in)
M	3	vertical battens	30x30mm (1¼x1¼ in)	265mm (10½ in)
N	2	capping timbers	25x15mm (1x½ in)	290mm (11½ in)
O	2	capping timbers	25x15mm (1x½ in)	405mm (16 in)
P	1	stop (not shown)	25x15mm (1x½ in)	150mm (6 in)

(see working drawing on next page)

Construction
First of all, check that the space in your garden allows for a frame of our dimensions and, if necessary, adapt the measurements to the area you have before buying the materials. Then estimate the cost from our Materials and Timber cutting lists so that you have an idea of the total outlay. It is as well to check the current prices with your local timber yard or do-it-yourself stockist.

The cold frame illustrated has been specially designed for home construction using simple wood-working joints only. The finished job, however, presents a spacious and rugged structure capable of giving many years of service.

The timber sections specified in the cutting list are standard stock sizes kept by most timber yards, but if you experience any difficulty in obtaining a particular size, then the next available larger size may be used provided that the necessary dimensional adjustments are made to the various parts.

For ease of construction and to make the frame completely portable, it is built as five separate assemblies. The main frame consists of front, back and two sides, each assembled as a panel and then fixed together with wood screws at the corners. The sides, being slightly higher than the front and back, form a recess into which the glazed top frame is dropped. Runners (part 'K') are fitted to the inner side of the end members (see left-hand inset in the drawing on the next page) and these allow the top to slide back for interior ventilation or for working inside the main frame.

The unit shown is designed around standard sized sheets of horticultural glass to avoid the need or expense of specially cut glass sizes. The design may, however, be re-sized to suit individual needs simply by amending the lengths of the panels affected.

Whether building to the sizes shown or to amended sizes, it is as well to work so that one panel is completed before the next is made, and in the order shown. This should help to ensure that any variations in timber sections or sizes are automatically catered for as work proceeds. Waterproof wood glue is recommended for all permanent joints to ensure a rigid structure.

The instructions given provide a frame measuring 1350 x 915mm (4 ft 5 in x 3 ft), standing 430mm (1 ft 5 in) high at the back, coming down to 330mm (1 ft 1 in) at the front. Before starting work, be sure to read through the following stages of construction.

Stage 1 – glazed top

Cut parts 'C' to length and then notch the ends (see drawing) to present a snug fit to parts 'B'. Use a tenon saw to cut the notches. Cut parts 'B' to length, remembering to allow for any variations in sectional timber sizes. Assemble the frame by screwing parts 'B' to parts 'C', after drilling pilot holes for the screws.

Taking measurements direct from the assembled frame, cut parts 'A' and 'D' to length and glue and nail them in position. Parts 'A' provide an edge stop for the glass, and parts 'D' a ledge upon which the glass rests.

Stage 2 – front and rear panels

Parts 'E' and 'F' must be approximately 6mm ($\frac{1}{4}$in) longer than the overall length of the completed top frame to allow this to run smoothly between the side members, so before cutting these parts check the length (parts 'B') of the top frame. Now reduce the depth of part 'E' by cutting a 15mm ($\frac{1}{2}$in) strip from the top edge to provide clearance for the sliding top frame, using a panel saw.

Cut parts 'I' and 'M' to length. These parts form the vertical jointing battens for the main cladding, parts 'E' and 'F', and are fixed centrally and at either end of the front and rear panels. Study the right-hand inset section on the drawing and note that the side pieces must be set back sufficiently to accommodate parts 'J' and 'L' of the end panels. Use a piece of the timber from which these parts will be cut to determine this distance. Assemble the front and rear panels by glueing and nailing to the battens 'I' and 'M', then reinforce each butt joint with a 30mm ($1\frac{1}{4}$in) screw.

Stage 3 – side panels

It is vital when building the side panels to be sure to make an opposite 'pair' and not two identical pieces.

Cut parts 'G' and 'H' to length and note that these should be approximately 50mm (2in) shorter than the overall length of the side pieces (parts 'C') of the top frame. Mark an angled line to parts 'H', allowing the full 150mm (6in) width of the board at the higher back edge and reducing to 30mm ($1\frac{1}{4}$in) for the lower front edge. Cut to the line – remembering to make a pair.

Assemble the side frames by glueing and nailing, then reinforce each joint with a 30mm ($1\frac{1}{4}$in) wood screw. Note that parts 'L' and 'J' must overhang the sides 'G' and 'H' by approximately 15mm ($\frac{1}{2}$in) to provide a fixing point for the capping timbers, parts 'O' and 'N' (see right hand inset section). Add the top frame runners (parts 'K') and then trim the tops of parts 'L' and 'J' flush to 'K'. Finally add the capping timbers, parts 'O' and 'N', by glueing and nailing.

Stage 4 – final assembly

Drill two 4mm ($\frac{3}{16}$in) holes to parts 'I' and 'M' as clearance holes for the 50mm (2in) main assembly wood screws (see drawing). Hold the frames firmly together and, using a bradawl through the holes, bore pilot holes in parts 'J' and 'L' for the screw threads. Fix the frames together, but do not apply glue to the joints; in this way the assembly can be easily dismantled for re-siting.

Try the sliding frame and plane it as necessary to achieve a neat sliding fit. Part 'P' (not illustrated) is then fitted as a 'stop' under the central part 'C' to butt against part 'M' when the frame is fully closed.

At this stage the assembly must be dismantled and given a thorough soaking with a horticultural-type wood preservative. When the preservative has dried, the handles should be added (see drawing) and the glazing fitted and secured by panel pins. To do this, lay the glass in position and with the hammer head lying sideways on the glass, gently tap the pins halfway into the timber frame.

Rest the frame on a row of loose-laid bricks, thus providing a neat finish and also helping to preserve the woodwork by keeping it clear of damp earth.

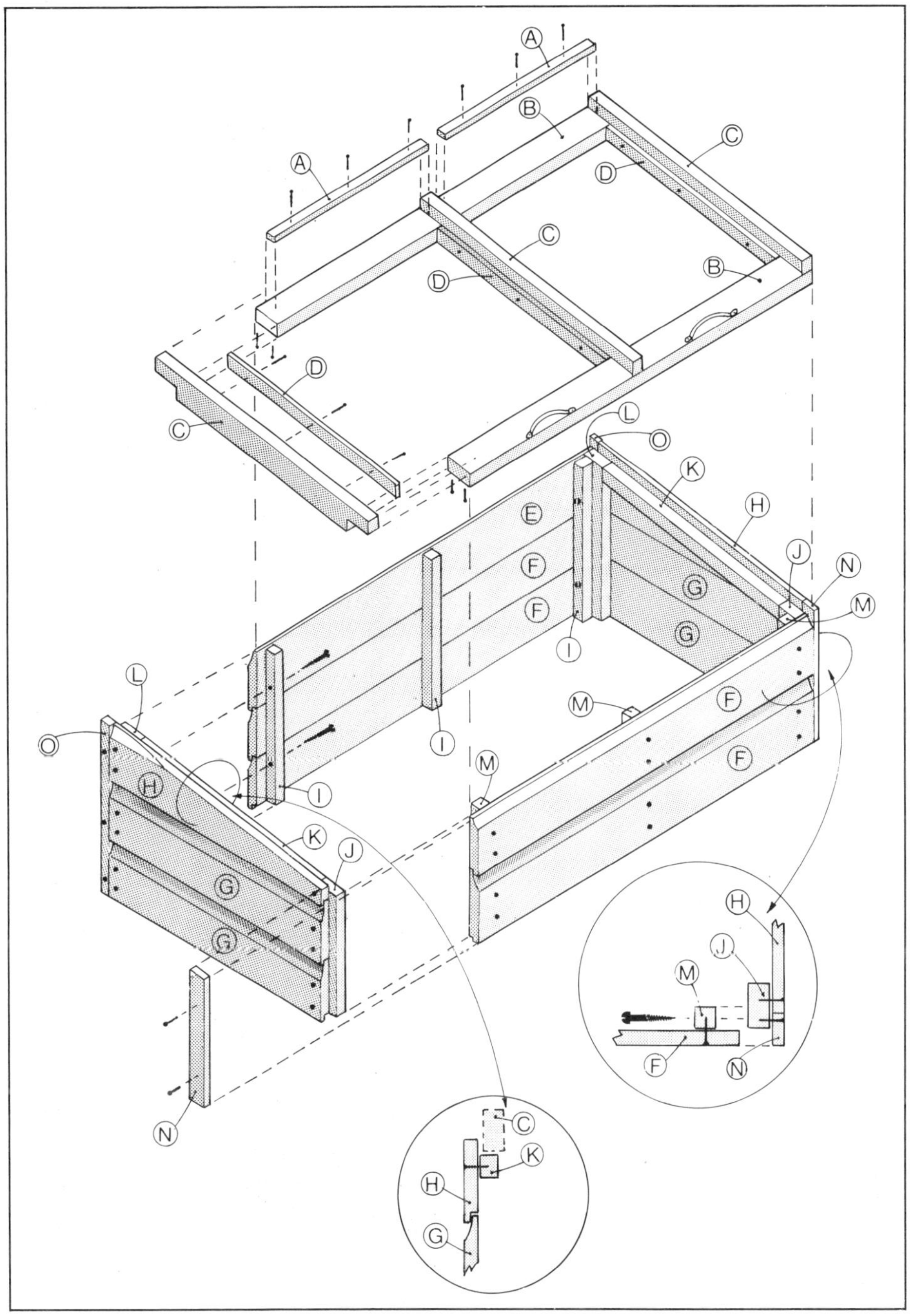

USING CLOCHES IN THE VEGETABLE GARDEN

The value of cloches lies not only in the sunshine they draw and the warmth they generate beneath them, but also in their ability to shield crops from cold winds – particularly in winter and early spring – and give protection against birds. Here we describe the main types available today before going on to look at the use of cloches throughout the year and at the crops that benefit.

Good cloches are not cheap to buy, but their cost should be reckoned against the number of years they can be expected to last and the value of the crops they will protect. When this is done, a row of cloches will be seen to be a very good investment indeed.

The main types

In recent years, glass cloches have lost ground, in terms of popularity, to the newer polythene and plastics models, but glass is still the most durable. At one time, packs of these cloches were on offer, but today it is customary to buy the fittings and glass separately. The obvious disadvantage of this type is that glass breaks, but with care and experience breakages can be kept to the minimum.

The most usual types of glass cloche are the 'tent' and the 'barns'. The first has two sheets of glass 60 × 30cm (24 × 12 in); the low barn has two sheets 60 × 30cm and two sheets 60 × 15cm, and the large barn is made up of four 60 × 30cm sheets. The latter are big enough to protect tomatoes, melons, sweet peppers, cucumbers and aubergines, at least for part of their growth.

Polythene cloches are usually of tent or tunnel design, and need to be firmly anchored so that the wind cannot carry them away. Plastics designs come in many different forms. A useful one is corrugated, bent to a half-circle and secured with hoops pushed into the soil. These cloches can be stacked flat when not in use, so taking up little space.

Some of the different types of glass, polythene and plastics cloches are also illustrated on page 12.

How to use them

In French, the word 'cloche' means 'bell', and the earliest cloches were, in fact, bell-shaped. They were used for striking cuttings or for protecting individual plants. Later, the 'continuous' cloche was invented, with open ends so that a number of them could be used together to make a row or 'run'.

Some cloches can still be used individually to protect particular crops

Open-topped, tunnel-shaped cloches not only make watering easier, they also make it more effective, the narrow base width concentrating water around the roots

such as a newly-planted cucumber or marrow. Single cloches can also be used for raising brassica seedlings. A low barn will take five rows 10cm (4 in) apart, and if the seedlings are thinned to 5cm (2 in) a single cloche will cover about 60 plants.

Whether used singly or as a run, the ends should always be closed with pieces of board or glass to avoid the creation of a wind tunnel. However, an exact fit is not necessarily essential.

Weeding and ventilation

The modern barn cloche has a detachable pane that makes weeding possible without removing the whole cloche; this pane can also be adjusted for ventilation purposes. Where this refinement is not available, ventilation can be given by leaving a slight gap between the cloches.

Watering

Watering is not the problem you might

Above left: a run of tent cloches in situ *over newly-planted seed*
Left: ventilation panels can be removed from barn cloches in warmer weather
Below: pots sunk into the soil will allow water to seep sideways beneath the cloche to nourish plant roots

expect, being necessary in spring and summer only. To get at plants growing in the centre, the cloche can be removed completely or the ventilating panel taken out, while for side rows watering can be done *over* the cloche: water runs down the side sections and into the soil, from where it seeps sideways beneath the cloche.

A good method of watering such plants as tomato, cucumber and melon is to sink plant pots about half their depth into the soil, approximately 15cm (6 in) from the plant stem, and then water into the pots.

The need for watering will be less if the ground is prepared well in advance – this should be kept in mind where a sequence of cloche crops is planned. If the soil is dug and manured in autumn or winter, it will retain moisture much better than a hastily-prepared site in spring. Failing this, fork in some good compost or well-moistened peat to the top layer of soil.

Layout

Where cloches are to be switched from one crop to another, a lot of effort can be saved if the strips are reasonably close together. Glass barn cloches, in particular, are heavy and moving them from one end of the garden to the other involves time and effort. Careful planning can cut this down.

De-cloching

Unless the weather suddenly becomes very warm, de-cloching of crops should be done gradually. Begin by removing the ventilating pane altogether or spacing the cloches a little farther apart. The next stage is to remove the cloches completely in the daytime, replacing them for one or two nights until the plants have become accustomed to the changed conditions.

Storage

With the possible exception of large barns, cloches are not usually required during summer months. Unused cloches should not be left lying about on the garden, for more breakages happen then than when they are in regular use. Those that are easily dismantled should be taken down and stored away. Tent and barn cloches can be stood on end and stacked one inside the other in a vacant corner or alongside a path.

Before using them in the autumn, give the cloches a wash so that the maximum amount of light is available to the protected crops, and to lessen the chances of harbouring pests and diseases.

Right: two types of barn cloche – the four-part (above) and the three-part model (below) with one ventilation panel

CROPS FOR CLOCHES

Previously we described the main types of cloche available, and also provided weeding, watering and ventilation details. Here we outline the range of crops that benefit from the protection afforded by cloches, giving the sowing or planting season in each case.

The gardener who has a run of cloches at his disposal will get off to a good start in the spring, for a crop with cloche protection for most or all of its growth will mature up to three weeks earlier than an unprotected one. This means that in many cases the same sowing strip can be used again – later in the year – for a different crop. Dwarf peas, for example, if sown under cloches around mid spring (middle of March), will be ready for picking in mid summer (June); as soon as they have been cleared, plant cabbage or cauliflower, or sow carrots or beetroot for pulling young in the autumn.

Spring and summer sowings

If you have any cloches to spare in late winter (January), put these in place and leave them for about a month to dry out and warm up the soil – this pre-warming is an important facet of cloche cultivation. Then, in early spring (February), you can sow lettuce, carrots, peas or broad beans there.

Another crop that benefits from growing under cloches in the spring is new potatoes. Tubers planted in mid spring (March), if already sprouting, will be through the soil well before the last frosts, and cloches will prevent damage. Give potatoes plenty of air during the daytime but close up the cloches at night. If the haulms are drawn up too quickly they will flop over when the plants are de-cloched.

By about late spring (middle of April) you can cover runner beans, dwarf French beans, or sweet corn, all these being sown *in situ*. This will give you about a month's start on the same crops sown without protection.

From early to mid summer (middle of May to early June) – according to district – tomatoes, sweet peppers, aubergines, cucumbers, marrows and outdoor melons will be ready for planting out under cloches. The cucumbers, cantaloupe melons, and some dwarf varieties of tomato can be covered throughout their growth if large barns are used, but smaller cloches are helpful for temporary protection. Even if you keep these tender crops under cover for just the first few weeks after planting, it will be worthwhile, for this is a critical period – especially if the nights are still cool.

Lettuce (above) will benefit from cloche protection in early spring

Continuing protection

When the plants are pushing at the roofs of the cloches, it is time to de-cloche, but a respite can be obtained for another week or two if the cloches are raised up on bricks.

In the case of cordon tomatoes, you can give continued protection by carefully tipping the cloches on end and standing them around the plants. Ideally, two cloches should be allocated to each plant, but if your supply won't run to this, use one cloche and leave the plant open on the south side. The cloches help to keep the plants upright; they also allow rainfall to reach the plants naturally, and enable you to pick the crop without first having to move the cloches. Do make sure, though, that each cloche is securely fastened to a cane pushed into the soil, or else a summer storm could bring disaster.

It is not always realized that cloches can extend the season at *both* ends. Late summer (July) sowings of beetroot, carrots, turnips and lettuce, if cloched in mid autumn (September), will continue to grow until early winter (November). The little lettuce Tom Thumb can be sown as late as early autumn (August) and still mature by early winter (November), provided you cloche it.

Ripening tomatoes

Cloches can be used for ripening tomatoes in the autumn. The weight of fruit growing on dwarf varieties pulls the laterals down. Flowering shoots continue to form, mostly at the top of the plants, but by mid autumn (early September) it will be too late for these to make anything and you can cut them out. You can then replace the cloches over the plants. Where the tomatoes have been grown as cordons, cut them from the supporting

canes, lay them carefully on a bed of straw or black polythene, and cover them with cloches. Ripening will then continue well into late autumn (October).

Drying off bulbs

Cloches are also useful for drying off onion, shallot and garlic bulbs. Spread them out in a narrow band just less than the width of the cloches, and cover. This gives the bulbs the full benefit of the sun, while keeping the rain out. Leave the ends of the cloches open so that the wind can blow through.

Autumn and winter sowings

All your cloches should be occupied throughout the autumn and winter. Lettuce of the Suzan type can be sown in mid autumn (September) and cloched a month or so later. Thin them to about 5cm (2 in) when they are large enough to handle, and thin them again around early spring (February) to 13–15cm (5–6 in). These thinnings can be transplanted. In late spring (April) take out every other plant for use and leave the others to heart up properly. For an overwintering cos lettuce, try Winter Density. To keep botrytis at bay, give ventilation in all but the coldest weather.

Both endive and corn salad will give better and cleaner crops if they are given cloche protection, and this is also true of spinach beet. A sowing of round peas – Feltham First is a good choice – can be made in late autumn (October), and one of broad beans in early winter (November). All these overwinter successfully.

If you have had difficulty growing spring cabbage, it is worth trying it under cloches, for these give complete protection against marauding wood pigeons.

A year's programme

There are many variations on the cloche theme that you can try out for yourself, but here is one suggestion for a run of large barn cloches throughout the year:
Mid autumn (September) – sow Premier or Suzan lettuce. A barn cloche will take three rows 20cm (8 in) apart.
Late autumn (October) – cover.
Late spring (middle of April) – de-cloche. Sow two rows of dwarf beans 30cm (12 in) apart, and cover at once.
Early summer to late autumn (end of May to October) – cover dwarf tomatoes, sweet peppers, cucumbers or melons.

Tent cloches (above left), and the ventilation panels of barn models (left), can be removed from dwarf French beans during the day in early summer
Far left: drying off shallot bulbs

ORGANIZING AND EQUIPPING THE GREENHOUSE

CHOOSING A GREENHOUSE

Greenhouses come in all shapes and sizes – and today no garden need be without one, however small, for there are many simple and easy-to-erect models as well as more elaborate and decorative ones.

The acquisition of a greenhouse opens up an exciting new area of gardening, where you don't have to worry about extremes of weather or damage from cold, wind or excessive rain. You can regulate the amount of water your plants receive and, because fertilizers are not washed away by rain, you can feed them correctly.

Temperature and ventilation can be adjusted and, by applying shading, even the light may be altered to suit plant preferences. Pests and diseases are easier to combat and the plants are protected from damage by birds and small animals.

Which type?

Most greenhouse styles offer the choice of a glass-to-ground or a base-wall design. The glass-to-ground type allows very efficient use of space for growing. When staging is fitted, there is enough light beneath for the accommodation of a varied selection of plants. The all-glass house is also ideal for tall subjects like tomatoes and chrysanthemums. By arranging your space carefully you can grow many different kinds of plants together. For example, you can grow tomatoes along the south side, followed by chrysanthemums – putting the pots on the floor. Your staging can then run along the north side, providing a surface on which to grow a variety of pot plants, with some space below for plants that like a certain amount of shade (as do many house plants). On the end wall you can train climbers bearing either beautiful flowers, or edible crops like cucumbers.

But for some purposes a greenhouse with a base wall of brick, concrete or timber boards (usually called a 'plant house') is preferable. Plants liking deep shade can be grown below the staging. This design is more economical to heat artificially and therefore is preferable when the greenhouse does not get much sun. It is also a good choice where high temperatures have to be maintained for propagation or for tropical plants (many of which do not demand much light). Greenhouses with a base wall at one side and glass-to-ground at the other are also available. These should be oriented east-to-west with the base to the north.

Planning ahead

Before buying your greenhouse, make sure that you are not infringing any rules or regulations by erecting it in your garden. If you are a tenant you should seek your landlord's permission; should you move, you can take the greenhouse with you. If you are a freeholder and wish to have a permanent structure (like a lean-to against the house wall) you will almost certainly require planning permission from your local council.

You must also do some advance thinking about the foundations of the greenhouse. You can lay old railway sleepers or concrete footings, or build a low, cemented brick wall on which the greenhouse can be free-standing or screwed into position. Do have a path of concrete, brick or paving stones down the centre of the house, for dry feet and clean working.

The best positions

Freestanding, rectangular greenhouses get most benefit from the sun if you orientate them east-to-west, with the long sides facing north and south. The 'high south wall' greenhouse *must*, in fact, lie this way to catch as much winter light and sun as possible. Staging, if used, should run along the north side.

With a lean-to, you may have no choice in the siting, but what you grow in it will depend on which way it faces. An east- or west-facing lean-to is usually fairly versatile since it gets some sun and some shade. If north-facing it will be very shady and is best devoted to pot plants (such as cinerareas, cyclamen, primulas and calceolarias) and house plants for permanent decoration. A south-facing lean-to can become very hot in summer and, unless you want to install shading, you should choose sun-loving plants like cacti and succulents.

Types of material

You should consider the cost of subsequent maintenance as against initial outlay when choosing your materials.

Glass or plastic? Glass has the unique property of capturing and retaining solar warmth. It also holds artificial warmth better. Polythene has a limited life and for long-term use a rigid plastic (like Novolux) is the wisest choice. Plastic surfaces are easily scratched by wind-blown dust and grit, causing dirt to become ingrained and a loss of transparency over a period of years. Plastic also becomes brittle with weathering and may disintegrate.

However, plastic is advisable if the site is likely to be the target for children's games or hooligans out to break glass, or where quick erection or portability is desirable, or where temporary weather protection is all that's necessary. Moulded fibreglass greenhouses are also available, but tend to be expensive and the fittings have to be free-standing.

Aluminium frames Aluminium alloy (often white-coated) is now tending to replace timber for the frame as it has many advantages. It is lightweight yet very strong, and prefabricated structures are easily bolted together. Sophisticated glazing, using plastic cushioning strips and clips instead of messy putty, means that the greenhouse can easily be taken apart for moving. There is no fear of rot, warp or trouble from wood-boring insects, or need for maintenance, like painting or treating timber.

A 'vertical-sided 'barn' or 'span' model (far left) with timbered base walls on three sides. The 'Dutch light' house (left) is always a glass-to-ground structure; it has sloping glass walls which are designed to trap the sun's rays.
A 'lean-to' (below) can be set against a garden or house wall, where it can double as a conservatory or home extension

Timber frames These may look better in a period-style garden. Select one of the more weather-resistant timbers such as cedar, teak or oak, but remember that all timber needs painting or treating with a wood restorer or preservative from time to time.

Providing shade

If your greenhouse receives plenty of sun you will need shading in the summer.

Slatted blinds, run on rails over the exterior of the roof, are efficient but costly. They also have to be made to fit. Interior blinds are far less efficient in reducing temperature, since the sun's heat-producing rays have already entered the greenhouse, though they do help to prevent direct scorch.

The simplest and cheapest effective method of shading here is with an electrostatic shading paint that is not washed off by rain but can easily be removed by wiping with a dry duster. You apply and remove it like a blind.

All year round ventilation

Ventilators are usually fitted in the roof and sometimes in the sides as well, reducing excess heat in summer and controlling humidity at all times.

Types of heating

It makes sense to heat your greenhouse, if only to keep out frost, since this greatly widens its usefulness. Your heating need not be costly if you don't waste it.

Oil heaters Both oil and paraffin are easy to store and portable heaters are particularly valuable as supplementary heating in periods of extreme cold or during power cuts. Use paraffin heaters that are specially designed for greenhouses; the blue-flame design is best.

Electricity is trouble-free and gives accurate temperature control, but it can be expensive if used wastefully. Fan heating is very effective providing the fan and heat output are controlled together (preferably with a separate, rod-type thermostat); avoid a heater with a continuously-running fan. Ventilation becomes almost unnecessary with this system, and if you line your greenhouse with polythene to form a kind of double glazing you can cut fuel consumption by up to half.

Convector heaters and electrically-heated pipes are also efficient when used together with an accurate thermostat.

Natural gas There are special greenhouse heaters using natural gas, with good thermostatic control. They can also be adapted to work from bottle gas, though this makes them more expensive to run.

Natural gas, oil and paraffin, when burned, all produce carbon dioxide and water vapour. The carbon dioxide is beneficial to plants, but the water vapour can be a nuisance in winter when you will do better to keep the greenhouse dry. You will need some ventilation to keep down humidity and supply air for the fuel to burn, but this cold air does mean that some of the heat is lost.

Other types of heating Solid fuel (with the heat distributed by hot water pipes) and oil-fired boilers are still relatively cheap methods of heating. Hot water pipes, linked to a boiler, maintain high temperatures but are costly to install.

Heated propagators You will need some form of heated propagator so that you can germinate seeds without heating the whole greenhouse to a high temperature. Electrically-heated models are simple and cheap to run.

Automatic watering

There is a wide choice of equipment here. The water can be fed to the plants by overhead sprays, trickle-feed pipelines, by capillary sand benches or capillary matting. In the case of capillary watering, the sand or matting under the pots is kept constantly moist by whatever automatic system is installed.

Artificial lighting

A paraffin lamp will give you enough light in the evenings for most jobs, but if the greenhouse has an electricity supply you can install either a lamp-holder and lamp bulb or a fluorescent tube.

ERECTING AND SITING A GREENHOUSE

To be the owner of a successful greenhouse, you need to spend at least as much time and thought on where to site it as on which type to choose. Equally, attention to detail when laying foundations and erecting the structure will amply reward the extra time spent.

In most cases it is wise to choose an open position for the greenhouse where it will get as much sunshine as possible. This generally means that you should try to position the unit with one of the longest sides facing south. It is a simple matter to shade the glass when you want to reduce light entry, but it is difficult to increase light without the trouble and expense of artificial lighting.

Remember that, in winter, nearly all plants will enjoy plenty of sunlight – even summer shade-lovers. Winter sunlight also means plenty of free warmth and your heating costs will be reduced.

Shady and windy sites

Avoid, where possible, a site that is near large trees (especially evergreens). Falling branches may break the glass, and spreading roots may upset the foundations. Falling leaves and exuded gums from some species dirty the glass, and you may also find that the roof is covered with bird droppings. Evergreens cast shade all year round, and many trees harbour numerous pests and diseases that can attack greenhouse plants and crops.

Small shrubs and trees are not usually a menace; these can even be planted (far enough away so that they do not cast shade) to act as windbreaks in windy areas. Strong, cold winds, usually from the north and east, can add greatly to the fuel bill. Other suitable windbreaks are fences, walls and hedges – as long as they are not too high.

Low ground and hollows

When choosing a site for your greenhouse, look carefully at the ground contours of your garden. In all cases where the site is at the foot of a hill there is a danger of frost pockets forming. Cold, frosty air can run off a slope almost like water, and surround a greenhouse that is set in a hollow. Where no other site is available, a low brick wall can help to deflect icy air currents.

In hollows and on low ground, water may collect or the ground may become very damp. These conditions are particularly unhealthy in winter when the greenhouse should be as dry as possible.

Sites near the house

Many people put their greenhouse at the far end of the garden – some distance from the house. There is often no good reason why it should be tucked away out of sight. Modern structures are rarely 'eyesores' and some designs are very attractive, especially when filled with decorative plants. There are many advantages in having the greenhouse within close reach of the house. Both water and electricity can be run to the greenhouse easily. Electricity, even if you don't want it for heating, may be needed for automatic aids or lighting; you may also wish to run natural gas from the house.

When the greenhouse is to be heated by solid fuel or paraffin, remember that the fuel will have to be carried to the greenhouse and, in the case of solid fuel, the ash carried away – yet another reason for avoiding remote sites. If you don't want to see a greenhouse from the windows of your home, you can always screen it with low shrubs or small ornamental trees.

In some cases greenhouses can be heated economically by an extension of the same central heating system used in your home. In this case the greenhouse should, preferably, come into contact with the house wall, and a lean-to is usually the best design. Where high temperatures are required it is always an advantage if the greenhouse can be set against a house wall, or a south-facing garden wall. Such a wall usually absorbs warmth from the sun during the day and radiates it at night, thus saving fuel and acting as a kind of free storage heater.

Laying the foundations

Most modern, prefabricated, amateur greenhouses are easy to erect single-handed, though with the larger sizes you may need assistance. The ground must always be firm and level, so laying a shallow foundation (by digging a trench and filling it with a fluid concrete mix that finds its own level) is often a wise move. However, some greenhouse manufacturers recommend their own base plinths and the small additional cost of these is well worth while. Some designs do not need elaborate foundations but are secured by 'ground anchors'. A separate hole is dug for each anchor and the framework is then bolted onto these before the glazing is put in.

Brick or concrete base walls, if required, are best constructed by a professional builder – unless you are reasonably expert in this sort of work. Greenhouse manufacturers always provide a detailed groundplan of the structure, so follow this closely when putting in foundations or base walls.

When erecting your greenhouse, use a spirit level and plumb line to make frequent checks on levels and verticals.

Fitting the glazing

Stand glass panes in a dry, covered place until you are ready to use them. If they get wet they are very difficult to separate and you risk breaking them. Glazing is best done when the weather is not too cold or your fingers may be too numb for careful handling. Do any metal or timber painting before the glass is put in. If you are using putty, only put it below the glass as a bed for the panes – not over the top as well, as in ordinary domestic glazing.

Plastic greenhouses

Be especially careful, when erecting and siting plastic greenhouses, to avoid possible wind damage. The suppliers usually issue special anchoring instructions and recommendations. When plastic is to be fastened to a timber framework, don't use creosote preservatives on the wood. Some plastics will become weakened by contact and all will be severely discoloured, making the greenhouse most unsightly. Moreover, creosote fumes are harmful to plants. For the same reason creosote should not be used on any timbers in close contact with plants in a confined area – such as in greenhouses or frames. Instead use one of the proprietary horticultural timber preservatives on the market.

Tending the site

The surroundings of your greenhouse should be kept tidy and weed-free. Weeds will harbour many troublesome pests; for example nearby stinging nettles may bring you an infestation of whitefly.

Incorrect siting

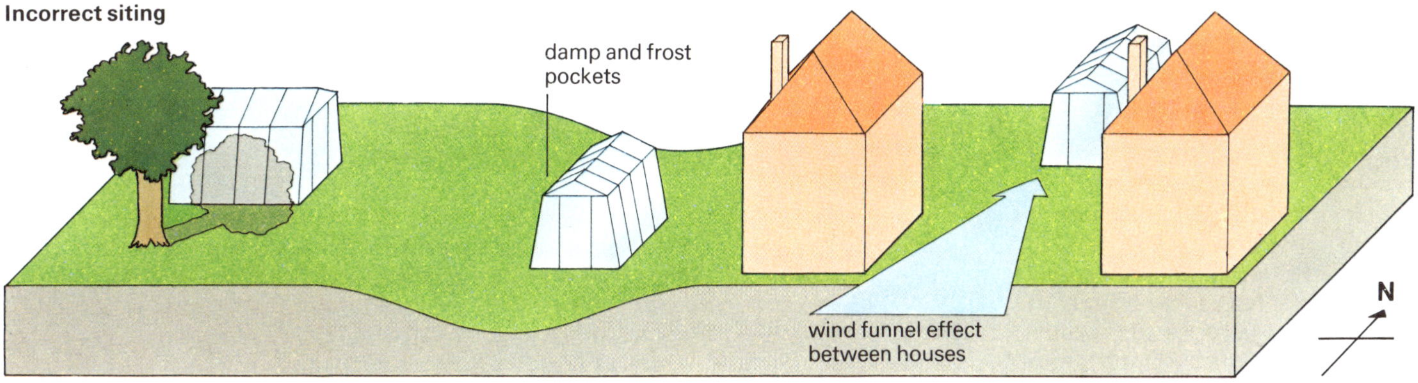

Correct siting

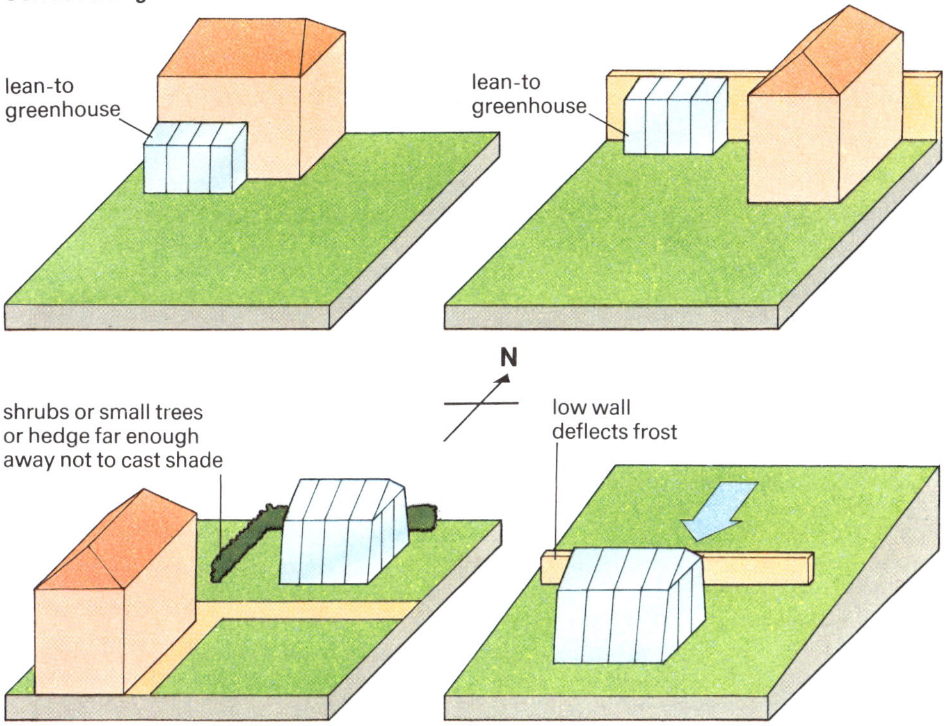

Types of plinth

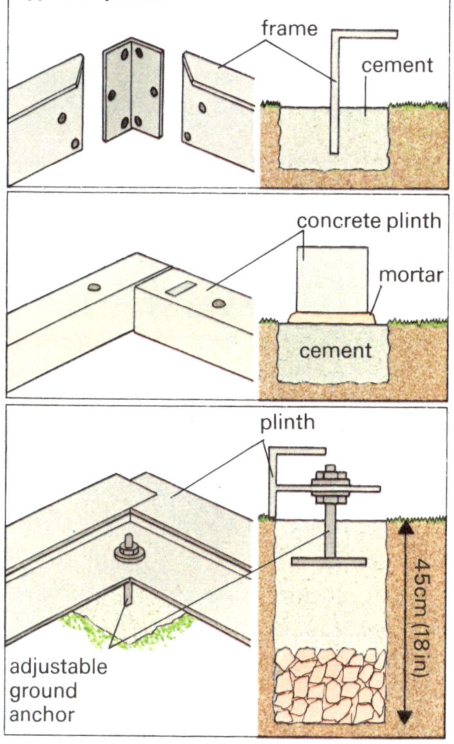

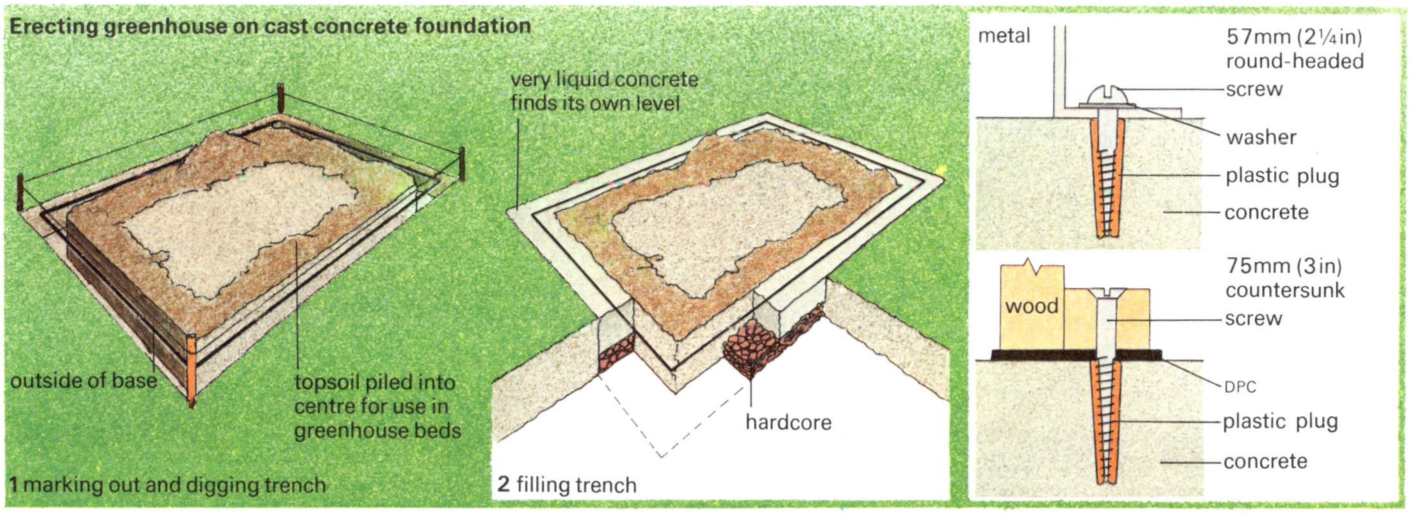

Top: avoid shade, damp, frost and wind – enemies of the greenhouse
Centre left: use house or garden walls for economical lean-to greenhouses; make use of low-growing shrubs or low walls to help protect against wind and frost

Bottom left: dig trench on a firm, level spot, remembering to place soil in centre for future use. Concrete over hardcore provides a solid base for the greenhouse that can be anchored with the right type of plugs and screws (bottom right)

Centre right: ready-made base plinths in in metal or concrete need only very very simple foundations, and are easy for the amateur to put together. The adjustable ground anchor system requires a solid concrete base

BASIC EQUIPMENT FOR THE GREENHOUSE

When you buy a greenhouse the price usually covers only the structure. All other items – sometimes even the ventilators – have to be bought as 'extras'. But this does allow you considerable choice of interior and exterior fittings. There are also many tools and gadgets available, in a variety of designs and price levels. Some of these are essential basic equipment and others can be bought as you need them for particular jobs.

In many greenhouses staging and shelving will be found useful at some time or other. Staging is often thought of as a permanent fixture but it need not be so. There are some small units now available that can be easily assembled and dismantled, moved about from place to place in the greenhouse, and extended to increase staging space if required. This form of staging makes the greenhouse very versatile and is specially useful in a glass-to-ground structure where a wide variety of plants of different heights can be grown and viewed.

Staging materials

Probably the most important aspect of your staging is the top surface. For most purposes a solid surface, strewn with some kind of moisture-retaining material, is the best surface for the warmer months. In winter it is an advantage if the staging top is of an 'open' nature to allow for air circulation around plants and, in warmed greenhouses, the distribution of heat; for this, slatted staging is suitable. However it is not common practice to change your staging according to the seasons, nor is it necessary. If you install open-type staging, it is a simple matter to cover it with polythene or asbestos sheeting, and then in mid spring (March) to cover this with a layer of moist shingle or other moisture-retaining material. You can then remove it all in mid autumn (September). This process helps considerably to maintain air humidity.

Instead of the conventional timber slats modern staging, particularly when constructed from metal angle strips, often has a top surface of wire or plastic mesh.

A really solid, substantial staging, made from bricks or concrete has an advantage worth noting in these days of fuel economy. Where a greenhouse receives a good amount of sunshine during the day, the bricks and concrete will store heat and evolve (radiate) it during the night. Sometimes enough warmth will be given out to keep the greenhouse frost free, and it will certainly be enough to keep the temperature more even. It is particularly valuable where rather high temperatures are being maintained for propagation or for growing sub-tropical plants, and where a relatively high warmth and humidity are needed all year round.

Portable shelves

Shelving is always useful – even more so if it is portable. Depending on how the basic greenhouse structure is designed it can be fitted to the sides or suspended from the roof – or both. If buying the brackets and the shelving material separately, then thick plate glass shelves are worth considering instead of the conventional planking or slats. Glass is a good choice if your greenhouse is very crowded as it allows more light to reach the plants below. Strips of strong plate glass can sometimes be purchased relatively cheaply as off-cuts from scrap.

Below left: staging – **1** *and* **2,** *metal frames with open wood tops, and* **3,** *wire mesh stretched over wood frame, allow good air circulation, while the more solid combinations in* **4** *retain heat*
Below: shelving – **1** *suspended by metal straps from roof;* **2** *fixed with an angle bracket;* **3** *bolted-on aluminium type*

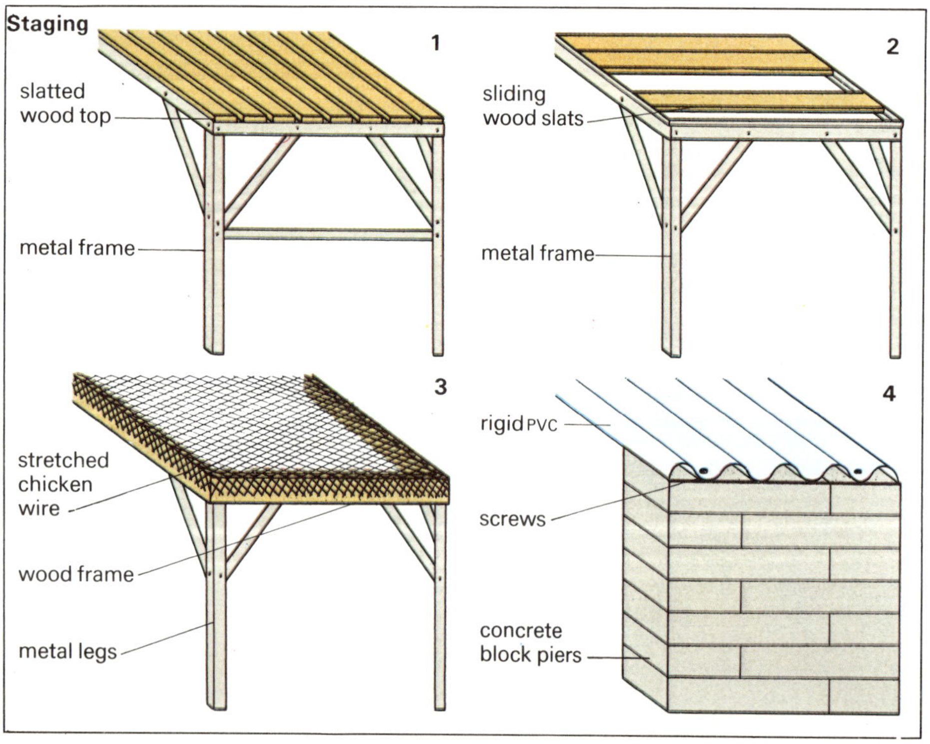

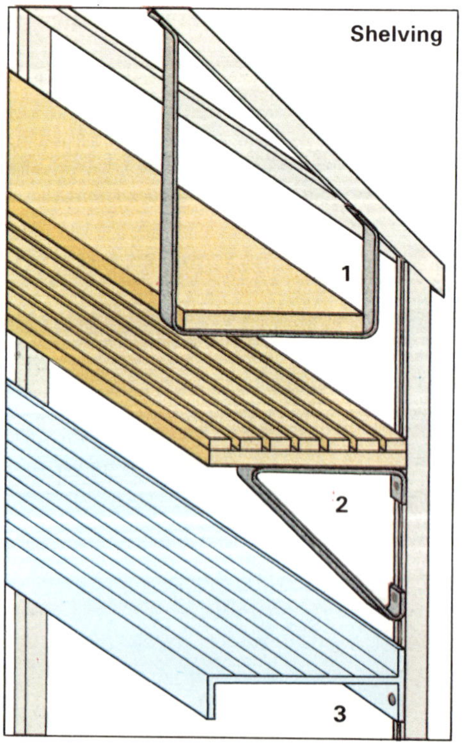

Types of thermometer

Thermometers are absolutely indispensable to proper greenhouse management. You will need at least one maximum and minimum thermometer in the greenhouse interior. Others may be useful for interior or exterior frames and outside the greenhouse. In all cases do buy a quality instrument, as this will give you accurate readings and last far longer than a cheap one. Tiny temperature indicators show the highest and lowest temperatures that have been reached; these are usually set with a magnet supplied with the instrument. Designs are now made that can be gravity set, and there are also pushbutton types. You may also want a frost forecast thermometer; this is a kind of hygrometer (for measuring humidity) but it has a scale indicating the possible chance of frost. Advance warning will enable you to check heating equipment, close vents and so on.

Watering and spraying equipment

Even if you intend to install automatic watering, a watering can will be useful at some time, even if only for applying liquid feeds. Choose one with a spout that will easily reach to the back of the staging and one that's not too heavy for you to lift when it is full. Some designs have extendible spouts. If your greenhouse is fitted with a water tap, then you can use a watering lance that is controlled by a finger-operated valve. Get one with a nozzle that will deliver a fine spray for damping down, as well as a normal flow.

Ideally, you should also buy two hand sprayers. One should have a fairly large capacity for damping down or spraying foliage with water, and for applying pesticides. Another small sprayer, holding about 500cc (1 pt), is useful for treating the odd plant (when it is not necessary to make up a vast amount of pesticide). Don't forget that foliar feeds can also be applied with sprayers. A special feature to look for when buying a sprayer is a nozzle that can be directed upwards as well as downwards, and that will reach between the plants easily. This will ensure thorough coverage of the undersides of leaves when spraying pesticides; most pests first congregate under the foliage. The pump-up or pneumatic type of sprayer is convenient and economical.

Potting benches

A very useful piece of equipment is a portable potting bench. This is a tray with one side missing that can be placed on the staging when needed. Use it for mixing compost, sowing, pricking out and potting jobs, and store it out of the way when not in use. You can easily make a bench using a sheet of aluminium (available from most do-it-yourself shops, often as off-cuts). Bend three of the edges upwards with pliers to prevent compost being pushed off the sides and back. Aluminium is one of the best materials to use because it is easy to clean and sterilize and is resistant to the hard wear caused by trowelling, cutting operations, and mixing. It is also lightweight and easily made into the shape you want.

Plastic and clay flowerpots

Keep a selection of flowerpots to hand. Plastic is easy to clean, but a few clay pots (if you can get them) are handy from time to time – some plants prefer them. The most useful sizes to keep in store for a wide range of pot plants are 8 or 9cm (3 or 3½ in) and 13cm (5 in).

Thermometers and frost detector

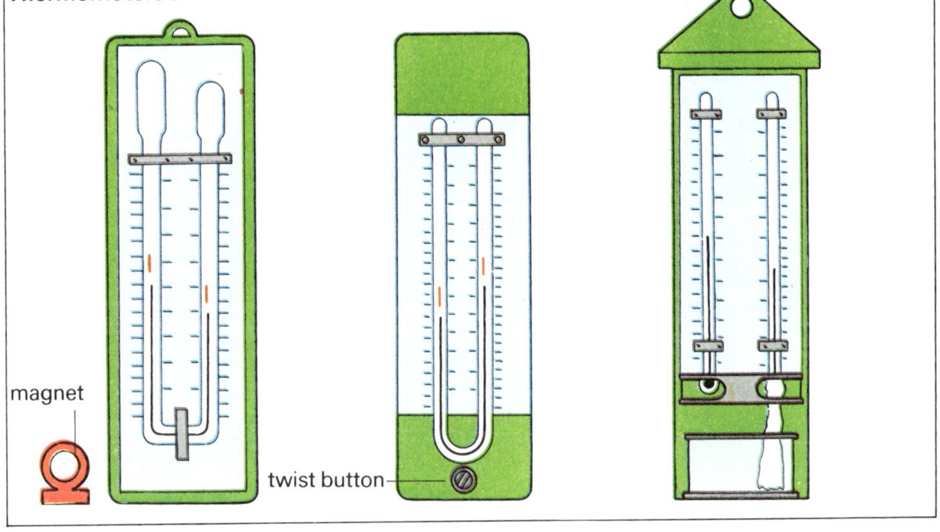

Watering equipment

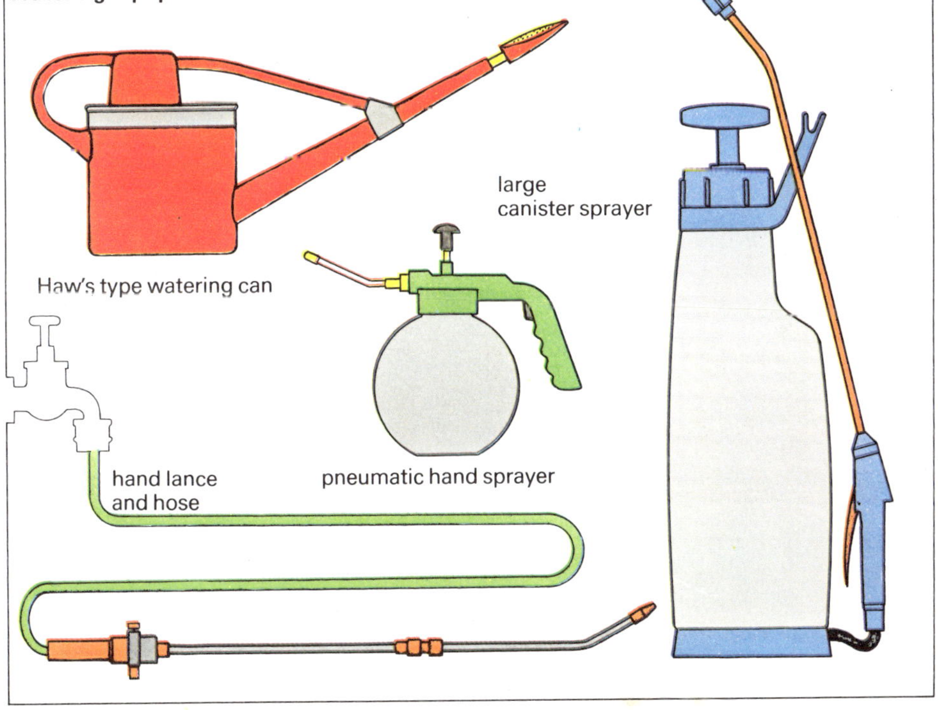

Above left: two different types of thermometer, with magnet or twist-button setting, and frost detector (similar to a hygrometer) to help give you valuable warning of a cold snap
Left: some of the basic equipment to cope with different watering needs

SHADING THE GREENHOUSE

Don't leave attention to shading until it is too late. You will find that correct shading, ventilation and damping down, are essential in the greenhouse for the cultivation of strong and vigorous plants.

Excessively high temperature in summer, coupled with lack of shading, is a common cause of failure among beginners in greenhouse and frame gardening. There is also still much misunderstanding about the subject, even where professional gardeners are concerned.

It is an advantage to site a greenhouse in an open sunny position, because this gives much free warmth in winter but, because of the heat-trapping effect of glass, shading will invariably be required in summer. Often it may be necessary much earlier than this during sunny periods, when temperatures can be sent rocketing, even in spring (February or March). Plants that are not used to bright sunlight and warmth, having just been through the winter, may wilt. The numerous greenhouse plants that flower in spring, such as cineraria, calceolaria and primula, will last much longer if kept shaded and cool. Seed sowings will also need shading at this time.

In summer an unshaded greenhouse, especially one that is badly ventilated and watered, may become an oven. Temperatures over 50°C (120°F) can be easily reached and even tropical plants will be shrivelled by the end of a day. Plastic greenhouses should be less of a problem in summer, because the solar heat is not trapped to such a great extent as with glass, but shading will still be necessary.

How much light?

A knowledge of the light requirements of the plants you grow is essential. In a mixed greenhouse the plants can then be placed accordingly. Deep-shade lovers, like many sub-tropical and house foliage plants, can go under the staging. Those preferring less can be sited in the natural shade of taller plants on the staging or under climbers. Plants demanding maximum light can go on shelves or under parts of the roof left unshaded or only slightly shaded during summer.

The effect of too much light and sun will be seen as bleached foliage, which in severe cases can become literally scorched brown. The plants will wilt, and if you have been watering them from above there may be brown spotting of the leaves. Droplets of water act as minute lenses, focusing the sun's rays and causing these burned spots. Plants with hairy or furry foliage are particularly prone to this kind of damage because the water droplets are supported just above the leaf surface and the focus is then much better. Plants commonly affected are saintpaulia, gloxinia, smithiantha, and others of the gesneria family with hairy leaves.

High temperature dangers

Greenhouse fruits, such as the tomato, can become blistered by excessive sunlight. Brown to grey watery 'scald' marks appear on the fruits. In the case of tomatoes high temperature is a frequent cause of failure, and shading is nearly always important during the ripening stage. At temperatures over about 32°C (80°F) the red pigment of the tomato fails

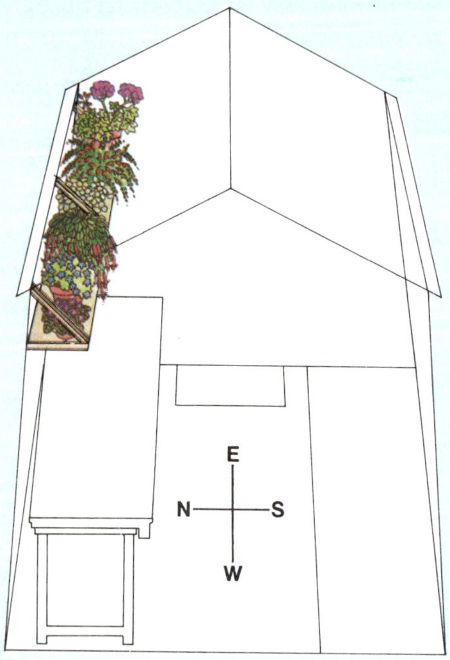

By placing your plants in different positions in the greenhouse, you can suit all their requirements for warmth and light. Small heat- and light-loving plants, such as Columnea gloriosa, *will do well if placed on a high shelf*

Larger heat- and light-loving plants can be placed on the staging. Plants which will thrive in this position, and provide an attractive display, include gloxinias, regal and zonal pelargoniums, primulas, cinerarias, calceolarias and hydrangeas

Some plants, especially many foliage plants, prefer shade; and those with variegated leaves, such as Tradescantia virginiana, *can lose their colour if left in bright sunlight. The best place to keep them is underneath the staging*

to form properly and the yellow persists. In addition there may be numerous other ripening faults, such as 'greenback', where the fruit is unevenly ripe and patched with red and yellow or green. Ventilation and white shading should be used to keep down temperatures during hot sunny weather.

The necessity of shading

Once the sun's rays have penetrated the glass or plastic lights of a greenhouse or frame, a part of them is converted into heat after striking the interior. This heat cannot readily pass back through the glass and so is 'trapped' inside. It is obvious therefore that for shading to be most efficient it must stop the sun's rays before they penetrate the glass. Exterior blinds are very effective, but remember that they also will absorb heat from the sun; so that this heat is not transferred to the glass or plastic roof the blinds should be a few inches above it. This will allow air to circulate and carry away heat.

Well-designed greenhouse blinds rest on runners and generally the slatted type of blind is best. These can be made of timber or of bamboo, and have to be made specially for your greenhouse and to the measurements you give the makers; they are lowered or raised by cords in the conventional manner. It is also possible for the blinds to be photo-electrically controlled, giving automatic operation.

Slatted blinds will of course let some direct sunlight pass through, but this light does not remain in one spot for long, owing to the sun's movement across the sky. Hessian or plastic sheeting and other materials are also sometimes used as blinds, but are very easily blown away.

In recent years interior blinds have come onto the market. These types are convenient because they stay clean and are not in danger of blowing away. However, they are of little use in keeping down temperature.

Shading paints

For very many years shading paints, applied to the exterior glass, have been used as a cheap method of shading during summer. Various mixtures of flour, whiting, glue and chalk have been suggested – often messy and even damaging to structures. Serious accidents have occurred, such as putting an arm through the glass when trying to scrape off such mixtures at the end of the season. Proprietary preparations of this kind were often tinted green, and even some modern methods of shading still employ the colour green.

Research both in Britain and in Holland has shown that white is the best colour, as it reflects back a much wider range of the sun's spectrum. Green actually absorbs much solar energy (indeed, this is the principle of photosynthesis of plants) and so a green-shaded greenhouse becomes considerably hotter than a white-shaded one. Plants also seem to grow better in a white-shaded house and there is a better rendering of flower and foliage colours as well as more sturdy growth. Remember that the shade cast by green leaves, such as in a wood or under shrubs, is not the same as that cast by a green-painted glass roof.

A remarkable modern invention is an electrostatic type of shading paint, which is marketed under the name of 'Coolglass'. This is specially formulated to reflect back as much of the sun's heat as possible but to let useful rays through. It can be sprayed or brushed onto the glass and diluted to give any degree of shade needed. It has the curious property of staying firmly on the glass even during heavy rain, yet being easily wiped off with a dry duster. This type of shading has given very good results with crops like tomatoes, cucumbers, fuchsias, begonias, carnations, orchids, chrysanthemums, foliage plants, and most frame crops.

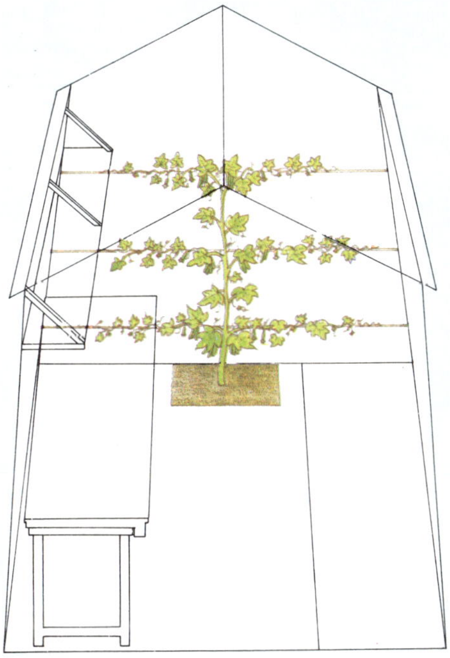

An end wall is a good site for climbing plants. The east wall is the best place, in this greenhouse, for a cucumber vine. It likes a draught-free position – well away from the door – and plenty of heat and light without being in direct sun

Some plants, like tomatoes, need plenty of heat and sun. The ideal place for them is along the south side of the greenhouse. However, even sun-loving plants need shading on very hot days when excessive temperatures can scorch their foliage

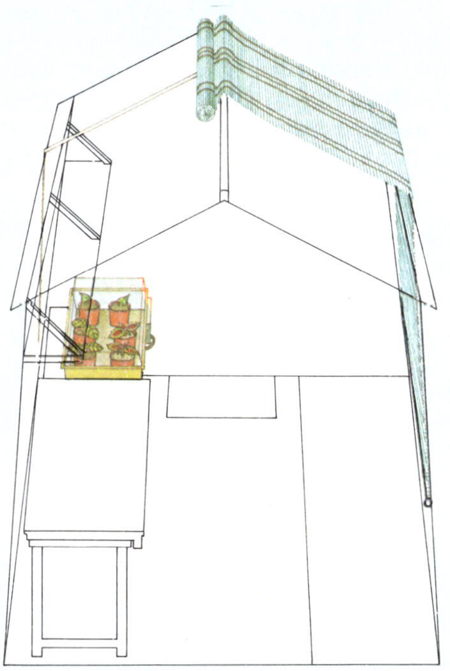

Two important pieces of greenhouse equipment concerning heat and light; a propagator, for providing the high temperatures needed by cuttings and germinating seeds, and an exterior blind for the most effective shading

AUTOMATIC WATERING IN THE GREENHOUSE

The majority of home gardeners have to leave their greenhouse to itself during the day and most people have to be absent from the garden now and then. It is on these occasions that watering can become a real problem, especially if the summer happens to be very hot and sunny. Automatic watering can solve this.

Apart from the problems of absence, automatic watering will be invaluable if you have lots of plants to look after. Moreover, it generally keeps plants constantly moist and encourages the humidity essential to healthy growth. This eliminates the chore of damping-down, and avoids extreme changes between dry and waterlogged soils or compost. Erratic watering is the cause of many troubles like dropping of buds and flowers, and cracked fruit in tomatoes.

The first attempts at automatic watering were usually improvised wicks – textile lamp wicks or blotting paper, with one end dipped into a tank or bucket, and the other end in the soil around the plant roots. Such arrangements usually have the disconcerting habit of drying up, or ceasing to work, as soon as your back is turned. Alternatively they may flood the plants.

Watering through sand

The first really successful system was introduced by the National Institute of Agricultural Engineering and is called the capillary sand bench. This system relies on the capillary action of water rising through any fine material like textile fibres or sand, but the water is always below the level of the plants and there is no risk of flooding. The plants are potted in plastic pots, with large drainage holes, that are kept clear of any obstruction. The pots are then stood on staging spread with a few centimetres of sand, preferably of what builders call 'washed grit'. The pots are pressed down firmly, so that the sand comes into direct contact with the compost in the pots through the drainage holes. The sand is kept constantly moist, by any one of several methods, and the compost in the plant pots will then take up moisture as

Automatic watering equipment

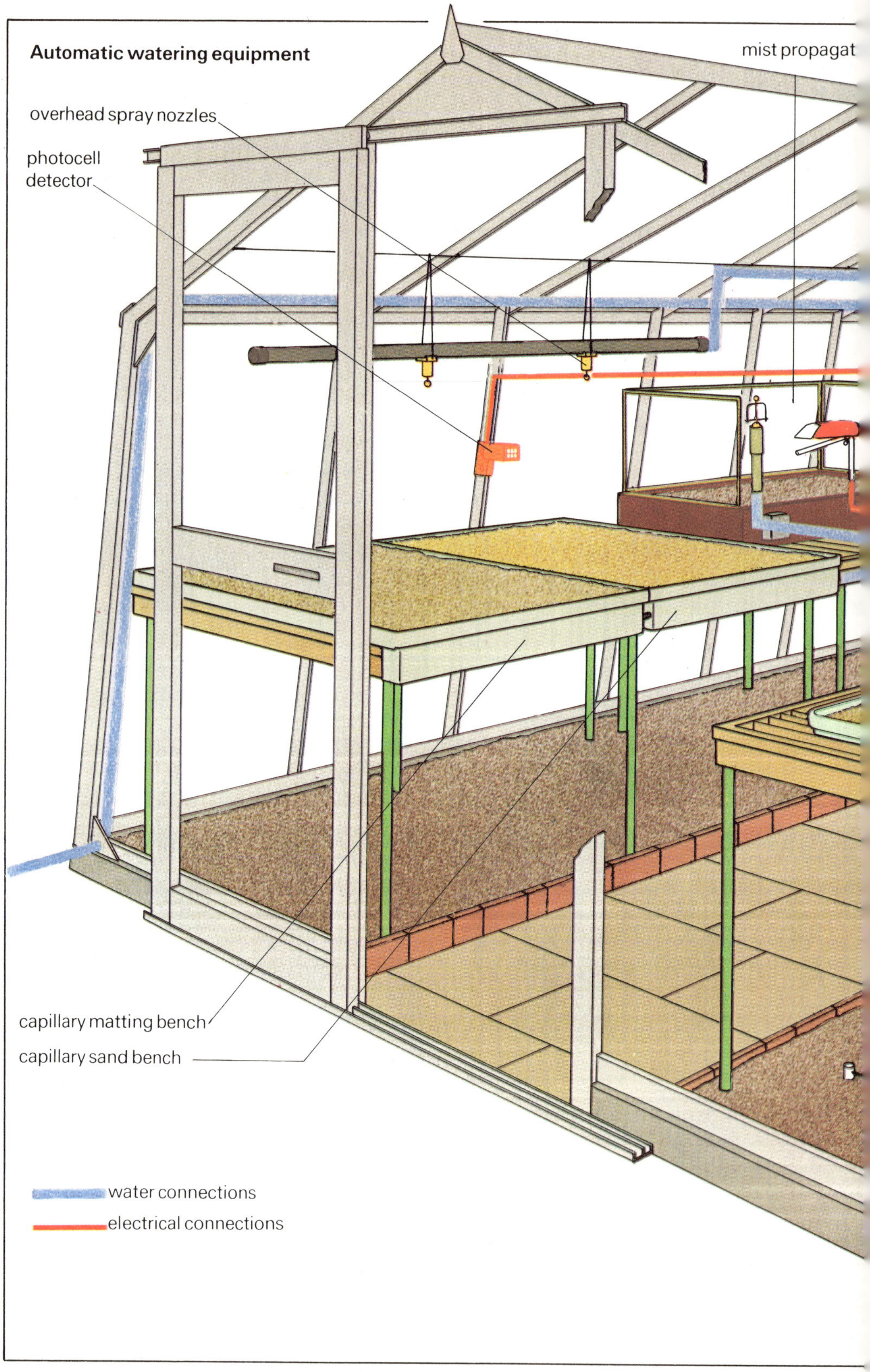

required. The amount taken up will vary automatically with the needs of the plant and temperature and humidity conditions – provided the sand layer is always well supplied with water. One other important condition is that the potting compost must be nicely moist when potting, otherwise there will be no flow between the moist sand and the compost.

Regulating the level

Originally an ordinary ball valve cistern was used to provide a constant water level for the sand layer, a perforated plastic pipe being connected to the cistern and running the length of the sand bench. You can make such an arrangement yourself, but proprietary equipment specially designed for this purpose can be bought.

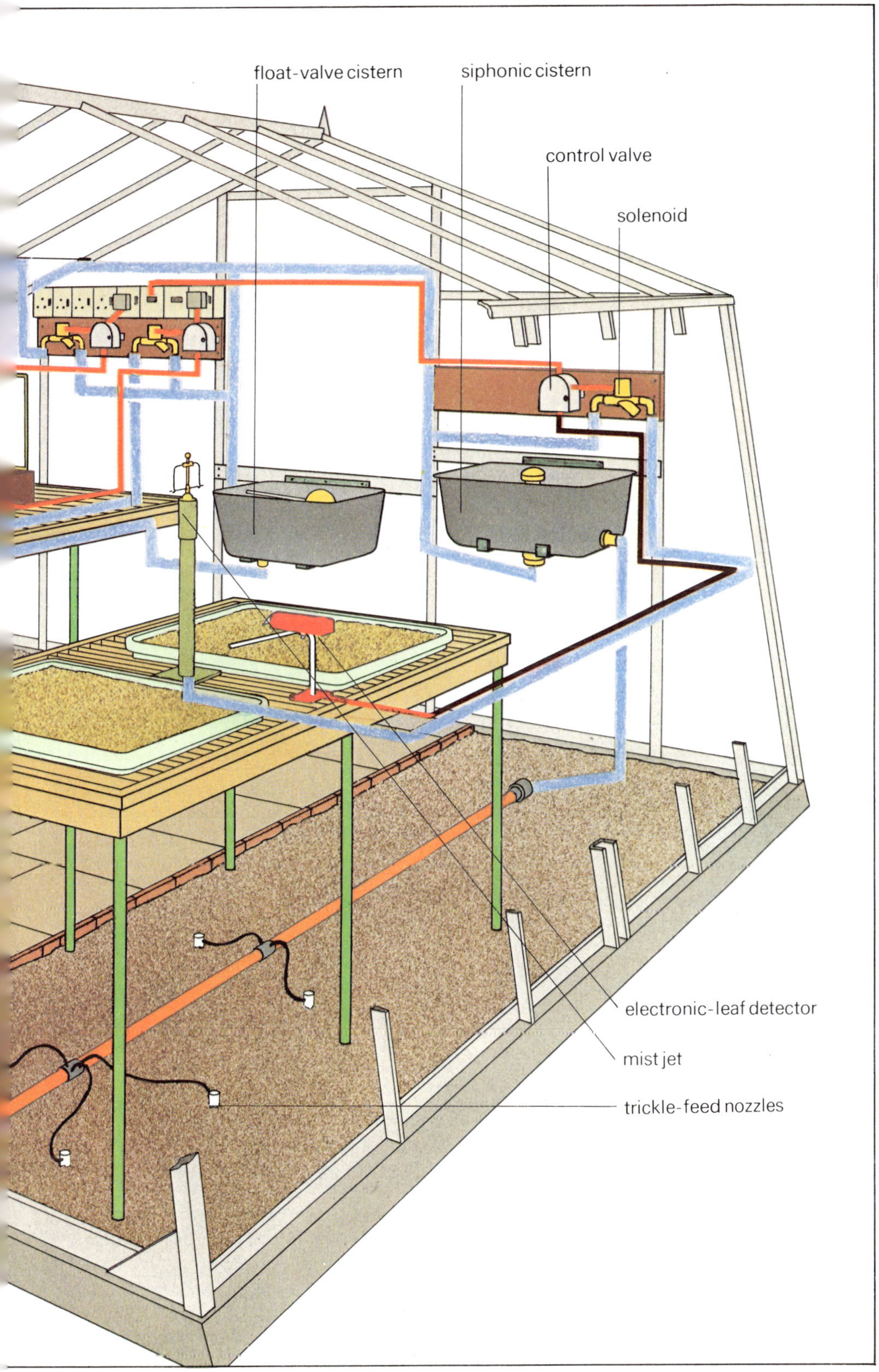

This is usually in the form of units that can be connected together as you require to extend the system. Instead of ball valves, neat little plastic float valves are available, with full instructions for installation. The sand has to be spread on plastic sheeting if ordinary slatted greenhouse staging is used for the bench, and the water level has to be just below the sand. The water is led into the sand by means of glass fibre or plastic wicks several centimetres wide. A good way to convey water along a considerable length of staging is to run plastic guttering against the edge; the gutter is kept constantly filled with water by means of the float valve connected to the mains or a tank, and the wicks are laid in the sand and dipped in the gutter at intervals along the bench.

Capillary sand bench: compost in plastic pots takes up moisture from sand bed

Plastic matting

A modern development instead of sand is a special kind of plastic porous matting. This is lightweight and very convenient to use. It can be cut and tailored to fit any shape of staging and even cleaned in a washing machine at the end of the season. It can be spread on polythene sheeting laid over the staging, and the edge dipped in a run of guttering as already described.

All capillary materials, such as sand, vermiculite, plastic matting, glass wool wicks, and so on, must be thoroughly moistened when being set up, otherwise the flow of water by capillary action may not start.

A neat little arrangement for simple distribution of water semi-automatically, which has now been in use for some years, is the siphon system. This has a small plastic tank fed with a drip feed valve connected to the mains or other source of

Above: plastic float valve cistern attached to wall at far end provides constant water level for sand layer in upper bench
Below: lower bench is supplied with water from auxiliary cistern at its own level

water supply. The valve is a sensitive one and by hand adjustment the rate at which the tank fills can be regulated. When full the tank siphons its water into plastic piping fitted with nozzles at intervals. These can be set over pots or along rows of plants, or along a sand or plastic matting capillary bench if desired. Of course with this arrangement you have first to experiment with the filling rate and adjust the amount of water according to the plants' needs or the area to be watered. Various other proprietary systems using trickle-feed pipe lines and nozzles have also been introduced.

Electricity

Electrically-controlled systems are, as you would expect, extremely accurate and efficient. Water flow in this case is governed by a water valve operated by electromagnet, and the water can be fed to nozzles or spray jets.

Two methods are now used to control the electromagnetic valve. The first is called an 'electronic leaf'. There are several designs, but they basically estimate the drying rate of a surface and switch the valve on and off accordingly. The second is an important innovation using a photoelectric cell to estimate the solar energy reaching the greenhouse. An electronic circuit then controls the valve to issue the right 'dose' of water. At night or during very dull weather no water, or very little, will be given. On a bright sunny day, however, the photocell will 'instruct' the valve to water at frequent intervals. This photoelectric system can be adapted to almost any kind of watering – capillary bench, trickle-feed nozzles or overhead spray. It can also be used for mist propagation and when connected to mist jets can be further used for automatic damping-down. A selection of application methods can be controlled by one photoelectric cell if desired, and the system is as automatic as you can get. Once set up it requires virtually no attention.

Slimes and algae

With all automatic watering there is usually trouble sooner or later from slimes and algae. Good light encourages their growth, so remember never to use transparent plastic tubing to convey water. Unused areas of sand benches can be covered with black polythene. Fortunately, there are now products available, such as Algofen, that will keep water systems free from slimes and algae. This has been cleared as safe by the Ministry of Agriculture and can be used freely *according to label instructions* even where there are edible crops.

CONTROLLING CONDITIONS IN THE GREENHOUSE

VENTILATION AND HUMIDITY IN THE GREENHOUSE

One of the advantages of growing plants in a greenhouse is that the condition of the atmosphere can be controlled. Unfortunately many beginners seem to give this little consideration. Here we explain how best to regulate the circulation and humidity of the air in your greenhouse.

The vital constituents of the air – carbon dioxide, oxygen, water vapour and nitrogen – are visible. The old saying 'out of sight, out of mind' applies! Yet air should be considered a 'fertilizer' because it is essential as a plant food. In photosynthesis, carbon dioxide (CO_2) in the atmosphere is used by plants, in the presence of water and light, to make starches, sugars and celluloses, and many other chemicals of which they are composed. Oxygen is also used and exchanged, and some plants – such as the pea family – make use of certain beneficial bacteria in their root nodules to take in nitrogen directly. Normally nitrogen is taken up only as nitrates from the soil.

The humidity of the air, the moisture it contains, is also unseen – but its presence becomes apparent when drops form as condensation on the greenhouse structure. A high humidity can be bad in winter and good in summer, so this also has to be controlled.

Adjustment of ventilators

Make sure that there are plenty of ventilators in the greenhouse structure. There is no need to be afraid of having too many, since you don't have to use them all at the same time. Although there should be a generous number they must fit tightly: ventilation does not have to mean *draughts*. Many times in the winter the vents may have to be kept closed, and even a small icy draught will counteract any benefits a heater may give. Sliding doors, now commonly fitted to greenhouses, are useful for extra ventilation in summer. They can be adjusted easily and will not slam. Both side and roof ventilators should be fitted, preferably on both sides of the greenhouse. This enables them to be opened on the side away from the prevailing wind. Where to position side vents is a matter of some controversy. Often there may be little choice, especially if the greenhouse has a base wall. However, in summer, vents set as low as possible will give good air circulation, since hot air rises rapidly and draws cool in from below.

Adjustment of ventilation will affect both temperature and humidity. Apart from the obvious cooling effect of the air change, a flow of air increases evaporation of water from the greenhouse. When water evaporates it absorbs energy, in the form of heat, from the surroundings. If the greenhouse interior is well damped down and watered in summer this will have a further cooling action. On the other hand, a fast flow of air may hasten evaporation excessively and you will have to be constantly watering to keep the air moist and the plants from drying out. Ventilation must therefore be given in moderation, and the amount you give will depend on the type of plants you grow and the outside weather conditions.

Humidity

In summer most plants prefer a moist atmosphere since this reduces the rate at which they lose moisture from their leaves – the process called transpiration. This, in turn, lessens the rate at which the roots dry out, and so the plants are able to absorb nutrients through their roots more easily. A moist atmosphere in summer also discourages red spider mite, a very common pest when the air is hot and dry.

In winter the aim is quite different – every attempt must be made to keep down humidity. In most home greenhouses the rule is, the drier the air, the better. When conditions are cool, perhaps cold, and daylight poor, many fungoid diseases flourish when the air is humid. These include moulds, mildews, and fungi causing stem and storage organ rots (of bulbs, corms, tubers, and the like). Ventilation again becomes very important, but many beginners are reluctant to give it. However, there are many winter days in Britain when the outside air is well above freezing, and you can then ventilate freely. Again, much depends on the plants you are growing, but in most home greenhouses a temperature higher than

Ventilating and humidifying equipment

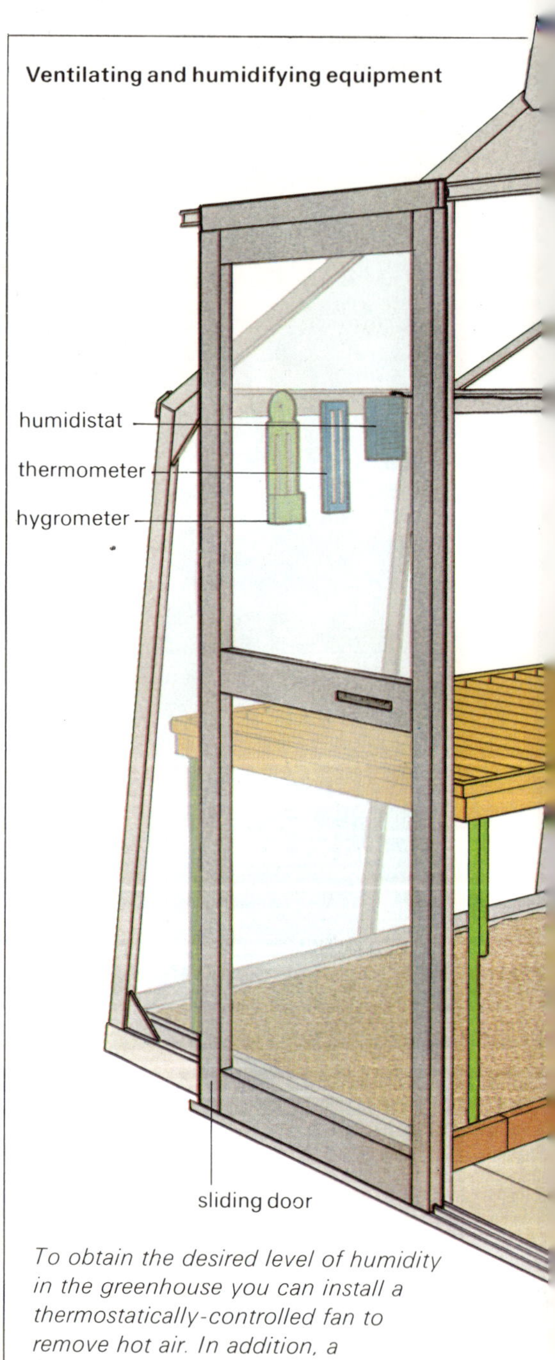

To obtain the desired level of humidity in the greenhouse you can install a thermostatically-controlled fan to remove hot air. In addition, a humidifier, controlled by a humidistat, will dampen the air when humidity is low
For adequate ventilation at all times it is advisable to have automatic roof ventilators that will open or close, depending on the temperature within the greenhouse

5–8°C (40–45°F) is rarely necessary.

In winter the air is further kept dry by *not* damping down and by watering, sparingly, only those plants that are still growing. Dormant plants should require no water at all. Staging that is kept moist automatically in summer, or covered with moist peat or grit to maintain humidity, must be allowed to go dry.

Use of heaters

Paraffin wick heaters are very popular and are probably the most widely used method of warming a greenhouse. Unfortunately, they are also frequently associated with winter plant troubles attributed to fumes. Typical symptoms are browning of leaf edges, leaf shrivelling, and scorched spots. Often this is caused by oxygen starvation, due again to lack of ventilation. Oil must have oxygen to burn properly. If a greenhouse is tightly sealed, with an oil heater burning, the time will come when the air becomes short of oxygen. The oil will not burn properly so that oil vapour and other results of incomplete combustion – harmful to plants – are produced. Where oil heaters

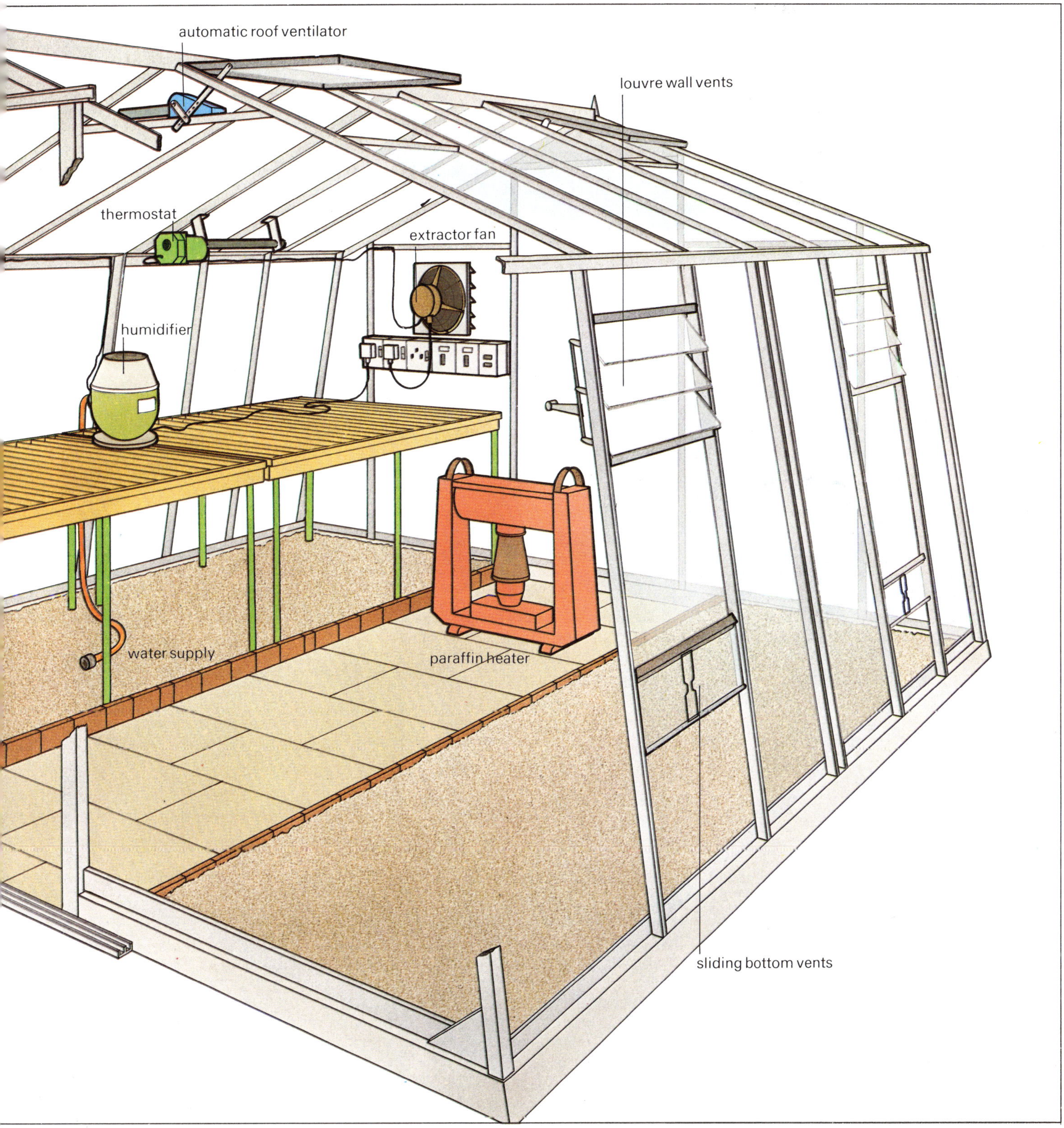

Above: easy to fit automatic roof, or side ventilator works on a special unit filled with a mineral that expands or contracts with temperature changes, activating a push rod to lift the vent
Below: fix extractor fan, controlled by rod thermostat, high up to remove hottest air, and if placing thermostat high up, set it to allow for temperature difference between plant level and its height

are used there must *always* be some ventilation, however cold the weather. Because oil forms its own volume of water, as water vapour, when it burns. This contributes to humidity and is another reason for carefully checking your ventilation.

Condensation

When the weather is cold some condensation is normal and indeed inevitable. If there is so much that drips form everywhere and the glass (or plastic) is coated with droplets, ventilation is seriously at fault. You are also probably overwatering. Plastic greenhouses are particularly affected by condensation because the water forms droplets instead of a film as it does on glass. The droplets interfere with light entry so that plants may become pale and weak. Efficient ventilation is the answer, together with reduction in quantity of water applied.

Watering

In summer it is a good idea to water early in the morning. This keeps up humidity during the day and there is adequate moisture for the plants at their time of greatest need – during bright daylight when photosynthesis is most rapid and plants are growing quickly. In the night there is little growth and little water requirement. Moreover, a high humidity during the cool of the night can encourage diseases like grey mould even in summer, something you may often see in tomato houses. High daytime humidity is good for tomatoes, aiding pollination.

Fan ventilation is now popular in greenhouses in summer owing to the ease with which it can be operated by a thermostatic control. It is wise to have some form of automatic humidification in conjunction with fan ventilation, prevent rapid drying out of the house. Over on the next page we tell you more about humidity and the most desirable levels according to the plants grown, how to use a wet and dry bulb hygrometer to help measure the changing levels of humidity in your own greenhouse; automatic humidifiers described on page 30 help cut down manual watering.

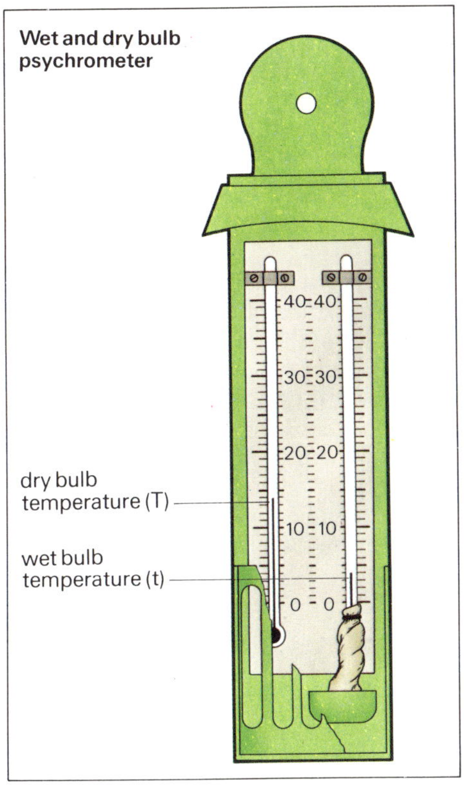

Above: two examples of a wet and dry bulb psychrometer. The diagram on the left shows the greenhouse type, while the one on the right, protected by louvred screens against the elements, is one you might spot in public parks or seaside places

Below: damp down greenhouse paths regularly during hot, dry spells; this helps to contain evaporation in the surrounding atmosphere

The temperatures recorded on the dry bulb thermometer (referred to as T) and the wet bulb thermometer (t) are noted, and by reference to tables supplied with the instrument, the relative humidity of the air can be found. The relative humidity, called RH for short, is the measure usually used. An RH of, say, 60 per cent – a roughly 'normal' figure, means that the air contains 60 per cent of the water that it is possible for it to hold at the temperature when the reading is taken.

The direct-reading hygrometer is simply a dial calibrated in RH, and usually also has sections marked 'dry', 'normal' and 'moist'. It works by the expansion and contraction of a special fibre that moves a needle on the scale, but the instruments are rarely accurate at the extreme ends. Fortunately for the greenhouse this does not matter. For most purposes, readings from about 35 to 50 can be considered 'dry', 50 to about 70 as 'normal', and 70 to 85 as 'moist'. In summer the RH should generally be kept not below about 70 per cent and in winter not below about 50 per cent. This is because the humidity level must relate to the outdoor temperature.

Regulating humidity

By siting plants carefully in the greenhouse it is possible to provide a single plant (or a small group) with its own microclimate. Trays of moist sand placed near, or on, an automatic capillary watering bench, will give localized moist air. Plants needing drier conditions can be put on shelves, near vents or on slatted staging. In summer many of the subtropical species can be freely sprayed with a fine mist of water to moisten the foliage thoroughly. The water should be clean and lime-free; if the mains tap water is limey, use clean rainwater instead so that the leaves do not become marked with lime deposits. In summer nearly all plants, whatever their nature, will benefit if you damp down the floor and staging from time to time. How much damping down you do depends on the humidity requirements of your plants.

Most forms of automatic watering will also keep up humidity automatically. Special automatic humidifiers are obtainable and usually consist of a fan blowing air over a spray of water, this operation being controlled by a special switch that is sensitive to air moisture. The photoelectric method of automatic watering can also be adapted to control humidity by being connected to misting jets that damp down the floor or staging.

For hot-water pipes, and similar types of heat radiator, simple water reservoirs with wicks can be fitted (as is done with domestic radiators). But when the heating is in operation in winter it is often desirable to keep humidity down. For the same reason the 'humidity' trays fitted to some older designs of paraffin oil heater should rarely be used.

ESTIMATING GREENHOUSE HEATING NEEDS

Before buying heating equipment for the greenhouse it is essential that you know roughly how much heat is necessary to maintain the temperature at the desired level during cold weather. To this end, you must first calculate the rate of heat loss.

Heating greenhouses is still a very misunderstood subject and much of the equipment available is far from perfect. It is not unusual for beginners to buy heaters that are quite unable to cope during severe cold spells. What may seem a financial saving on equipment and fuel can lead to a great deal of waste.

Once you have calculated how much heat the plants in your greenhouse will need during the coldest spells, you can decide whether or not a heater is necessary, and – if it is – you can work out an approximate figure for fuel consumption. However, even the most expensive fuels need not be a serious burden in the average small greenhouse.

When assessing heating requirements, there is an important basic point that should be borne in mind: the higher the temperature in the greenhouse compared with that outside, the faster heat will be lost – and the faster your heater will have to develop heat to maintain the temperature you want.

Clearly, you must aim for the lowest necessary temperature for fuel economy, and take all precautions to avoid waste. Heating equipment should distribute heat evenly, so that no part of the greenhouse structure is raised to an unnecessarily high temperature. Many beginners tend to have excessive levels in winter, whereas nearly all the common popular greenhouse plants are perfectly happy with about 4–7°C (40–45°F).

Assessing heat loss

To find out approximately how much heat your heater will need to produce, you must first get an idea of how fast your greenhouse will lose heat when the temperature outside is at its lowest, and that inside at the desirable minimum. Armed with this knowledge, you can choose equipment with the output to balance the loss; only if the outside temperature continues to drop (as in a very severe winter) may some form of extra heating be needed.

Construction materials like glass, wood and brick have widely different thermal conductivities and rates of heat loss. The area of these materials, and the heat loss through the floor, are additional factors to take into account.

Summing up, to calculate how much heat your greenhouse will lose at any desired interior minimum temperature, when the temperature outside is at its lowest, you need to know the following points:

1 The desired interior minimum temperature.
2 The expected exterior minimum.
3 The area of construction materials.
4 The area of the ground covered.

Let us assume that **1** is 7°C (45°F) and that **2** is −7°C (20°F) which is a good few degrees of frost. Various methods of calculation can be used to estimate heat loss, using factors to take into account the thermal conductivity of the different construction materials. However, they

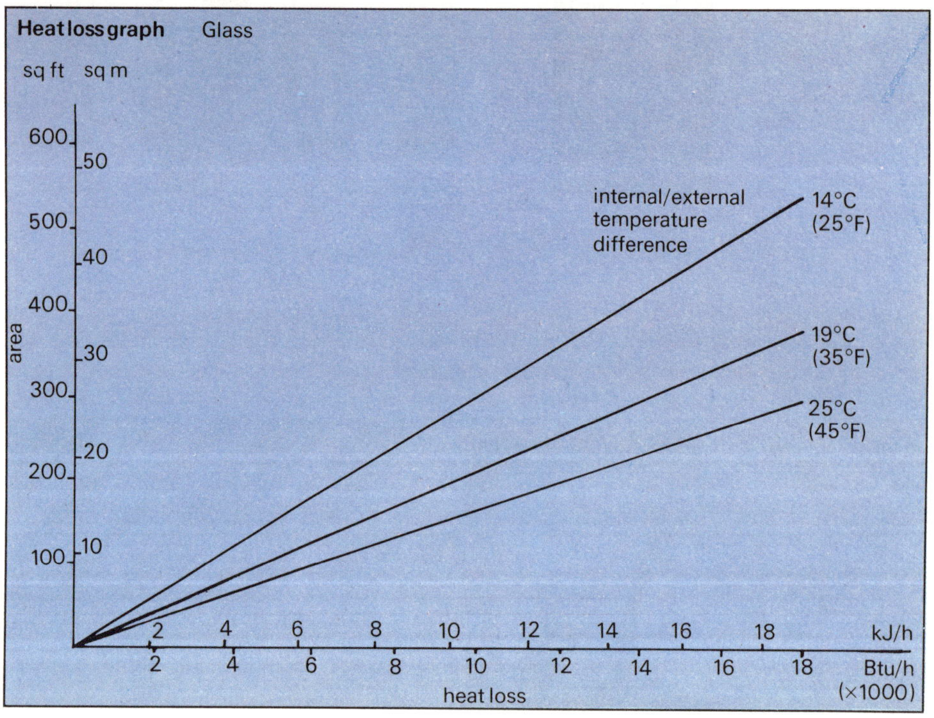

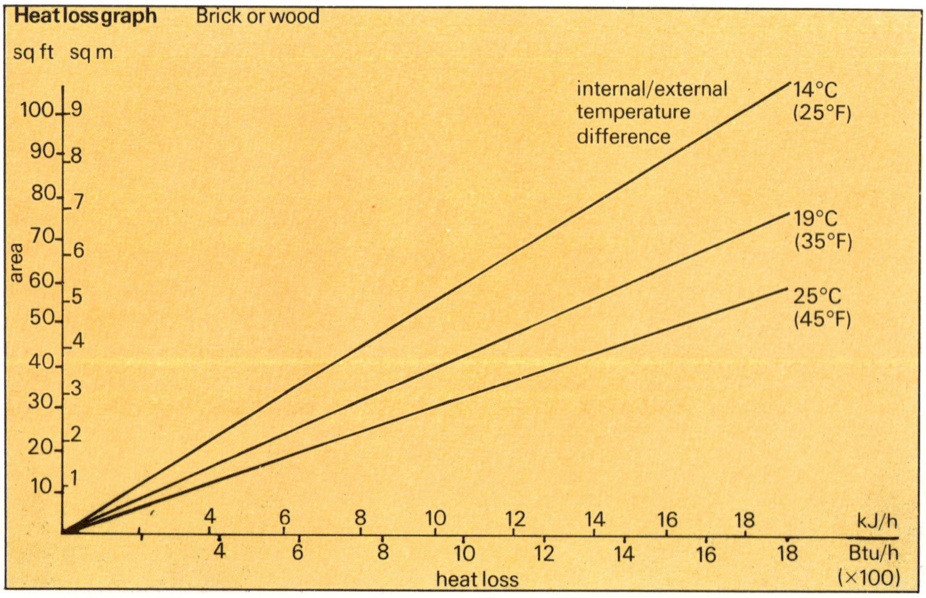

To use the graphs appearing on the facing page it is necessary first to calculate the areas of the glass, and wood or brick, that go to make up your greenhouse. The example below shows how this can be done

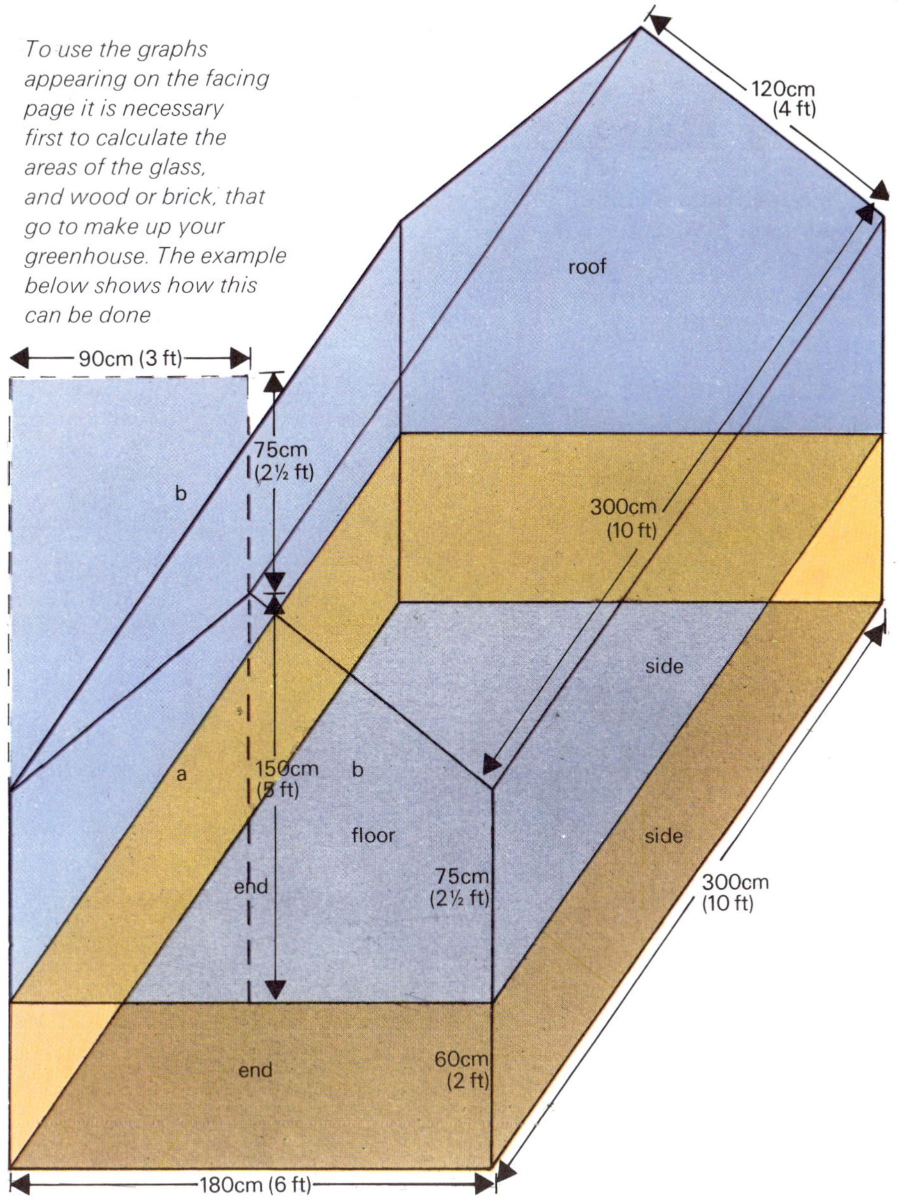

Calculating areas

Glass				
roof	120×300cm	(4×10 ft)	(×2)=7.2m²	(80 ft²)
sides	75×300cm	(2½×10 ft)	(×2)=4.5m²	(50 ft²)
ends (a+b)	225×90cm	(7½×3 ft)	(×2)=4.05m²	(45 ft²)
			total=15.75m²	(175 ft²)
Base walls (brick or wood)				
sides	60×300cm	(2×10 ft)	(×2)=3.6m²	(40 ft²)
ends	60×180cm	(2×6 ft)	(×2)=2.16m²	(24 ft²)
			total=5.76m²	(64 ft²)
Floor	180×300cm	(6×10 ft)=5.4m²		(60 ft²)

The graphs to the left enable you to discover the maximum heat loss rate that your greenhouse is likely to experience during the winter – and thereby choose heating equipment of the appropriate output. As well as the more likely temperature difference of 14°C, graphs are also included for 19°C and 25°C (25°F, 35°F and 45°F)

are often lengthy and complicated. Here, we give a method involving simple graphs that are based on figures already worked out for indoor/outdoor temperature differences of 14°C (25°F), ie 7°C inside and –7°C outside; 19°C (35°F); and 25°C (45°F).

The graphs give an estimate of the heat lost from glass, and brick or wood (that are more or less the same in this respect), for any section of the greenhouse. There is no need for a graph for heat lost through the floor, since this is near enough 100 × its area in sq m (10 × the area in sq ft), the figure obtained being kilojoules, or British thermal units, per hour (kJ/h or Btu/h). All good-quality heating equipment should be rated in terms of these units – don't buy any unless this is specified by the manufacturer. The area of glazing bars can be ignored, being quite small in comparison with the main areas of construction materials.

An estimate to within about 950 kJ/h (900 Btu/h) is good enough – equal to about 250 watts in electrical terms. Any figure of kJ/h can be converted to watts by dividing by 3·6 (3·4 in case of Btu/h).

Take the example of an average-sized greenhouse of 1·8 3m (6 × 10 ft), with a wooden base wall, glass sides and roof, to explain the calculation.

By referring to the graphs, we find the following:

For glass, 15·75 sq m (175 sq ft) equals about 6100 kJ/h (5800 Btu/h).

For brick or wood, 5·76 sq m (64 sq ft) equals about 1100 kJ/h (1050 Btu/h).

For the floor, 5·4 sq m × 120 (60 sq ft × 10) equals 650 kJ/h (600 Btu/h).

This gives a final total of 7850 kJ/h (7450 Btu/h).

From this it is seen that if there is about 7°C (12°F) of frost outside (–7°C or 20°F), to keep the temperature at 7°C (45°F) inside, a heater giving about 7800 kJ/h (7500 Btu/h) must be installed. If this figure is divided by 3·6 (3·4), we get about 2·2 Kw for an electric heater: a 2 Kw or, to be safe, 2½ Kw electric heater should therefore be installed.

Although these graphs assume the popular 7°C (45°F) minimum, and the average 7°C (12°F) of frost, it should be realized that most plants will be quite safe should the temperature in the greenhouse fall for short spells to merely frost-free.

Provided the heating equipment has some form of thermostatic control, no heat should be wasted if the equipment is overrated. In fact, it is wise to err on the side of equipment that when turned on full, gives a higher heat output than necessary, rather than risk an under-estimate.

GREENHOUSE HEATING SYSTEMS

Having explained how to estimate the heating requirements of your greenhouse, here we look at various ways of producing that heat.

The wrong choice of greenhouse heating equipment can mean high fuel bills, so make sure you pick the right methods for your particular needs.

Paraffin wick heaters

The most widely-used form of heater seems to be the paraffin wick type. This is convenient and portable but the necessity for manual control can lead to fuel being wasted. In recent years attempts have been made to automate combustion, but the designs are prone to fume and still need further improvement. Another disadvantage of this thermostatic type of heater is that it continues to give off considerable heat and consume much paraffin *after* it has been turned off.

Many very small heaters are sold, but often they are quite incapable of providing enough warmth, so always check the kilowatt (or Btu) output, and also the paraffin capacity. If a heater is to provide enough warmth it will have to burn adequate paraffin, for you cannot get heat from nothing.

It is important to choose a heater that is designed for the greenhouse, as some domestic types give off fumes that can harm plant life. Generally, the 'blue flame' type of heater can be recommended where a good growing temperature needs to be maintained. With this type, extra air can get to the wick – promoting more efficient combustion – and there is little or no fuming.

A paraffin heater should preferably have hot-air tubes to distribute the warmth more efficiently, otherwise a current of warm air will rise directly upwards and be cooled by contact with the greenhouse roof. This means that a considerable amount of heat is lost before the warm air gets a chance to circulate properly. This rule, incidentally, applies to other forms of greenhouse heater as well, so always try to distribute the heat evenly around the house.

Other constructional features to look for include a stainless steel lamp chimney, a copper tank (that will not rust and leak), and a reservoir of reasonable size so that filling is not a chore. Some designs are fitted with a humidity water trough, but this is both unnecessary and undesirable.

Heating equipment

Combustion of paraffin produces too much water vapour as it is, without adding to humidity by filling a water trough. If a trough is fitted, leave it empty.

An especially useful feature is that some designs can be kept topped-up automatically with paraffin from a large drum, thus enabling them to burn for long periods without attention.

Paraffin wick heaters can be used in greenhouses with a floor area of about 1·8 × 3·7m (6 × 12 ft), but in this case the maximum-output heater is usually necessary, or else two or more heaters, depending on temperature requirements. Where high temperatures are needed it is better to choose some other form of heating equipment.

Natural gas

This has now become a popular fuel, but for the type of heater where combustion products are released into the greenhouse, you should exercise the same care over ventilation as in the case of paraffin lamps – otherwise you will have trouble with condensation and unsatisfactory combustion of the fuel.

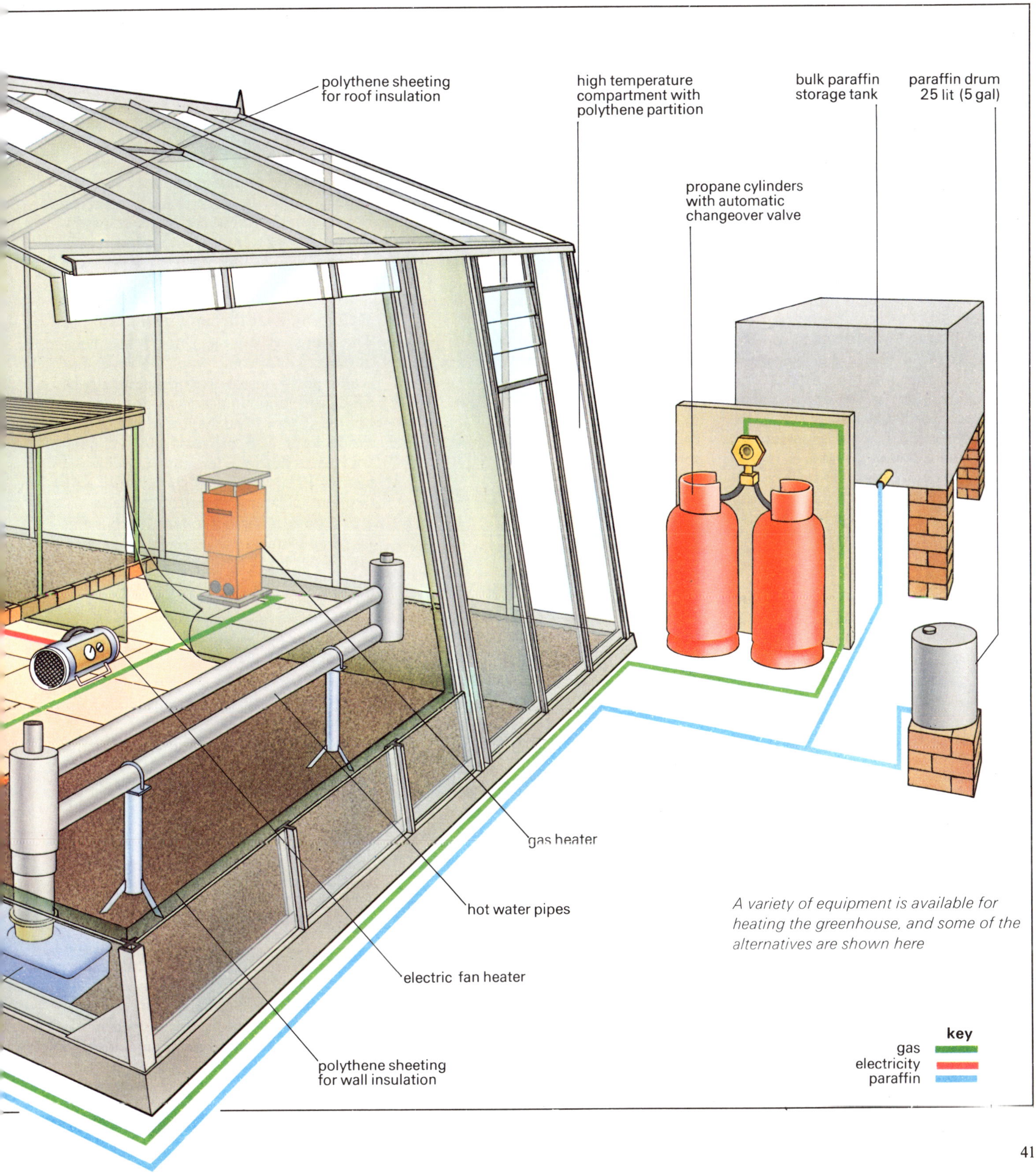

A variety of equipment is available for heating the greenhouse, and some of the alternatives are shown here

With natural gas there is better thermostatic control, hence less waste of fuel. Where it is impossible to run a piped main, a bottled source can be used, though this tends to be expensive. Continuous burning can be achieved by using a pair of bottles with an automatic changeover valve that comes into operation when one bottle is empty.

Hot water pipes

These were one of the first forms of greenhouse heating, but unless high temperatures are required or the greenhouse is very large – exceeding the average amateur size – installation and running can be expensive. Water pipes hold heat for a long time and are difficult to control accurately by thermostat. At high temperatures heat exchange is more rapid and control better.

Modern equipment is designed for easy installation and maintenance. Hot water pipes are an especially practical proposition when the fuel used is the same as that employed for domestic heating, for bulk buying at a cheaper rate is then possible.

Although solid fuel is the cheapest for hot water pipe heating, liquid and gaseous fuels are more easily and accurately controlled by thermostat.

It is important to have as generous a run of pipes as possible, and preferable to convey the heat around three sides of the greenhouse.

Don't put the pipes too near the glass – you may find it best to run them along each side of a central pathway.

Electricity

This need not be expensive unless wastefully employed – as in the case of using an immersion heater to warm hot water pipes. Electricity is most economical when heaters with a low heat capacity – and hence immediate response to thermostatic control – are used to distribute the warmth. It has the advantage of not giving off water vapour, that could otherwise cause trouble in winter months.

The most suitable appliances are fan heaters, tubular heaters, and convectors.

Fan heaters These should have the fan and heating element switched on together by a separate, rod-type thermostat. Moving air will quickly transfer the warmth from the heater to the greenhouse sides. Once these are warmed, it is best to let the air remain relatively still.

A rod thermostat between the power point and the heater will give more sensitive temperature control – provided the heater's own thermostat is on its highest setting.

Tubular heaters These are designed to hold little heat and are hollow inside. They should be spread out around the greenhouse and not all banked in one or two positions.

Convectors These are best put under staging if possible so that the rising warm air is better distributed.

Never let any one small area of the greenhouse structure become hotter than really necessary. The greater the heat gradient between the inside and the outside, the faster heat will be lost.

Dividing into compartments

A greenhouse can be divided into compartments of different temperature with advantage. A permanent partition with a door, or a temporary polythene one, can be used. An extra warm section should preferably be a middle one – or the end farthest from the door. Lining a greenhouse with polythene can cut heat loss by up to 40 per cent – if done correctly. Allow some 13–25mm ($\frac{1}{2}$–1 in) of static air between the polythene and the glass.

Retaining heat through insulation

The value of double glazing has been appreciated for some years. However, the sealed-glass variety used domestically is expensive and impractical for greenhouses. Extra glass panes added to the inside have also proved far from convenient because condensation and dirt get behind them in a very short time, and frequent cleaning is not easy when a greenhouse is full of plants. Polythene sheeting is much easier to manage, and can be put up in autumn and left for the winter months only; it is simple to take down, roll up and store for the summer.

The insulation effect of polythene is quite dramatic. At least 40 per cent can be cut from the normal heat loss figure – and this means a corresponding reduction of fuel bills. Lining is especially suited to greenhouses with electric fan heaters or other 'dry' forms of equipment. Where paraffin or gas is burnt – and there is no flue – condensation may be a problem, for considerable water vapour is produced during combustion. In all cases, however, the vents should be separately lined so that they can be opened to permit generous and free ventilation whenever the weather permits.

Remember that the sun is a valuable source of free heat, so any insulation arrangements you may put into operation should not obscure light longer than necessary. Only a little winter sunlight will shoot up greenhouse temperatures even when it's well below freezing outside.

Left: old carpeting put on greenhouse roof at night conserves heat when cold

EFFECTS OF LIGHT ON PLANT GROWTH

The first part of this section on the use of artificial light examines the principles behind the effects of light on plant growth. We go on to deal with the techniques and equipment for growing plants with artificial light that can be adapted from commercial practice for use in the home or greenhouse.

Most gardeners are familiar with seed potatoes that have been chitted up in the light – the sprouts are sturdy and blue-green in colour. Now compare these with potato sprouts that have been stored for several months in a sack in a dark corner of a shed. They are etiolated – pale and sometimes up to 15cm (6 in) in length. This is a very clear example of what happens to plants when they are deprived of natural light.

Unfortunately the problem of making up a plant's light deficiencies cannot necessarily be solved by simply suspending an ordinary light bulb over it. The reaction of different species and varieties of plants to light is very complex – no two species react in the same way; some plants prefer full sun while others like shade (sometimes even heavy shade) and some flower in summer while others flower in spring, autumn or even winter, each one adapting itself to particular environmental needs and conditions.

Before you can use artificial light intelligently with the object of supplementing daylight and assisting plant growth, you will need more precise knowledge of the principles of light and the effects of light on plant growth. You will then also be able to appreciate why some sources of artificial light are better than others.

The effect of latitude

The difference between the amount of solar light radiation (sun's energy reaching the Earth) that is received in summer

Below: a colourful group of popular house plants thriving under the beneficial influence of a Grolux tube

and winter is due largely to latitude. The farther from the equator your garden lies the lower the amount of radiation it receives. In Britain, even in the extreme south of England, the sun never rises more than 15 degrees above the horizon in mid winter (December); as it then has to penetrate a much thicker layer of the Earth's atmosphere its power is reduced. In fact the total solar energy supplied in a winter month may be only 10 per cent of that experienced in a summer month.

In addition to the effect produced by latitude there are also local conditions to take into account. Cloud cover, for instance, which can vary over quite a short distance, and industrial pollution, can be important factors in reducing solar radiation. Taking the average figures for the British Isles as a whole, there is not sufficient natural light (not enough daylight hours) to grow many plants effectively between late autumn and mid spring (October and March).

Early experiments

In the late 1940s W. J. C. Lawrence of the John Innes Institute noted that serious light deficiencies existed during the winter months and he started using artificial light on tomato seedlings, not only to produce better plants but to shorten the time between pricking out and planting. Although the results were rewarding, the cost of the lamps used at the time (high pressure mercury) did not convince growers that the expense was worthwhile.

Since that time more efficient lamps have been produced, commercial growing rooms introduced and the technique of inducing plants (chrysanthemums in particular) to flower throughout the year has become established practice.

Principle of light

Any source of radiation – whether the sun or an artificial radiator (lamp or heater, for example) – emits a certain amount of energy consisting of electromagnetic vibrations (such as visible light, radio waves or gamma rays). The wave motion of these vibrations has a constant speed but the length of the waves may vary, and it is the length of the waves that determines what kind of energy is produced. Some wavelengths – the relatively narrow waveband between 380nm and 780nm (one nm, or nanometer, is one millionth of a millimeter) – are visible to the human eye. It is this visible part of the spectrum that is called light.

Below 380nm comes ultra-violet radiation; this causes the skin to tan and can be dangerous to plants. Above 780nm is infra-red radiation (heat).

Within the visible spectrum the wave length of the radiation determines the colour of light. As the wavelength increases you see the following sequence of colours – violet, indigo, blue, green, yellow, orange and red. 'Beyond' red is far-red – partly outside the visible spectrum but important to plants. For convenience the spectrum can be simplified into four spectral divisions: blue 400–500nm, green 500–600nm, red 600–700nm and far-red 700–750nm.

Light can be considered not only as a wave motion but also as a flow of light particles. Each of these light particles represents a certain amount of energy that depends upon the wavelength (shown by colour) of the type of light; the shorter the wavelength the higher the amount of energy per light particle. Thus a blue light particle contains a greater amount of energy than a red one.

Plants react to light in three ways: to the intensity of light, to the duration of light and to the colour of light. Each of these reactions will now be considered in greater detail.

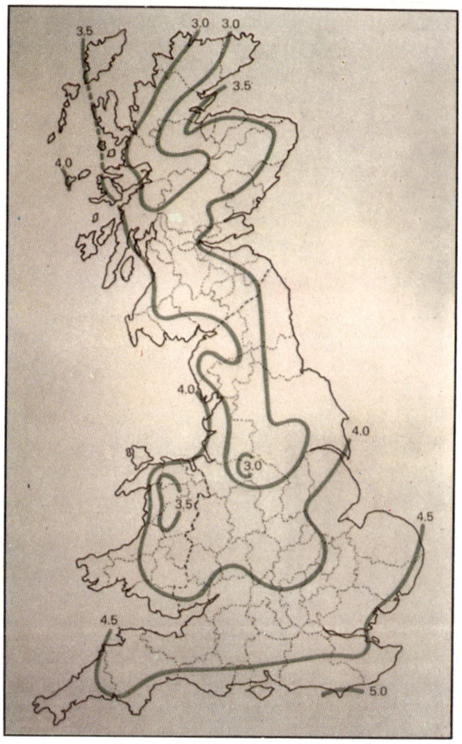

Right: map showing the average means of daily duration of bright sunshine (in hours) in Great Britain

Below: diagram showing how energy level decreases with increasing wavelength

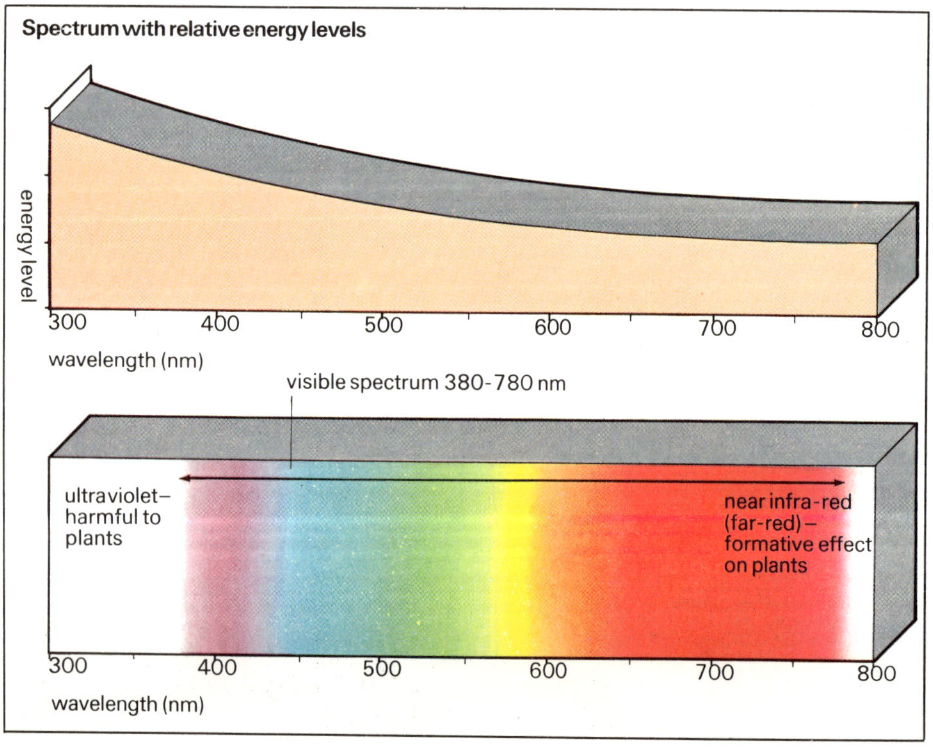

Light and photosynthesis

The energy necessary for plant growth is almost all derived from the radiant energy that is absorbed by the parts of the plant growing above ground. The carbon required by the plant for food and for cell structure is derived from the carbon dioxide in the air. Photosynthesis is the process by which light energy is used to reduce this carbon dioxide to sugars that can later be converted to a variety of different structural and food materials. Photosynthesis is dependent on the particular pigments (the chlorophylls)

Above: mixed varieties of year-round pot chrysanthemums – those in flower on the right received supplementary artificial light, the others did not

that produce the basic colour of the green leaves. Chlorophylls absorb mainly blue and red light; green is largely reflected.

Not all the light available to a plant is absorbed by the leaf; a proportion of it is reflected at the leaf surface and some light is transmitted through the leaf without being absorbed.

Allowing for this wastage, for photosynthesis to take place a great deal of light must fall on the leaf surface. Although this is likely to happen in summer, in winter the amount of sunlight available to greenhouse plants is greatly reduced.

In commercial practice the aim is to maintain between 5,000 and 10,000 lx (the amount of light falling on an area one metre square is measured in lx or lux). This will be dealt with in more detail in the following sections when we look at different kinds of lamps and their uses.

Light and photoperiodism

Photoperiodism is the effect of day-length on plant development. It has been known for more than 50 years that the flowering habits of some plants depend on the relative length of day and night and that these habits vary widely from one kind of plant to another.

This knowledge has led to a broad classification of plants into three groups. First there are those that will only flower (or will flower more readily) when the daily period of light exceeds a certain critical minimum; these are known as 'long-day' plants. In the second group are those that will flower only when the day-length is less than that critical minimum – 'short-day' plants. The third group contains plants that flower equally readily in any day-length – 'day-neutral' plants.

The position for individual plant species, however, cannot be stated quite so simply. Some plants require a certain day-length for bud initiation and a different period for flower development (short-day/long-day plants or long-day/short day plants). In others, sensitivity to day-length varies with temperature. The effects of relative day-length on flowering behaviour first drew attention to the phenomenon of photoperiodism and it is in the control of flowering that artificial lighting techniques have so far been used most successfully.

Sufficiently long photoperiods can be provided during naturally short days by using artificial light to shorten the night. This can be done by switching lights on at dusk to lengthen the day or turning them on for a few hours before dawn to produce the same effect at the opposite end of the day, or using them for a short period during the middle of the night – known commonly as night-break.

Only relatively low illuminance levels are needed to achieve the desired effect, the actual level depending on the type of plant concerned. Simple tungsten-filament lamps (domestic light bulbs) are generally used. You need not be too fussy about the arrangement of the lamps over the growing area so long as it provides the required illuminance as evenly and cheaply as possible. Generally a minimum of 50–100 lx is considered adequate.

Light and photomorphogenesis

The rate at which photosynthesis can take place depends on the number of suitable light energy particles received. Red light contains more light energy particles per unit of energy than any other suitable wavelength. From this it could be assumed that a pure-red light source would be the most beneficial for good plant growth. But there are other light requirements (in addition to photosynthesis) that must be taken into account if the plant is to develop satisfactorily. As well as red light (about 660nm), blue light (about 450nm) and far-red light (about 735nm) also exert controlling influences on plant development; this is known as photomorphogenesis – the effect of different light wavelengths on plant growth. Plants grown entirely in blue light have a suppressed, hard, dark appearance and are inclined to 'rosette', while those grown in red light tend to be softer, and suffer some degree of stem elongation. Red light can also suppress the elongation or etiolation that occurs in darkness, but far-red light cannot. Thus the effect of light on vegetative growth (stems and leaves) is complex. This, then, is the reason why the careful choice of a light source for growing plants in the greenhouse – or the house – is so important.

Right lamps for the light

Suitable lamps for artificial illumination are expensive and it would be unfortunate if you chose the wrong lamp for the lighting technique you had in mind. Photosynthesis, photoperiodism and photomorphogenesis are only three, albeit extremely important, factors to be taken into consideration. There are others, such as temperature, size of greenhouse, bench or bed widths, height of roof above the growing area, and number, type and stage of development (seedling or mature stage) of the plants and the proximity of other plants in the growing area. These aspects will now be covered in more detail.

USING ARTIFICIAL LIGHT IN THE GREENHOUSE

Having seen how plants react to light the next step is to make use of this knowledge to determine how much irradiation greenhouse plants need and the most effective ways of providing it.

The commercial grower uses light to grow plants to a certain stage in the quickest possible time. He is, therefore, prepared to meet the cost of providing the high level of irradiance (the energy emitted by the lamp – including light) and temperatures necessary to give him optimum growth response. Furthermore he grows, in many cases, tens of thousands of plants at a time, which enables him to install the lamps in blocks at least four lamps square – making a minimum of 16 lamps. He can also double-batch – treat two batches of plants at the same time by moving the lamps every 12 hours from one batch to the other.

The grower uses artificial light to start plants early; for example he will propagate tomatoes in the middle of winter ready for planting out in the greenhouse from late winter to mid spring (early January to mid March), while cucumbers are planted out before this and lettuce are cropped from late autumn to mid spring (October right through to March). He also uses light to extend daylight – by turning the lamps on at dusk or before dawn, in the middle of the night or from dusk to dawn.

Home greenhouse uses

The amateur gardener may be interested in these techniques but will also want to provide extra light during dull winter days to ensure that plants (such as saintpaulia, or other houseplants) continue growing and flowering during the months when the average natural light is not strong enough to promote normal plant development.

The amateur gardener, therefore, does not need to be too concerned about the commercial growers' exacting growing conditions. You can, however, use artificial light effectively by starting later in the season, say at the beginning of spring (early to mid February), so that once the propagating stage has been completed the plants can be set out in their growing positions at a time of the year when natural light is improving and outside

Isolux diagram
2400mm (8ft) 125W lamp
Height: 400mm (16in)

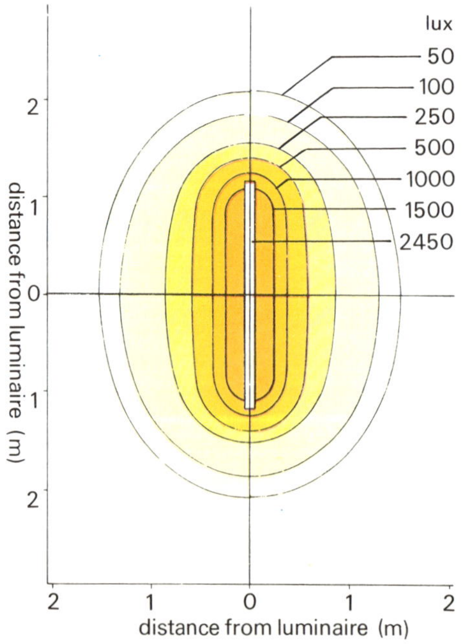

Above: the area under the greenhouse staging can be made use of by installing supplementary lighting that is mounted under the bench
Left: diagram showing the illuminance distribution from a 125W fluorescent tube

temperatures are rising, and when it won't be too costly to maintain a minimum temperature of 13°C (55°F) throughout the night.

However, during the period from seed germination to planting out you will have to keep temperatures up to around 18°C (65°F) during the day, dropping down to 16°C (60°F) at night. To heat the whole greenhouse to these temperatures would be very expensive, but fortunately there are ways of keeping the heating bills under control. The first step is to reduce the heat losses from the house to the outside air. A 250-gauge polyethylene sheet attached to the inside of the glazing bars will effectively save up to 40 per cent heat loss. Next, as only a few plants will be irradiated, use a plastic curtain (500-gauge polyethylene) to partition off the propagating area. This area must have some means of ventilation, but if the greenhouse has fan ventilation do not include it in the propagating area – a single roof vent should be adequate for this. You can, however, use a small fan to circulate air among the young plants, and help deter grey mould (botrytis). But if you are already using a fan heater to boost the air temperature, then an additional fan will not be necessary to provide ventilation.

Uniform illuminance

Before choosing and installing one of the lamps readily available, there is one more factor that needs to be considered – the evenness of illuminance that the lamp provides. How this evenness varies can be seen from isolux diagrams; an isolux is a line joining equal levels of illuminance. These figures vary appreciably according to the type of lamp and luminaire (reflector) used. The diagram (left) shows the illuminance distribution from one 2400mm (8 ft) 125 watt fluorescent tube mounted at a height of 400mm (16 in). Observe that the lines are more or less oval and that the illuminance falls more rapidly as the distance from the lamp increases. As commercial growers must have illuminance that is as even as possible across the growing area (to ensure uniform plant growth), the aim is to provide an illuminance within 10 per cent plus or minus of the recommended illuminance. For example: if an illuminance of 5000 lx is stipulated then the illuminance across the growing area should not be more than 5500 lx or less than 4500 lx; the latter illuminance level is generally referred to as the cut-off figure.

It can be clearly seen that the cut-off for a fluorescent tube is only a few centimetres, so to irradiate an area more than 150mm (6 in) in width it will be necessary to use two or more tubes. You can see that immediately under the lamp the illuminance is 2450 lx but at a distance of 1m ($3\frac{1}{4}$ ft) on either side it has fallen to about 200 lx – less than one-tenth. Note also that the light output at each end of the tube drops by nearly one half (to 1250 lx), so you could not expect the same plant response beneath the area 150mm (6 in) wide at either end where the illuminance is less, as you would from the remaining 2130mm (7 ft) length of tube.

To take an example: supposing you wish to provide 2450 lx at plant level with two 2400mm (8 ft) tubes fixed 400mm (16 in) above the growing area, it would then be necessary to install the tubes approximately 300mm (12 in) apart – the distance being measured from the centre line of each lamp. If you then decided to increase the illuminance to 5000 lx, the distance from the centre line of each lamp would be reduced to 50mm (2 in).

Advantages of fluorescent tubes

Despite the apparent complications in setting up a lighting installation with fluorescent tubes, this light source has several advantages. First, being a linear source of light, an even illuminance can be expected over the growing area. Secondly, fluorescent tubes need very little headroom compared with mercury and sodium discharge lamps and so are ideal for the modern small greenhouse, where the height of the eaves level above the bench is only 760mm ($2\frac{1}{2}$ ft), and also for use under the staging.

As a general rule the area under greenhouse benches is too dark during the winter months for the majority of plants to grow normally, even if temperatures higher than 7°C (45°F) are maintained. However, two fluorescent tubes under a 760mm ($2\frac{1}{2}$ ft) high bench will transform this normally unproductive area into one that will grow many plants, even in the middle of winter. But extra precautions

Diagrams showing the arrangement of 125W tubes to give illuminances of 11000 and 8000 lx at various different heights above the greenhouse staging

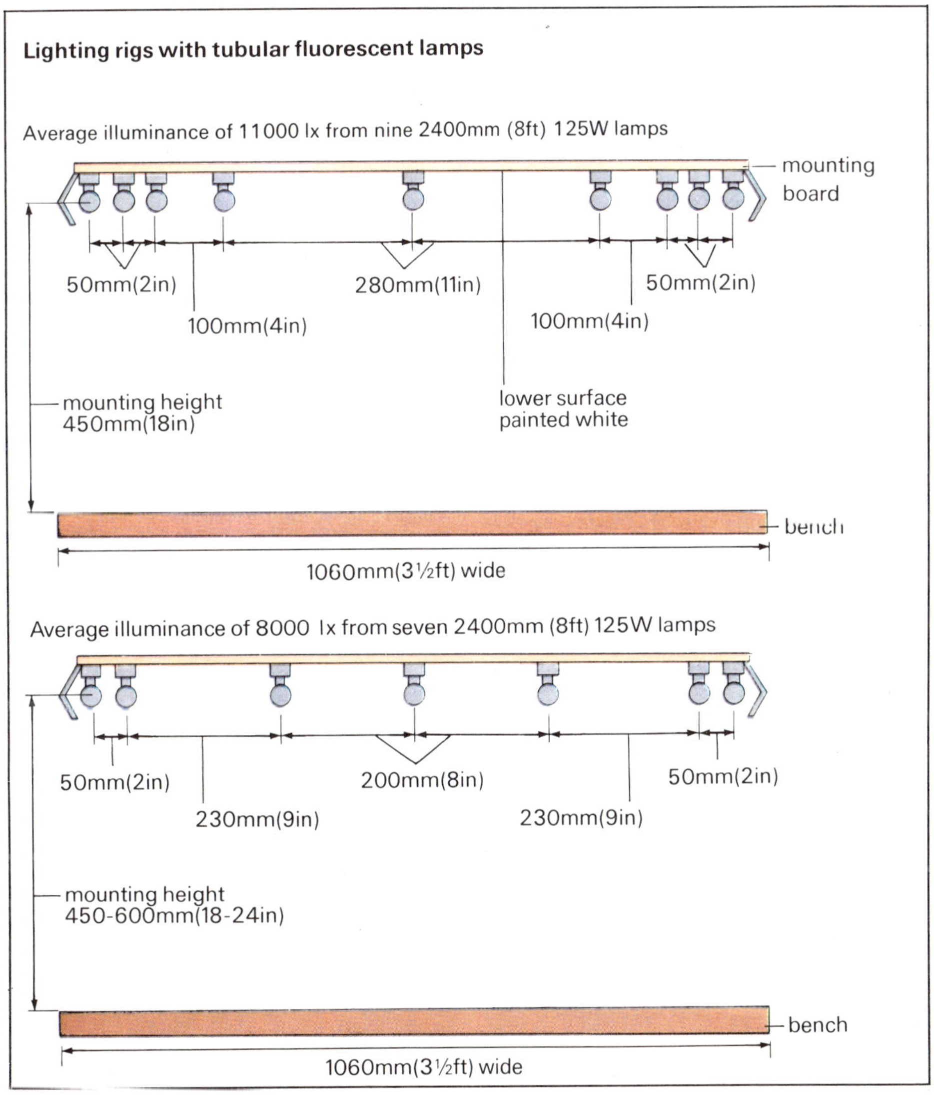

will be needed to ensure all the electrical fittings under the bench are protected from water seeping through from the bench above.

The third advantage of the fluorescent tube is that it radiates much less heat than would mercury and sodium discharge lamps used to irradiate the same amount of bench area.

Other kinds of lamp

To appreciate the advantages of the fluorescent lamp, compare it with other available sources of artificial light, for instance the MBFR/U (mercury fluorescent reflector), SOX (low pressure sodium) and SON (high pressure sodium) lamps.

The first to consider is the 400 watt MBFR/U. Instead of the light being distributed evenly along a 2400mm (8 ft) length, as in the case of a 125 watt fluorescent tube, it is concentrated at the bottom of a lamp that has a diameter of only 180mm (7 in). Unlike the oval isolux of the fluorescent tube, the MBFR/U isolux are circular. Again the illuminance falls off rapidly so that to cover any sort of area at all a minimum of two lamps would be required; to achieve the ideal, you would need four lamps, which would emit heat equal to that of a 1720 watt electric fire (1600 watts from the lamps and another 120 watts being generated by the control gear). Two lamps would effectively cover an area of 1250 × 760mm (4 ft 2 in × 2½ ft). To overcome any problems with cut-off near the edges of the bench where plants will not be receiving the desired amount of light, these plants can be changed over – with those in the centre of the bench – halfway through the irradiation period. This also applies to SOX and SON lamps. Two lamps should successfully irradiate the average small greenhouse bench 760mm (2½ ft) wide if they are installed over the bench centre line. Four lamps would be required to cover a bench 1070mm (3½ ft) wide, the centre of the lamps being suspended 150mm (6 in) from each bench edge. Similar results can be expected from the 310 watt SONR (high pressure sodium reflector lamp) in comparable conditions.

The 180 watt SOX lamp is a linear source. The lamp is very efficient and will produce an illuminance of 6000 lx when hung 1200mm (4 ft) above the growing area. The lamp's cut-off point is again marked, in fact light output falls appreciably towards each end of the tube; nevertheless two lamps should effectively irradiate a bench 1070mm (3½ ft) long, 760mm (2½ ft) wide. Again, due to the narrow cut-off, it is necessary to install the lamps parallel to the centre line of the bench, and suspended about 150mm (6 in) in from each edge of the bench.

The 400 watt SON/T (high pressure sodium tubular lamp) with the Camplex luminaire produces a quite different isolux pattern. In this case 'tubular' indicates the fact that although the lamp is tubular in shape it is only 338mm (13 in) long, so it can be considered to produce a spot light source. The lamp is usually suspended horizontally and, with the luminaire, produces a dumb-bell shaped isolux pattern.

This is an efficient light source that even at a height of 1500mm (4 ft 11 in) gives an illuminance of 4500 lx at bench level. However, the cut-off is quite marked, there being a 25 per cent fall in illuminance at 500mm (19½ in) from a point immediately below the centre of the lamp. Compared with the other types of lamp the 400 watt SON/T produces a very high illuminance (45,000 lumens at 2000 hours) so this lamp should be suspended 1500mm (4 ft 11 in) above the growing area, which would make it impractical for the small greenhouse unless the plants being irradiated were positioned on the floor. One lamp of this type should be sufficient for most gardeners' requirements.

Protecting other plants

Plants have a tendency to grow towards a strong light. As an example, if you were to place a plant on a south-facing windowledge you would observe that after a period of time the stems would be bending over towards the light. This property is known as phototropism. In a small greenhouse or, in fact, in any greenhouse where plants are grown in the vicinity of a powerful lamp, phototropism will occur, especially during winter months. To prevent this it is advisable to hang a sheet of aluminium foil between the lamp and the plants being grown in natural light only.

Similar precautions should be taken when long-day treatment is given in one section of the greenhouse, as even this low level of overspill (less than 50 lx) could have an adverse effect on the untreated plants. You can imagine what would happen if the light from lamps used for plants receiving long-day treatment was to spill over to plants that you wanted kept in short days.

Left: this type of fluorescent tube lighting can be used to maximum effect because one batch of plants can be moved and replaced by another
Below: 400W SON/T lamps in a commercial setting

GROWING PLANTS WITH ARTIFICIAL LIGHT

In the preceding pages we have shown that both the amount and the colour of light influence plant growth and development. We have also discussed various methods of installing lamps.
Now we explain the techniques used for growing popular greenhouse plants under artificial light.

Above: check that night-break lighting will not disturb your neighbours

Many plants raised in greenhouses can benefit from extended day lighting and/or supplementary lighting. Supplementary lighting is the use of artificial light to supplement poor natural light during winter months. The object is to encourage plants to start into growth sooner and come into crop or flower earlier.

Night-break lighting provides an additional period of light in the hours of darkness. This often proves an economical way of lengthening the plant's day hours. Times given for night-break lighting are centred around 1.00 am.

The following paragraphs discuss a wide range of plants, from tomatoes to antirrhinums.

Tomatoes

Tomatoes need a minimum night temperature of 13°C (55°F). They also need plenty of light, and in the early months of the year natural light is not strong enough to produce sturdy, well-developed plants. So under normal cool house conditions of 7°C (45°F) it is not possible to start picking until mid summer (June). By then shop prices will have fallen and the effort and expense in producing the crop may seem hardly worthwhile. The ideal, therefore, is to use artificial light to start them cropping earlier.

Sow the seeds in pans in early spring or even late winter (February or January), and germinate in a temperature of 21°C (70°F) – an electric propagator provides the right condjtions. As soon as the seeds are large enough to handle, prick out into 9cm (3½ in) pots and grow on under artificial light. The total average illuminance should be 10,000 lx so, as only about 12 plants will be needed in the average gardener's greenhouse, a 400 watt MBFR/U lamp mounted 970mm (3 ft 2 in) above the plants should be adequate. Two 1500mm (5 ft), 65 watt warm white fluorescent tubes, each of them mounted 380mm (15 in) above the plants, would also be effective. Three weeks' irradiation can be sufficient; during mid spring (March) the lamps can be turned off on clear sunny days. Tomato plants should never be irradiated longer than 16 hours each day or growth and flowering may be retarded. You can start before early spring (mid February) but you would then have to maintain a continued minimum night temperature of 13°C (55°F) after the propagating period.

Aubergines and sweet peppers

These vegetables can be grown out of doors during a warm summer but cropping may be disappointing. For better results start them early, perhaps in a propagator in early spring (February), and treat them as you would tomatoes. You can cut your running costs by irradiating the young plants at the same time as the tomatoes.

Lettuce

Lettuce is a major commercial greenhouse crop during the winter months, but under normal light conditions it may take six weeks or more before the young plants are ready for planting out in the greenhouse border or heated frame. To speed things up sow pelleted seed individually in 5cm (2 in) pots with a peat-based seed compost and germinate them in a temperature of 10°C (50°F). If you irradiate the seedlings 24 hours a day for 14 days immediately after germination, planting out time can be advanced by up to four weeks. In this way you can grow and clear a lettuce crop before the border is needed for tomatoes. An illuminance of 5000 lx is adequate. If, however, you have problems in blacking out your greenhouse at night so as to avoid disturbing neighbours, irradiate for 12 hours daily at 10,000 lx.

Bulbs

Daffodils and other narcissi, hyacinths,

Above: these fine calceolaria show the benefit of supplementary light
Right: the larger cucumber plant, grown in supplementary light, is well in advance of one grown in natural days

tulips and crocuses can be forced successfully under 40 watt general service lamps installed on a frame on the basis of 2·5 lamps per square metre or yard.

As the foliage and flower-stalks increase in height so the frame is raised accordingly. Completely darkened sheds and cellars are adequate for forcing as long as you can maintain a temperature of not less than 16°C (61°F). Store the bulbs in boxes in mid to late autumn (late September) and stand them in a cool place outdoors, such as by the north side of the house or wall, and covered with 15cm (6 in) of straw or 10cm (4 in) of moist peat. Make sure the straw and peat are kept moist. Towards mid winter (end of November) when the shoots are about 6·5cm ($2\frac{1}{2}$ in) long the bulbs will be ready for forcing.

Daffodils and other narcissi need 16°C (61°F) and if pre-cooled bulbs (bulbs specially treated for forcing) are used. successive batches can, with a careful selection of varieties, be forced to provide a continuous supply from mid winter to late spring (December to April). For tulips 18°C (64°F) should be the aim until buds are showing, then drop to 16°C (61°F) until flowering. Keep hyacinths in the dark for the first 1–7 days depending on the variety. Temperatures need to be higher than for narcissi or tulips; start off with 24°C (75°F) and then, when colour shows, drop to 18°C (64°F). Hyacinths need a relatively high humidity, but still follow the general watering rule for all bulb flower crops – restrict it to just enough to ensure good, firm growth.

If you have space under the greenhouse bench, then you can force them there, provided you exclude daylight with black polyethylene sheeting. Keep up temperature by means of a small fan heater if necessary, and pay careful attention to ventilation. The daily lighting period can be restricted to 12 hours and this can be done at night to economize on heating.

Chrysanthemums

Although considerable success has been achieved in producing good quality blooms during the winter months, those being produced between late winter and mid spring (January and March) were inferior to those flowering in or before mid winter (December). As a result of research, growers are now using supplementary lighting as well as the normal night-break techniques, to maintain bloom quality throughout the winter. For the purpose of all-year-round production, chrysanthemum varieties are divided into response groups: for example a 10-week variety is one that requires only 10 weeks from commencement of short days (when night-break lighting is finished)

Illuminance requirements for various plant species

Plant species	Illuminance lx (MBFR/U)	Irradiation period	Irradiation time per 24 hours in hours	Purpose and further details
Aechmea fasciata (urn plant)	2000	early winter to early spring	8–10 (night-break)	promoting vegetative growth of seedlings
Antirrhinum majus (snapdragon)	4000	for 4–5 weeks after appearance (sown early winter)	day-lengthening to 16	flower advancement by approx 4 weeks
Aphelandra	367	early winter to early spring	6–8 (night-break)	promoting vegetative growth; at higher irradiance levels also earlier flowering
Begonia Elatior	67	late autumn to late spring	8 (day-lengthening)	suppressing bud formation; more and earlier cuttings
Begonia Lorraine	33–67	in winter; for 40 days after taking leaf cuttings	8 (day-lengthening)	preventing flower-bud initiation; improved sprouting
Begonia rex	100	from the end of mid autumn	8 (night-break) mid winter 2 (night-break) autumn and spring	improving vegetative growth of young plants; better foliage
Begonia semperflorens	2000	mid winter to early spring	10 (night-break)	improving vegetative growth and earlier flowering
Bulbs: tulip, daffodil and other narcissi, crocus	1000	mid winter to early spring	12 (no daylight)	flower forcing
hyacinth	1667	mid winter to early spring	12 (no daylight)	flower forcing
Calceolaria hybrid	333	after flower-bud initiation	4–5 (day-lengthening) 8 (night-break)	acceleration of flowering
Callistephus chinensis (China aster)	733	from mid autumn	8 (night-break)	stem elongation and flowering advancement (to mid spring)
Campanula isophylla (bellflower)	333–667	early winter to mid spring; for some weeks after stopping	8 (night-break)	flowering in spring instead of summer; more cuttings
Carnation (dianthus)	433	middle of late winter to end of early spring	all night	increasing flower crops
	433	early autumn to late spring	6–12 (night-break)	extending flowering time
Chrysanthemum	300	in winter	day-lengthening to 16	year-round cultivation; to prevent bud initiation in winter critical day length: 14·5 hr
	100	third week of early autumn to late spring	night-break (from 2–5 each night depending on time of year)	year-round cultivation; to prevent bud initiation in winter critical day length: 14·5 hr
	833	early autumn to late spring	7 (night-break)	stock plants; to promote vegetative growth for cuttings
Cineraria (or Senecio) cruentus	367	after flower-bud initiation, for about 2·5 months	9 (night-break)	flower advancement by 2–4 weeks in a period of 2·5 months
Cyclamen persicum	2000	early winter to early spring	8–9 (night-break)	promoting vegetative growth of seedlings
Dahlia	1333	in winter	2 (night-break)	flowering advancement
Euphorbia fulgens (scarlet plume)	67	early autumn to late winter; for 5–7 weeks	8 (night-break)	earlier flower crops critical day length: 12 hr
Euphorbia pulcherrima (poinsettia)	100	from the beginning of late autumn; for 2–3 weeks	2–3 (night-break)	retarding flower initiation (eg till mid to late winter)
Euphorbia (splendens) milii (crown of thorns)	367	late autumn to late spring	4 (night-break)	improving vegetative growth; year-round flower production
Ferns	2000	early winter to early spring	10 supplementary during the day	improving vegetative growth
Fuchsia	400	mid to late autumn	4 (night-break)	flowering promotion

Illuminance requirements for various plant species

Plant species	Illuminance lx (MBFR/U)	Irradiation period	Irradiation time per 24 hours in hours	Purpose and further details
Gerbera	2000	early winter to early spring until 2 weeks after planting out	15 supplementary during the day	improving vegetative growth of young plants
	2000	next 6 weeks	6 supplementary during the day	improving vegetative growth of young plants
Kalanchoe	1333	late winter to mid spring	10–12 supplementary during the day	early crop
	3333–6667	late winter to mid spring	10–12 supplementary during the day	improving vegetative growth
	333–667	from late autumn	8 (night-break)	flower retarding
Lilium (lily)	3333–6667	mid winter to mid spring	day-lengthening to 12	promoting bud initiation by day-lengthening
Matthiola incana Column (stock)	4000	late winter to early spring; until planting out	16 supplementary during the day	flower initiation
	2000	late winter to early spring until planting out	8 (night-break)	improving vegetative growth
Regal pelargonium	133–200	from mid winter, after flower-bud initiation	2–4 (night-break)	earlier flowering
Saintpaulia (African violet)	2000	in winter	day-lengthening to 16	improving and advancing flower production
	6667 (beneath greenhouse benches)	in winter	24 (no daylight)	improving and advancing flower production
Saxifraga cotyledon	133	middle of early spring; for 3 weeks	3–4 (night-break)	flowering advancement (1–4 weeks)
Sinningia speciosa (gloxinia)	2000–3333	early winter to early spring	8 supplementary during the day	improving vegetative growth of seedlings
Stephanotis floribunda (Madagascar jasmine)	267–400	mid autumn to mid winter	day-lengthening to 14	second flower crop in autumn and winter
Strawberry	117 (cyclic; 15 min/hr) or 67 (continuous)	from middle of late winter; for 40 nights	8–9 (night-break)	earlier and larger crop by flower promotion
Vriesea splendens (flaming sword)	2000	early winter to early spring	8 supplementary during the day	improving vegetative growth seedlings

The Gardener's Seasons

early spring	(February)	early autumn	(August)
mid spring	(March)	mid autumn	(September)
late spring	(April)	late autumn	(October)
early summer	(May)	early winter	(November)
mid summer	(June)	mid winter	(December)
late summer	(July)	late winter	(January)

to flowering. The night-break lighting is used between early autumn and late spring (August and April) to prevent premature flower-bud development and encourage vegetative growth, and varies from two hours each night in early autumn (August) to five hours in mid winter (December). As the first two weeks of short days are critical, so far as quantity of daylight is concerned, it is necessary to supplement this with artificial light between the beginning of winter (November) and the end of early spring (February). For this purpose 400 watt MBFR/U or warm white fluorescent lamps are used to produce 7200 lx, which will be enough to give gratifying results.

Saintpaulia (African violet)

So long as temperatures can be maintained at 18–21°C (64–70°F) these plants will grow normally under the greenhouse bench. Two 1500mm (5 ft), 80 watt warm white fluorescent lamps 380mm (15 in) above the plants will be adequate for a space 760mm ($2\frac{1}{2}$ ft) wide and 1400mm ($4\frac{1}{2}$ ft) long. The daily lighting period should be 12–14 hours.

Antirrhinums

Special greenhouse forcing varieties should be used. Sow between late autumn and early winter (October and early November). Plants are grown in a temperature of 10°C (50°F) and high temperatures should be avoided. Make quite sure you remove all sideshoots. In a propagating case or under mist with a bottom heat of 21–24°C (70–75°F) germination should take place after three days. Five days later the seedlings can be placed under a 400 watt MBFR/U lamp or warm white fluorescent tubes from 1700 hours to 0700 hours. This lighting should be switched off after about two weeks. This period of long days will enable you to have an early show of flowers.

PLANTS IN THE GREENHOUSE

STOCKING THE GREENHOUSE WITH PLANTS

When you buy and erect your first greenhouse it will look depressingly bare, and you may wonder how you will ever fill it with plants, Do not despair, however; bear in mind that most greenhouse gardeners eventually find themselves at the other extreme and cry out for more room.

Don't be too impatient to fill your greenhouse. Take your time about selecting plants, and choose those that will be happy together (sharing the same, or very similar, conditions of light, temperature and humidity) and suited to the environment created by your particular greenhouse and site.

If you want some quick colour you can always grow annuals from seed while planning your long-term plant selections.

Mixing and matching plants

There are a number of growing routines that you can adopt using groups or successions of popular plants. For example, you may want to use the greenhouse for raising bedding plants early in the year, followed by tomatoes and then chrysanthemums. Alternatively, you might want to specialize in vegetables such as cucumbers, melons or climbing French beans, or in flowers such as carnations or orchids. Any other plants must then be chosen to fit in with these.

Your scope for mixing plants is very wide since, by positioning them carefully, you can largely satisfy their individual requirements. For instance, you can shade the glass immediately above plants needing deep shade or else put them under the staging. Put plants demanding plenty of light as near the glass as possible and well away from others that might cast shade. Stand plants preferring high humidity on moist shingle, and keep those that like drier air on slatted staging.

Trouble arises, however, when you try to put together plants with widely differing demands, such as mixing tropicals, sub-tropicals, alpines, succulents, semi-aquatics, sun or shade lovers and hardy plants. Of course there are always a few examples of these groups that seem more tolerant of conditions that are abnormal to the group as a whole. For example *Aphelandra squarrosa* (zebra plant) is from warm parts of Brazil, yet it can be acclimatized to a quite cool greenhouse. Numerous succulents also make themselves at home in fairly moist conditions.

Using the whole greenhouse

When stocking your greenhouse, you must also remember that plants have many different habits of growth. It is not only their height that varies; they may become bushy, grow erect, trail or hang, climb, or be capable of being trained into standards or other shapes. It is by exploiting the many different and exciting shapes of plants that a really attractive greenhouse is created.

The greenhouse should be able to cope with these variations, if you arrange to have shelving that can be set at different heights and make provision for pots or baskets to hang from the roof – remembering that such containers can be very heavy when filled with moist compost. You can also install staging of various heights and leave parts of the greenhouse clear so that plants can be grown from floor level to the full house height. For climbers, wires or plastic netting fastened to one side (particularly in a lean-to) may give you further scope.

All-year-round interest

You should be able to plan your greenhouse so that there is as much 'going on' in winter as in high summer. Plants like cinerarias, calceolaria, primula, browallia, schizanthus and annuals such as salpiglossis will give colour from late winter to late spring (January to April), especially if batches of seed are sown in succession. Remember that variety may greatly influence the time of flowering and by choosing several varieties you may enjoy the same type of flower for a longer period. For example most of the compact-growing cinerarias will flower early, perhaps even in mid winter (December), while the large, exhibition kinds usually flower much later in spring. The same can be said for calceolarias, of which the newer F.1 hybrids are remarkably quick-flowering. In the case of bulbs, too, there are specially-prepared kinds that you can force gently for early flowers, keeping their untreated counterparts for later blooms.

In the decorative greenhouse or conservatory evergreens will provide attractive foliage through winter, but select them carefully to avoid creating too much shade. This is especially important when choosing and siting evergreen climbers.

Better house plants

The present-day range of house plants provides many exciting evergreens and some gloriously exotic foliage. Although popularly described as 'house plants' they often do far better in the greenhouse because of its higher humidity. However, these house plants must always be selected with their minimum temperature requirement in mind. Avoid buying those needing more warmth during the winter. Unfortunately many come onto the market in mid to late winter (late December) and they may have been standing in chilly, draughty florists' shops for some time. These plants take some weeks to show the effect of such treatment, so don't be surprised if they suddenly wilt or drop their foliage after being transferred to your greenhouse.

Acquiring healthy plants

Be critical about accepting plants and cuttings from other gardeners. These may have been passed on because the originals were rampant and weedy. Many poor-flowering impatiens (busy Lizzy) are acquired this way. It is better to wait for plants of which you know the botanical origin, and the variety and name. Remember that there are many specialist growers who sell only healthy plants that are correctly named. These are the people from whom to buy plants like orchids, carnations, alpines, begonias, streptocarpus, achimenes, pelargoniums, fuchsias, virus-free fruit (including strawberries), cacti and other succulents, bulbs and other storage organs, and the many other popular favourites for growing under glass.

Growing from seed

All greenhouse gardeners should make themselves familiar with the techniques of growing from seed. Numerous delightful and uncommon plants can be obtained this way. As well as the good selection of popular greenhouse plants that you can order from the general seedsmen, there are rare and unusual plant seeds to be obtained from specialist seedsmen.

Many house plants can also be raised from seed, including palms and cacti.

SEED SOWING AND PRICKING OUT

Many different plants are raised from seed sown in containers in a greenhouse: summer bedding plants, flowering pot plants, and vegetables like tomatoes, lettuce, celery, cucumbers and marrows. But the techniques of sowing and subsequent care are similar.

Late winter and spring is the main period for most sowings; more precise timing is usually given on the seed packets. A heated greenhouse, or a propagator, is necessary for germination (that is, starting seeds into life).

Seed trays and pots

Seed trays, approximately 5–6cm (2–2½ in) deep, are available in either wood or plastic. Plastic ones last for many years, if well looked after, and are easy to clean. Hygienic conditions are important if you are to raise healthy seedlings, so clean the seed trays thoroughly before use.

For very small quantities of seed use plastic pots 9 or 13cm (3½ or 5 in) in diameter. These are also recommended for very large individual seeds, such as marrows and cucumbers. Again, wash all pots carefully before use.

Types of compost

Garden soil is not a very suitable medium in which to grow seedlings as it is full of weed seeds and harmful organisms, and it may not provide the correct conditions required by the seed for successful germination. Instead, buy one of the ready-mixed seed-sowing composts, the most popular being John Innes Seed Compost, consisting of loam, peat, sand, superphosphate and ground chalk.

Alternatively there are many brands of seed compost which consist only of peat with added fertilizers; these are known as 'soilless' composts because they do not contain loam. When using soilless compost you have to be especially careful with watering, for if it dries out it can be difficult to moisten again; over-watering may saturate it and cause the seeds to rot. With a little care, however, soilless compost gives excellent results.

Building in drainage

Be sure that surplus water is able to drain from all containers. When using John Innes composts it is essential to

Pricking out seedlings with a dibber

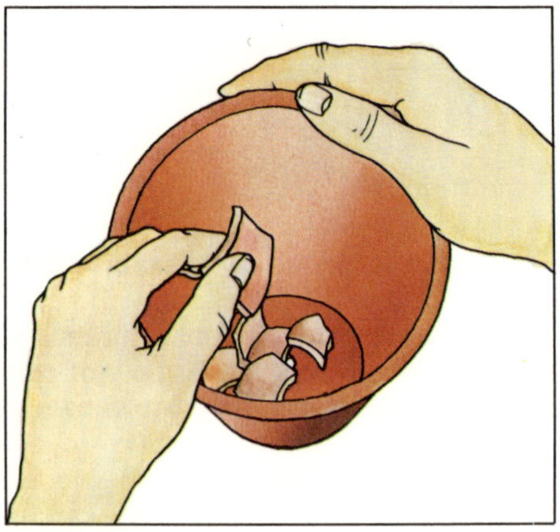

Place a layer of crocks in the bottom of flower pots to provide drainage

place a layer of crocks (broken clay flower pots or stones) at least 13mm (½ in) deep over the bottom of the pot. Cover the crocks with a little roughage, such as rough peat. If you use seed trays, crocks are not needed, just cover the drainage slits with some roughage.

Soilless compost can be used without any crocking – unless it is going in clay flower pots, in which case you must cover the large hole at the bottom with crocks.

Once you have arranged the drainage material add the compost to about 13mm (½ in) below the top of the tray or pot, to allow room for watering. Firm it gently all over with your fingertips, paying particular attention to the sides, ends and corners of seed trays. Make sure that the surface is level by pressing gently with a flat piece of wood that just fits into the tray or pot. Soilless compost should not be pressed hard but merely shaken down by tapping the container on a hard surface or lightly firming with the wood.

Very tiny seeds (like lobelia and begonia) should be sown on a fine surface. So before pressing down, sieve a layer of compost over the surface using a very small-mesh sieve. Alternatively you can sprinkle a thin layer of silver sand over the compost before sowing. Do not use builder's sand as this contains materials toxic to plants.

Water the compost lightly, using a fine rose on the watering can, before you sow.

Sowing the seeds

Seeds must be sown thinly and evenly otherwise the seedlings will be overcrowded and you will find it difficult to separate them during pricking out (transplanting). They will also have thin, weak stems and be prone to diseases like 'damping off'.

Small seed is usually sown broadcast (scattered) over the surface of the compost. Take a small quantity of seed in the palm of one hand – just sufficient to sow a tray or pot. Hold your hand about 30cm (12 in) above the container and move it to and fro over the surface, at the same time tapping it with the other hand to release the seeds slowly. If you move your hand first backwards and forwards and then side to side this will help to spread the seeds evenly. You may find it easier to hold the seeds in a piece of paper, instead of in your hand.

It is difficult to sow very small seeds evenly, some being as fine as dust, but if you mix them with soft, dry, silver sand (using 1 part seeds to 1 part sand) this helps to bulk them up and makes them easier to handle.

Large seeds, which are easily handled, can be 'space-sown' – that is placed individually, and at regular intervals, on the surface of the compost. Tomato seed, for instance, can be treated in this way.

Very large seeds, such as cucumbers, peas and various beans, are best sown at two per 9cm (3½ in) pot. If you use peat pots, they can later be planted, complete with young plant, into the final pot or open ground. When they have germinated, remove the weaker seedling, leaving the stronger one to grow on.

Pelleted seeds

This term describes seeds that are individually covered with a layer of clay which is often mixed with some plant foods. They are easily handled and can be space-sown in boxes or pots. The compost around pelleted seeds must remain moist as it is moisture which breaks down the coating and allows the seeds to germinate.

After sowing

Seeds should be covered with a layer of compost equal to the diameter of the seed. It is best to sieve compost over them, using a fine-mesh sieve. However, do not cover very small or dust-like seeds with compost as they will probably fail to germinate.

If you use John Innes or another loam-

1 *Cover drainage materials with compost, firming it gently with the fingertips*

2 *Level the surface of the compost by pressing with a flat piece of wood*

3 *Scatter a little seed into tray by tapping it gently from your open hand*

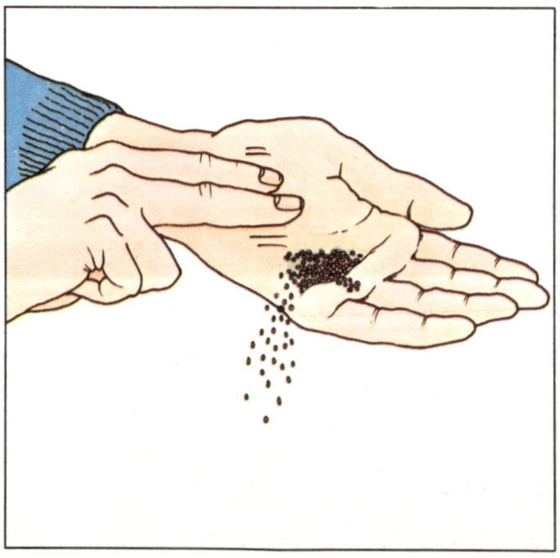

4 *With large seeds, sow two in a small pot and remove the weaker seedling*

1

2

3

1 Sieve compost over seeds; 2 Stand tray in water till surface looks moist. 3 Use a dibber to lift seedlings and transfer them to a new tray, where they will have room to grow on

containing compost the seeds should then be watered, either using a very fine rose on the watering can or by standing the containers in a tray of water until the surface becomes moist. (This latter method is not advisable for loam-less composts as they tend to float; moisten them well before sowing the seed.) Allow the containers to drain before placing them in the greenhouse.

A good, or even better, alternative to plain water is a solution of Cheshunt Compound, made up according to the directions on the tin. This is a fungicide which prevents diseases such as damping off attacking seedlings.

Aids to germination

Place the pots or trays either on a bench in a warm greenhouse or in an electrically-heated propagator. Most seeds need a temperature of 15°–18°C (60–65°F) for good germination. The containers can be covered with a sheet of glass that, in turn, is covered with brown paper to prevent the sun's warmth drying out the compost. Turn the glass over each day to prevent excess condensation building up on the inside. Water the compost whenever its surface starts to become dry. As soon as germination commences remove the covering of glass and paper, for the seedlings then require as much light as possible if they are to grow into strong, healthy plants.

Pricking out

Once the seedlings are large enough to handle easily prick them out into trays or boxes to give them enough room to grow. Generally, standard-size plastic or wooden seed trays are used that are 6cm ($2\frac{1}{2}$ in) deep; there is no need to put drainage material in the base. The trays are filled with compost in the way described for seed-sowing, again leaving space for watering. A suitable compost would be John Innes Potting Compost No. 1 which can be bought ready-mixed. It consists of loam, peat, coarse sand, John Innes base fertilizer and ground chalk. Alternatively, use one of the soil-less potting composts that contains peat, or peat and sand, plus fertilizers. Make sure the compost is moist before you start pricking out.

You will need a dibber for this job – either a pencil or a piece of wood of similar shape. With this lift a few seedlings at a time from the box or pot, taking care not to damage the roots. Handle the seedlings by the seed leaves – the first pair of leaves formed. Never hold them by the stems which are easily damaged at this stage.

Spacing out

The number of seedlings per standard-size box will vary slightly according to their vigour. Generally 40 per box is a good spacing (5 rows of 8). For less vigorous plants you could increase this to 54 per box (6 rows of 9).

Mark out the position of the seedlings with the dibber before commencing, ensuring equal spacing each way. Next make a hole, with the dibber, which should be deep enough to allow the roots to drop straight down. Place the seedling in the hole so that the seed leaves are at soil level, and then firm it in by pressing the soil gently against it with the dibber.

If only a few seeds have been sown in pots each seedling could be pricked out into an individual 7cm (3 in) pot. But if you have single seedlings, such as marrows, already started in 9cm ($3\frac{1}{2}$ in) pots, these will not need to be moved.

After pricking out, water in the seedlings (with a fine rose on the watering can) preferably using Cheshunt Compound. Then place them on the greenhouse bench or on a shelf near to the glass, as maximum light is essential. Continue to water whenever the soil surface appears dry.

Windowsill propagation

If you do not have a greenhouse, heated frame, or propagator, you can still raise seedlings in the house. Ideally the germination conditions should be as similar as possible to those which are recommended for greenhouse cultivation. Windowsills are the best places for raising seeds, and if they are wide ones you can use standard-size seed trays.

However it is usually possible to fit a few pots onto the narrowest of windowsills. For best results use trays or pots that are fitted with propagator tops. The temperature on the sill must not drop below the average room temperature and south- or west-facing sills are obviously best.

Make sure the seedlings are never deprived of daylight or allowed to get cold at night. Never draw the curtains across between the plants and the warm room air on cold nights, if necessary bring them into the room. Finally, to maintain strong and even growth, turn all pots and trays around every day.

Use a pot with a propagator top when starting off seedlings on a windowsill

POTTING OFF AND POTTING ON

The basic terms used in potting are 'potting off', when young rooted cuttings or seedlings are moved from trays into pots, and 'potting on', when the more advanced plants are transferred to bigger pots.

Nowadays plastic pots are generally used in preference to clay, but whichever type you have ensure that they are clean and dry before using them.

POTTING OFF

As soon as cuttings have developed a good root system they should be carefully lifted from their trays and put into individual pots about 7·5–9cm (3–3½ in) in diameter. When seedlings are large

Before placing a pot-bound plant in its new pot, carefully remove old drainage crocks from the base of the rootball

enough to handle easily they can be treated in the same way (as an alternative to pricking out into trays).

For this first potting, use a fairly weak compost, such as J.I. No 1, or an equivalent soilless type consisting of loam, peat, coarse sand, John Innes base fertilizer and ground chalk.

Allowing for drainage

Drainage material is not necessary in plastic pots as the holes are devised so that the compost does not leak. Furthermore, there is a trend towards using less drainage material in the bottom of small clay pots. When there are some drainage holes provided, place a few crocks (pieces of broken clay pots or stones) over the drainage holes and cover with a thin layer of roughage such as coarse peat or partially-rotted leaf mould. If you are using soilless compost, crocks or drainage materials are not normally necessary. Place a layer of compost over the drainage material and firm lightly with your fingers.

Transferring the plants

Hold the rooted cuttings or seedlings in the centre of the pot, with the roots well spread out, and trickle compost all around until it is slightly higher than the rim of the pot. Give the pot a sharp tap on the bench to settle the compost well down and lightly firm all round with your fingers. Make sure the compost is pushed right down to the bottom.

Some soilless composts, however, require little or no firming, so check the manufacturer's instructions first.

Remember to leave about 13mm (½ in) between the surface of the soil and the rim of the pot to allow room for watering.

After potting off, water the plants thoroughly, using a fine rose on the watering can, to settle them in further. Then they can be returned to the bench.

POTTING ON

Plants need potting on to prevent them becoming 'pot-bound' (when the roots are packed very tightly in the pot). If this happens the plants will suffer from lack of food, growth will be poor and they will dry out very rapidly and require frequent watering.

However, it is worthwhile noting that some plants, such as pelargoniums, are more floriferous (bear more flowers) when slightly pot-bound.

Plants should be moved to the next size of pot, for instance from a 9cm (3½ in) to a 13cm (5 in), from a 13cm (5 in) to a 15cm (6 in) and so on. The reason for moving only to the next size pot is that plants dislike a large volume of soil around their roots because they cannot absorb water from all of it and, therefore, it is liable to remain wet. This can result in root rot and the possible death of the plant. Small moves allow plants to put out new roots quickly.

Composts and drainage

Richer composts (those containing more plant foods) are generally used for potting on. If you prefer the John Innes type, then use No 2, which contains twice as much fertilizer and chalk as No 1. Some plants (for example chrysanthemums,

1

2

3

4

To pot on a pot-bound plant: **1** *place crocks and drainage material in bottom of larger pot, then carefully remove plant from old pot;* **2** *half-fill new pot with compost;* **3** *hold plant in centre of pot, add more compost to within 2cm (½ in) of rim;* **4** *firm all round plant*

tomatoes and strawberries for fruiting under glass) like an even richer compost, such as J.I. No 3 – particularly when they are moved into their final size of pot).

Drainage material, as described under potting off, is generally advisable when using soil composts in pots that are 13cm (5 in) or larger. A layer of crocks about 2–3cm (1 in) deep should be sufficient, plus roughage.

Repotting the plant

Remove the plant from its pot by turning it upside-down and tapping the rim of the pot on the edge of a bench. The rootball should then slide out intact. On no account disturb this ball of roots and soil, but remove old crocks, if any, from the base. Scrape off any moss or weeds on the surface with an old wooden plant label or similar object.

Place enough soil in the new pot so that, when the plant is placed on it, the top of the rootball is about 13mm (½ in) from the top of the pot. This will allow for a light covering of compost with room for subsequent watering. Firm the compost lightly with your fingers and then stand the plant in the centre of the new pot. Trickle fresh compost all round the rootball until you reach the top of the pot. Give the pot a sharp tap on the bench to get the compost well down and firm it all round.

If you are using soilless composts, follow the maker's instructions for firming. You will probably need to add more compost to reach the desired height. Finally, water in the plants, using a fine rose on the watering can.

Potting on is best done when plants are growing actively in spring and summer – or in the autumn, although growth will then be slowing down. Plants potted in spring and summer will quickly root into the new compost because of the warmer weather.

RAISING ANNUALS FOR THE GARDEN

There are several advantages to raising your own bedding plants in the greenhouse, apart from the obvious one of saving money. Every year leading seedsmen offer a splendid range of seeds for popular and less common bedding plants, together with new varieties and introductions, and also F.1 hybrids that have greater vigour than ordinary strains.

When you grow your own plants from seed you have better control of their quality and timing. Bought plants are often damaged through overcrowding in their seed trays, or through having been kept in them too long before you are able to plant them out. Sometimes, also, they have not been hardened off properly.

All these disadvantages can be avoided when you raise your own plants in pots; this helps enormously when bedding out since there is less root damage and the plants grow away faster.

When to sow

Most of the favourite bedding plants can be sown in the greenhouse from about mid to late spring (March to April). Some, however (such as fibrous-rooted begonia and antirrhinum) are slow-growing and these should be sown as early as late winter (January), otherwise they may not be ready for reasonably early display. On the other hand, avoid unnecessary early sowing, or you will waste greenhouse space and heat; you may also spoil the plants if bedding out has to be delayed because the weather is too cold. Fast growers, like tagetes (marigolds), can be left until the very last.

In some cases it is a good idea to sow seeds from a packet over a period of time, and not all at once – especially when the quantity of seed is generous. Having several batches of seedlings in various stages of development means you will be able to enjoy a long flowering period.

Sowing techniques

How you sow can be varied to suit the cost, quantity and the size of the seed. Large seeds that are easy to handle (like zinnia) and that may also be expensive (as in the case of F.1 hybrids), should be sown individually in small pots. Finer seed can be sown in a tray or pan; prick out the seedlings into more trays when they are large enough to handle. If seed is cheap and very fine it can be mixed with a little silver sand, to reduce the density of distribution, and sown directly into seed trays. Instead of pricking out you can then thin the seedlings by pulling out the excess and discarding them. This may sound wasteful, but it saves considerably on time – also a valuable commodity.

For germinating seeds use a sterilized seed compost such as the John Innes Seed Compost or one of the many proprietary composts. See that it is nicely moist – but not wet – before sowing. A useful rule is to cover the seed with its own depth of compost. Very fine or dust-like seed, however, should not be covered. Many failures are due to deep sowing, to water-logged compost or (always fatal) to compost that is allowed to dry out after sowing and during germination.

Nowadays plastic seed trays are available; these are clean and easy to use. The standard size is 35 by 25cm (14 by 9 in) but smaller ones are useful as germination trays for the propagator.

Germinating the seeds

After sowing cover the seed containers with glass and then a sheet of brown paper, newspaper or translucent white paper. Or you can slip the tray into a polythene bag, to help to retain moisture.

Some form of propagator will be most helpful for germinating the seeds. For bedding plants high temperatures are not only not necessary, but quite undesirable. Too much heat will force the seedlings and they will become spindly, pale and weak. A temperature range of 7–18°C (45–65°F) is adequate for most parts; the lower temperatures will suit the more hardy plants (like antirrhinums) and the higher will be needed for more tender subjects like zinnias. But if you propose using a propagator for other greenhouse work then get one that can be 'turned up' for more warmth when required. Generally an electric propagator is convenient and, if fitted with a thermostat, is economical and allows of easy temperature control. There are also inexpensive, small electric propagators for warming only one or two seed trays, and designs that are heated by paraffin oil lamp. Many people manage to germinate the odd trays of seeds in their homes on the windowsill of a warm room. If you have a warm greenhouse used for warm house plants, you can also use it for seed germination. It will, however, be too

Newspaper provides a cheap and handy cover to shade seedlings. It is often better placed under the glass

warm – and probably too dark – a place for the seedlings to grow on happily.

Germination time may vary from a couple of days to about three weeks depending on the type of seed, and temperature – don't be tempted to hasten germination by using unnecessarily high temperatures. Make a daily check to see whether germination has occurred. Remove the container's cover when the first seedlings are through so that more light can penetrate. Exposure to bright sunshine in the early stages is, however, harmful and may result in scorching of the tiny seedlings, so put the container in a shady corner.

Pricking out seedlings

Pricking out should always be done as soon as possible – as soon as the seedlings are big enough to handle easily. In the case of very tiny seedlings, such as lobelia, small groups can be 'patched out' since it is impossible to separate them.

When pricking out, be generous with your spacing. Commercial growers often overfill their seed trays; the roots become entangled and suffer from the disturbance caused when the young plants are divided for planting out. After pricking out it is a sensible precaution to water in the seedlings with a Cheshunt compound (used according to maker's instructions). This will help prevent damping-off disease – a serious menace to seedlings. This fungus disease attacks the stems at compost-surface level and the seedlings then topple over. It occurs mainly where greenhouse hygiene has been neglected and will spread very rapidly unless promptly checked.

Hardening-off and bedding out

All bedding plants must be given a period of gradual acclimatization to the open air before planting out. This is called hardening-off and frames are especially useful for the process. In the greenhouse itself move the seed trays, gradually, to cooler spots. Then about three weeks before you plan to bed them out, move the trays to frames outside. Open the frame lights a little more each few days as the three-week period passes until, finally, they are fully exposed day and night. For the first week or so you may have to close the frames at night depending on weather conditions. Do not bed plants out until all danger of frost has passed.

Plants should be watered while hardening off in a frame – the last stage before planting out

If you have used peat pots, or pots of similar organic composition, for raising some of your bedding plants, do remember to keep them well watered after bedding out. Plants in these pots are intended to be planted pot and all to avoid root disturbance, but they will not rot down to allow the roots to grow out unless kept quite moist.

PLANTS FOR UNHEATED GREENHOUSES

Too many people deprive themselves of the pleasure of owning a greenhouse by thinking of the cost of heating it during the winter. But you can enjoy enormous benefits from protected cultivation without providing any additional heat. There is a wide range of plants that need only shelter from wind, excessive rain, frost or extreme cold, to give finer results and earlier crops or flowers than if grown in the open. Indeed, these plants will not do well in a greenhouse that is too warm – and so an unheated one is ideal.

This section on plants for unheated greenhouses looks at what types of greenhouses are suitable and suggests some plants that can be grown from seed and from bulbs to provide a display of colour all year round.

The degree of hardiness of the plants you can grow will vary according to the severity of winters normally experienced in the part of the country in which you live. In mild areas, for example, comparatively tender plants will survive quite easily. In colder regions you may have to be more cautious in your selection.

Below: tagetes germinate in natural warmth

Suitable greenhouses

To make the most of free warmth from the sun the unheated greenhouse should let in as much light as possible. A glass house will trap more warmth than a plastic one, but if you propose to grow only hardy plants then this will not be so important. Remember, however, that any extra free warmth may be useful for gentle forcing and early growth, even if the plants are completely cold-resistant. An all-glass (glass-to-ground) greenhouse will capture much natural warmth, and so will a lean-to structure set against a south-facing wall. In some cases such a lean-to will remain frost-free overnight as the rear wall can store warmth during the day and radiate it at night.

Don't choose a site shaded by buildings or trees if you are erecting a cold greenhouse. Nor should you put the house in a hollow or at the foot of a slope or hill; these sites are often frost pockets. Wet or waterlogged ground is also best avoided since plants in a cold greenhouse dislike an excessively humid atmosphere in winter, and are more prone to attack by fungus diseases.

Spring sowings

Probably very few home greenhouse owners use heating from about late spring (April) onwards. In spring a glass greenhouse will usually become sufficiently warm naturally to germinate most bedding plants, tomatoes and more exotic summer fruits like melons. These can be grown on to give useful summer and autumn cropping. Without warmth, or perhaps with just a small heated propagator, most of the more hardy and

Delicate annuals can give spectacular displays with the protection of a cold greenhouse. Below: Salpiglossis sinuata. *Bottom: schizanthus, the butterfly flower*

Left: double-flowered petunias
Above and above right: achimena, native of Central America, and Tecophilaea cyanocrocus, *the Chilean blue crocus*

quick-growing bedding plants can be raised. Tagetes (African and French marigolds) are extremely easy plants, and you can leave the sowing until quite late. Avoid slow developers that prefer congenial warmth (such as fibrous-rooted bedding begonias). But the slow growers like antirrhinum will do well since they are perfectly hardy and can be started as early as late winter (January).

Summer and autumn displays

During the summer and autumn the greenhouse can become a wonderland of colour for only the price of a few packets of seeds germinated from late spring to early summer (April to May) without artificial warmth. Outstanding for its colourful blooms is salpiglossis; stop the plants at the seedling stage (when a few centimetres high) to promote bushy growth. Pot on into 13cm (5 in) pots.

The new compact strains of schizanthus are also easy to grow and showy, and need no stopping or training. Many of the more choice garden bedding plants, especially F.1 hybrids, make splendid pot plants. F.1 hybrids of zinnias are spectacular when given weather protection, and you can produce magnificent columns of blooms if you grow the large-flowered antirrhinum as single spikes by removing all sideshoots.

The cold greenhouse is ideal for protecting delicate or double flowers that are prone to weather damage and summer winds and rains. Double petunias do very well, provided there is maximum light, and some varieties will fill the house with a clove-like scent that you won't notice outdoors. The recently-introduced variety of hibiscus Southern Belle, with its enormous, but papery-thin, flowers, is almost certain to be spoilt outdoors but will be seen in its full glory with greenhouse protection. Sow it in a warm place indoors and move the young plants to the greenhouse in about early summer (late April or May). From then on they make rapid growth and the plants will need 25cm (10 in) pots as a minimum size for their final homes.

Bulbs for summer and autumn

For summer and autumn display many bulbs or similar storage organs can be started in spring. These include begonia, gloxinia, achimene, polianthes (tuberose), hippeastrum, the glory lily, gloriosa (which, contrary to many warnings, can be started late and still flower well), canna (of which the best for the small greenhouse is the variety Lucifer – the earlier you start these the better), smithiantha and many lilies and nerines.

With nerines, use the named greenhouse varieties that are potted on in early autumn (August). Storage organs of most greenhouse plants that flower from summer to autumn can be stored dry over winter in a frost-proof place in the home, and started into growth again in the following year.

Winter and spring displays

Of special importance for the winter-to-spring display are hardy bulbs. An unheated greenhouse is the ideal place for them; and you will be amazed at how much more beautiful many of them are than you had previously realized. They usually flower much earlier under protected conditions and the flowers will often be more noticeably scented and unblemished. Choose unusual varieties with double or more delicate flowers.

As well as the popular hyacinths, daffodils and narcissi, grow a selection of the smaller, dainty bulbs generously grouped in bowls or pans. Such collections could include allium, babiana, bulbocodium, chionodoxa, eranthis (winter aconite), erythronium, fritillaria, galanthus (snowdrop), leucocoryne, leucojum (snowflake), muscari (grape hyacinth, of which there are some especially fine forms), puschkinia (striped squill), scilla (squill), tecophilaea and urginea.

Crocus, alone, can be had in an astonishing range of varieties and species from which you can choose a selection to flower over a long period. And under glass the birds cannot tear them to shreds. Tulips grown in pots provide a glorious display, especially the double varieties.

There are numerous other spring-flowering plants notable for colour. Polyanthus make fine pot plants and are easy to grow from seed. Coloured (and completely hardy) strains of primrose are now available and are particularly good for pots.

GREENHOUSE PLANTS FOR HANGING BASKETS

Hanging baskets, suspended from the roof, are an excellent answer to the eternal problem of dwindling shelf space in the greenhouse. And, in fact, many plants are seen at their best displayed in this way.

Do make sure, first of all, that your greenhouse roof will support the weight of your hanging baskets; remember that, after watering, a container may be very heavy. Hanging containers, and the type of plants put in them, should also be chosen in proportion to the size of the greenhouse and the height of the roof. Baskets over 25cm (10 in) in diameter are rarely suitable for the average $3 \times 2{\cdot}4$m (10×8 ft) home greenhouse, especially when the roof is rather low.

Plastic-covered wire baskets are now readily available, also some non-drip designs. And for some plants, particularly orchids, wooden baskets made from hardwood timber slats (usually teak) make pleasing containers.

Be sure to hang them where you can water and tend to them easily, and where the drips will not fall on other plants.

Preparing the basket

Mesh baskets look much more attractive if lined with sphagnum moss with the mossy side facing out. Over this place a few pieces of polythene before filling up with potting compost. The polythene will prevent water draining too fast and compost drying out rapidly, but make a

Above: cascading white blooms of Campanula isophylla *Alba*
Left: well-cared-for trailing lobelias can completely smother their container
Far left: massed planting to bring a welcoming splash of doorway colour, includes ivy-leaved pelargoniums, tagetes, alyssum and petunias

few slits in it to prevent waterlogging. In some cases a plastic lining should not be used – as with plants liking well-aerated compost (such as orchids and columneas) or when you want plants (usually bulbs) to grow out of the basket side through the moss itself.

Plants from seed
When it comes to filling the basket there are, for a start, several suitable plants that can be raised successfully from seed. Red or blue pendulous lobelias and *Thunbergia alata* (black-eyed Susan) are quick, easy and inexpensive to raise this way.

Thunbergia alata is really a climber, but you can use it effectively in baskets if you encourage the stems downwards by stapling them to the underneath of the basket as they grow. Easy from seed, too, is the lovely *Campanula fragilis* (not to be confused with the well-known *C. isophylla* that is similar but can only be grown from cuttings). However, *C. fragilis* will take about two years from seed to reach a size that will give a good display.

A little-known exotic lobelia with very large flowers that are a delightful shade of blue is *Lobelia tenuior*. It is, however, a little tender and is best not used for baskets that will be put outside during summer.

A charming foliage plant to grow from seed as an annual is *Cardiospermum halicacabum* (balloon vine). This, like thunbergia, is a climber, but it hangs well from suspended containers. Its small, graceful, vine-like leaves make an interesting change from the often-used *Asparagus sprengeri*. An additional attraction of the balloon vine is that it produces dainty, pale green, inflated seed capsules like those of physalis (Chinese lantern).

Striking flowers and foliage
One of the most impressive foliage plants for baskets is *Cissus discolor*, but it has the disadvantage of being deciduous in the average cool greenhouse. The foliage is gloriously coloured and marked and the plant should be given a container of its own. Well grown, it will hang down almost to the floor. In a cool greenhouse be careful to keep it on the dry side over winter.

Another good choice for baskets are columneas, although they need a winter minimum temperature of 10°C (50°F). According to species, columneas may have velvety or shiny foliage; but the flowers are all usually tubular and in showy shades of orange. Columneas are often a little 'difficult' since they demand a high humidity combined with a congenial temperature all year round. They also need an open compost made from fibrous peat and moss.

Among the best and (deservedly) most popular of basket plants are the ivy-leaved pelargoniums. As well as interesting foliage these plants have long-lasting flowers; these are produced freely from early summer (May) in the greenhouse, often continuing into the winter in frost-free conditions. There are many named varieties with single and double flowers in a wide range of colours. It is best to plant about three well-rooted cuttings to each 25cm (10 in) basket, but if plants have been saved and grown on from previous years only one may be needed.

Of similar merit are fuchsias, although the flowers tend to come periodically or may be delayed, and the blossoms can be spoiled by bad weather if put outside. When choosing fuchsias try to get varieties especially suited to hanging; you will usually find this information in the growers' catalogues. Varieties with extra long and large blooms, like Pink Flamingo and Mrs Rundle, and those derived from *Fuchsia triphylla* that have cascading clusters of long, tubular flowers usually in shades of rich salmon pink, look especially pleasing when viewed from below.

A similar effect is given by the pendulous begonias. These have quaint, tassel-like flowers in a selection of colours. Some bear masses of flowers

shaped like their large-flowered counterparts, only these are small and pendulous. Various types can be found described in the back pages of 'major' seed catalogues where bulbs and other storage organs are listed. Although you get much quicker results from tubers, you can also grow them from seed, but this must be sown early in the year if you are to enjoy a long display throughout the summer.

Bulbs and tubers

Attractive bulbs for planting from early to mid autumn (August to September) are lachenalia (Cape cowslip) of which the best for baskets is *Lachenalia bulbifera*, usually listed in catalogues as *Lachenalia pendula*. Plant the bulbs through the sphagnum moss of the basket, omitting any plastic lining. You will need about 8cm (3 in) of space between each bulb; plant a few in the top of the basket as well. In the cool greenhouse a basket so planted will become a 'ball' of tubular flowers coloured red, yellow and purple, from mid winter (December) onwards.

An exciting tuber to plant from mid spring (March) onwards is *Gloriosa rothschildiana* (glory lily). This is a climber, but can be most impressive if encouraged to hang over a suspended basket. Three tubers to each 25cm (10 in) basket give the best effect. The brilliant red and yellow flowers are like reflexed lilies. This is a plant best confined to the greenhouse since it is liable to damage if put outside.

Above left: a gay, mixed basket, with pelargonium, lobelia and tagetes
Above right: quaint, tassel-like flowers of the eye-catching pendulous begonia
Below: cross-section of a basket showing placement of sphagnum moss, polythene and compost

Plants for small baskets

Excellent for small baskets or similar hanging containers, and easy for the cool greenhouse is *Rhipsalidopsis (Schlumbergera) gaertneri* (Easter cactus) that flowers in spring. Flowering from about mid winter to early spring (December to February) is the Christmas cactus *Schlumbergera × buckleyi* with magenta-coloured flowers. *S. truncata* (crab cactus) comes in several colours, and is also winter flowering. All have a pendulous habit and quaint flowers shaped like Chinese pagodas. Cuttings root very rapidly and are often easy to beg from friends.

Good for small containers, too, is the dainty *Streptocarpus saxorum* (Cape primrose) with small velvety foliage and flowers like a miniature form of the giant-flowered, well-known hybrids. The stems are reddish and the blooms a violet colour. A winter minimum temperature of about 10°C (50°F) is needed.

BULBS FOR WINTER FLOWERING

Early bulbs can bring add to your home in winter. O them in early autumn (Au plant in bowls or pots indo or in the greenhouse in mid autumn (September).

Bulbs, corms and tubers that are generally grown in pots for early flowering are hyacinths, daffodils (narcissi), tulips, crocuses and cyclamen.

Choosing your bulbs

Always buy top-size bulbs for flowering indoors; you will get more and better blooms from these, and they are well worth the small extra cost. Top-size daffodils will have two or three 'noses' or growing points per bulb. Hyacinths are measured by their circumference, in centimetres, around the widest part of the bulb, and the top-size variety measure approximately 18–19cm (7–7½ in). 'Prepared' hyacinth bulbs, which give blooms about mid winter (December) are usually 16–17cm (6–6½ in) in circumference.

These 'prepared' bulbs grow much more quickly than untreated bulbs and flower in time for Christmas in Britain. The bulbs are refrigerated by the suppliers, a process that speeds up the period before flowering, but you must plant them as soon as possible after purchase. If not, the effect will wear off and they will then bloom later – probably in late winter (January).

Top-size tulips can also be recommended for planting in bowls: these measure about 12–14cm (4½–5½ in) in circumference. Crocuses should be no smaller than 7–9cm (2½–3½ in) round.

Inspect the bulbs before you buy them – or immediately upon receipt if you are buying from a mail order firm – to ensure

Far left: fragrant Cyclamen persicum
Left: tulips and hyacinths in wooden tub
Below left: Narcissus bulbicodium *Hamilton*
Below: Crocus chrysanthus *Advance*
Bottom: Crocus tomasinianus *Ruby Giant*

that they are not soft or infected with mould. Bulbs should feel firm to the touch and quite heavy in relation to their size. Bulbs that feel soft or very light are undoubtedly rotting inside and will neither flower nor grow properly.

There are many varieties of hyacinths, daffodils, tulips and crocuses – choose those that appeal to you. The Roman hyacinths are the earliest to come into flower, apart from the treated varieties. The narcissi varieties Paper White and Grand Soleil d'Or are extremely attractive for indoor planting arrangements, and the large-flowered Dutch crocuses, together with dwarf early single and double tulips can also be highly recommended for winter flowering in the home.

Materials for planting

You can buy special bowls for bulbs from garden centres and shops. The usual growing medium to use with these is bulb fibre, also easily obtainable from your garden suppliers. This is basically peat combined with a mixture of crushed charcoal and oyster shell. You can also grow your bulbs in ordinary plastic or clay flowerpots, provided you first cover the drainage holes with a layer of crocks topped with a thin layer of roughage. Use a conventional potting compost in pots, such as J.I. No 1, or a loamless (soilless) compost. They must be moist before use.

How to plant

Now to the method of planting the bulbs. First place a layer of fibre or compost in the bottom of the container and firm it lightly with your fingers. Then stand the bulbs on the growing medium, ensuring that their tips are level, or just above, the rim of the container. Then place the compost or fibre between and around them and lightly firm it with your fingers. After planting, the upper third of hyacinth bulbs should remain exposed and the noses of daffodils and crocuses must be visible. Plant your bulbs close together for the best flower display but do not let them touch each other. For example a 15cm (6 in) diameter bowl will hold two or three hyacinths, one daffodil, five tulips, or eight crocuses; and a 30cm (12 in) diameter bowl will contain seven to nine hyacinths, six to seven daffodils, twelve tulips or sixteen crocuses. These estimates are for top-sized bulbs.

Caring for your bulbs

After planting, place the bowls in complete darkness in a cool place – a cellar is ideal. Many people bury the bowls about 15cm (6 in) deep in a bed of ashes or sand in a cool part of the garden. Or you can put each container into a black polythene bag and place it in a cool, shady part of the garden. Try to keep the temperature below 9°C (48°F) at this stage.

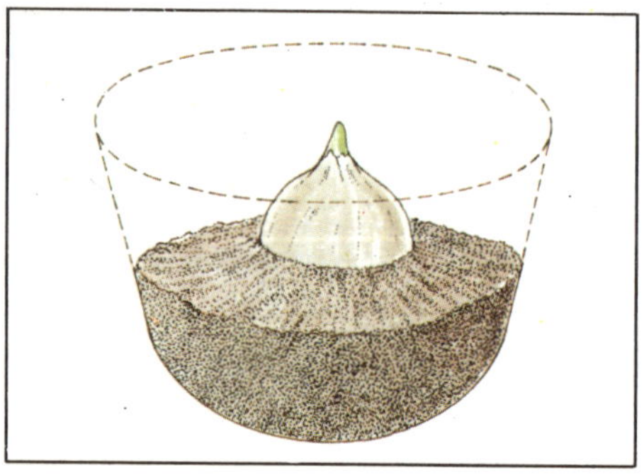

To prepare bulbs for indoor use, above: set bulbs in layer of peat fibre; above right: place more fibre over and around bulbs, and firm this down lightly; below: bury bowl for eight weeks in bed of ashes in cool part of garden; below right: dig up bowl and place for one week on windowsill in subdued light

Leave the bulbs in these conditions for a period of six to eight weeks (during which time roots will develop) until they start to produce shoots. Daffodils, hyacinths and tulips should be brought back into the light when their shoots are 2–3cm (1 in) long, and crocuses when they have 13mm ($\frac{1}{2}$ in) high shoots.

Above: while roots are developing you can store bowl in black polythene bag and place in cool, shady part of garden

To start with, place the bowls in subdued light, then, after a week, transfer them to full light and a temperature of 10°C (50°F). The temperature should not be higher than this until the flower-buds are well formed, at which time you can increase the temperature to 15°C (60°F).

Keep the compost or fibre moist at all times. Do not over-water bowls; remember that they have no drainage holes in the base, and so the fibre could become saturated. If this should happen, carefully stand the bowl on its side until the surplus water has drained away.

It should not be necessary to stake the flower-stems but if these do become top heavy, insert two or three canes and encircle them.

When the bulbs have finished flowering, stand them in a cold frame or a sheltered spot out of doors to complete their growth. Water and feed them until the leaves have completely died down. Then remove the bulbs, clean and dry them and store in a cool dry place until planting time in the autumn. You must not grow them indoors again, but you can plant them in the garden where they will make a good display during spring of the following year.

GROWING CACTI AND SUCCULENTS

Cacti and succulents add an exotic note to every collection of greenhouse and indoor plants. Once known as the 'Cinderellas of the plant world', their popularity is now assured. With a little care they can be induced to grow well and produce flowers of astonishing variety and colouring. Here we look at the different types of cacti and how they can be grown successfully.

Succulents are plants that have evolved with the ability to store water in their leaves, bodies and roots to enable them to survive periods of drought. They are more common than most people realize – in fact, most countries in the world have some form of succulent plant in their native flora. Even in Britain, sempervivum (houseleek) and sedum (stonecrop) are quite often seen even though the climate does not seem to warrant succulent growth.

One of the largest families in the succulent flora is the CACTACEAE, or cactus family. Cacti differ from succulents in having areoles from which their spines grow and from which, in many cases, the flowers are produced. These areoles look rather like small felt pin cushions; the spination of the other succulent plants resembles thorns.

It is believed that both cacti and other succulents originated from a common source before the continents of Africa and America parted in the continental drift many millions of years ago. Today cacti are native to North and South America, but succulents, though mainly indigenous to Africa, can be found growing native in many other parts of the world.

Types of cacti

There are two completely different types of cacti: the epiphytes and the so-called 'desert' cacti. Both groups require separate forms of cultivation as their habitat is so different.

The epiphytes (or 'jungle' cacti) that include such well-known plants as schlumbergera (formerly zygocactus), the Christmas and Easter cacti, epiphyllum, rhipsalis and so on, are flat-stemmed plants growing in the tropical rain forests of Central America. They do not live on the ground but on the branches of forest trees, in crevices and joints that have accumulated leaf mould and bird droppings. Their stems and roots obtain moisture from rain and they are continually shaded from the tropical sunshine by overhanging branches.

The second type is the so-called 'desert' cactus; the name is slightly misleading as the true habitat of these plants is not desert but a form of heathland with grass and small shrubs. They are native to North and South America but seem to adapt well in other places; too well in some cases – as in Queensland, Australia, where the opuntia (prickly pear) invaded vast areas of farmland and defeated all efforts at eradication until its natural predator, the caterpillar of the cactoblastis moth, was imported. These cacti inhabit areas of little rainfall but have

Serried ranks of cacti bristling with protective spines (previous page) or a mixed group of succulents (opposite) form a unique display. Below: opuntia (prickly pear) with seed pods. Bottom: schlumbergera, an attractive jungle cactus

powers to absorb water when it is available and retain it for future use when times are dry and hard. Sometimes they can absorb moisture from morning mists through their stems and spines.

General cultivation

In Britain most cacti are grown in greenhouses or garden frames, as the winters are too damp and humidity causes the plants to rot if they are planted outdoors. Cacti will withstand a habitat that has very cold, but dry, nights and winters, but cannot survive a damp, cold atmosphere.

Some gardeners still use clay pots for growing cacti, but most have now changed over to plastic, as these are lighter on the greenhouse staging and easier to keep clean, especially for exhibition purposes. Also, plants in plastic pots do not require watering so often.

Whereas the 'desert' cacti will grow well in full sun provided there is sufficient ventilation, epiphytes, being 'forest' cacti, require shading from sun from early summer to mid autumn (May to September), and can only be grown on top of the greenhouse staging during the winter months. Evidence of sunburn shows as red pigmentation on the stems; affected plants should be shaded at once. Never stand the pot in a container of water as they cannot tolerate bog-like conditions.

How much water?

How much water to give and how often to water are key questions with this group of plants, and it is difficult to give an easy answer. Common sense plays a great part here: if it is hot and sunny, plants growing under glass require a great deal of water. Those growing in clay pots may need water each evening. Be careful when watering not to leave any droplets on the crowns of the plants, as this could cause scorching when the sun comes out, and badly damage a plant; this is one reason for watering in the evenings and not during the day. If the weather is overcast or damp the plants will not require much water. Desert cacti rest during the winter months and need very little water then, although overhead spraying from time to time can be beneficial. Some succulents can grow in the winter and rest in summer, and it is as well to know the plant's habits and treat it accordingly.

Composts used for growing cacti and succulents must be particularly porous, such as J.I. No 2 or 3, to which you should add some very sharp sand, grit, or broken brick to ensure good drainage. This is very important, especially when growing in plastic containers. The pot size should be as large as the diameter of the plant with its spines plus a further 13mm ($\frac{1}{2}$ in) all round. The epiphytic cacti will require the addition of humus to the potting compost in the form of leaf mould, peat or well-rotted manure, and again the soil must always be well drained.

Cacti and succulents grown indoors should be treated as ordinary house plants; they will require watering during the winter (especially if there is central heating) otherwise they will dehydrate. Also if they are kept on a windowsill, and there is frost, bring them into the room, inside the curtains; cacti and succulents will not withstand damp frosts. A quite large plant will go to pulp overnight and is a heartbreaking sight next morning when the curtains are drawn back.

How much heat?

Cacti and succulents require heat during the winter, but remember that they hate a stagnant, stale atmosphere because it causes fungus and rot. So even during the winter provide the plants with some fresh air on a sunny day.

If you heat by paraffin, remember that for every 5 lit (1 gal) you burn, the same amount of water vapour is produced. Even so, many people find heating by this method satisfactory, providing that the appliance is well maintained, and not in a draught. It is very sad to see a collection covered in black, oily soot where a stove has flared. This is also very difficult to remove and it takes years for the plants to grow out of the effects.

Electricity is clean and easy, but unfortunately very expensive. Under-soil cables are very good, but costly to run and install for a complete collection; this method is favoured for seed-raising and for the propagation section, where plants are put to root. Fan-heaters create a very dry heat, so spraying will have to be done occasionally during the winter when it is sunny or the plants become dehydrated. With a special type of electric water heater that gives off steam when it boils, spraying is not required. Should there be a power failure for any reason, a certain amount of heat will be retained in the pipework, providing the power cut does not go on for too long.

Gas heating for the greenhouse is becoming very popular but be sure that you can obtain spare parts should anything go wrong. Laying a gas supply to the greenhouse could prove to be costly if it is any distance from the house, especially if it necessitates taking up cement paths as well.

Lining your greenhouse with sheet polythene provides a form of double glazing during the winter, and cuts down heating costs appreciably. If you do decide to fit this, make sure that the sheets are overlapped in such a way that the condensation will not drip onto your plants and cause rot, but run down safely out of harm's way.

GROWING CARNATIONS IN THE GREENHOUSE

Perpetual-flowering carnations of the size and quality sold in florists' shops are not easy for the beginner to grow successfully, but once you have mastered the right conditions for them in your own greenhouse, you will be well rewarded by the magnificent shape and varied colours of these show blooms. Here we look at aspects of the cultivation of perpetual-flowering carnations, including propagation by cuttings taken from your own plants, and list some of the most attractive varieties available today.

Greenhouse carnations of the kind seen in florists' shops are called perpetual-flowering carnations, and are the product of over a century of breeding in France, Britain and the United States. The Sim varieties, introduced just after World War II, are still by far the most popular, and should continue to dominate the world's markets as long as they are carefully protected from pests and diseases, and as long as research into methods of producing virus-free stocks continues. They originate from a scarlet self carnation, William Sim, that became a phenomenal market variety and produced sports in almost every other colour known in carnations, as well as innumerable new varieties.

Greenhouse requirements

The amateur gardener's greenhouse cannot compare with the huge structures of commercial growers, yet very successful results are produced, in spite of the drawbacks of fluctuation in temperature and humidity and the fact that plants often have to be left without attention for most of the day.

Heating Your greenhouse must allow the plants maximum light at all seasons, as well as full ventilation from the roof and both sides. To keep up flower production in winter, do not allow the night temperature to fall below 16°C (61°F). If this is too expensive, compromise by heating your greenhouse sufficiently to maintain a temperature of about 5°C (40°F) to keep out the frost. By this method some flowers can be obtained for about three-quarters of the year. Electric heating is cleaner and more convenient than any other method, and economical in that it can be controlled by a thermostat, power being consumed only as necessary. Fan heating is probably the most popular method of electric heating used in domestic greenhouses, and it is economical to install. The fan can generally be used independently of the heater, and is very handy to promote air circulation in the summer.

Above: carnations in a commercial greenhouse are supported by a wire grid. Red-edged Skyline (top), Laddie Sim (pink), Joker (crimson), William Sim (scarlet) and Yellow Dusty
Right: corset the bud with an elastic band to stop the calyx from splitting

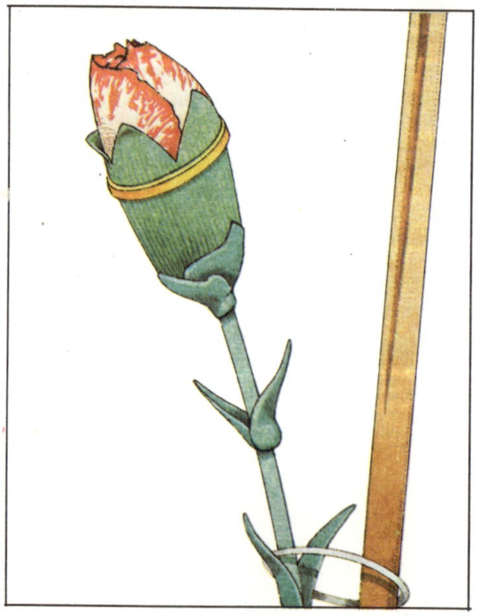

Staging This is simple to erect; make a base of breezeblocks and crossing timbers to support lengths of corrugated asbestos or galvanized iron. Cover the galvanized iron with polythene for protection, then put on a layer of pea shingle. Keep the staging low because some varieties, the Sim types in particular, eventually grow taller than the people who grow them. Young plants are obviously shorter than older ones, so keep them on the lighter side of the greenhouse.

Care and cultivation

The best time to buy plants that are 'stopped and broken' is mid spring (March). These have sideshoots and are bushy (as distinct from rooted cuttings that do not have side growths). They are taken out of the 8cm (3 in) pots they are grown in before being despatched for sale, or can be bought in small peat pots.

Potting Before you start potting, make sure that the roots of the young plants are moist. If they are not, immerse the rootball in water until the bubbles of air stop rising. Use 15–18cm (6–7 in) clay or plastic pots, with J.I. potting compost No 2. Push three or four canes into the compost and tie twine round them, to keep the growths within bounds. Alternatively, use circular wire supports that clip on to a central cane. Water newly potted plants only when they are growing strongly. Over-watering is the commonest cause of failure, so keeping the plants on the dry side usually improves them. The roots are very easily drowned.

Start feeding the plants about a month after potting, and repeat once every two weeks thereafter. Use any soluble fertilizer that has equal parts of nitrogen and potash, following the manufacturer's instructions for application. If the plants do not appear healthy for any reason, withhold fertilizer.

Disbudding and shading Flower-buds appear about two months after potting. Most growers disbud, leaving only the crown bud on each stem. This is usually corseted with a small elastic band to prevent the calyx from splitting when the flower expands. To disbud, hold the stem near the bud with one hand, and pull the bud and its stalk sideways with the other.

Lightly shade the greenhouse before the flowers unfold, to prevent scorching from strong sunlight. Coolglass is most effective for this, and can easily be rubbed from the glass with a dry rag or brush when it is no longer required.

Autumn and winter blooming It is always a problem to decide whether to leave the flowers on display in the greenhouse or to take them indoors to beautify the house. If you take the latter course you can encourage flowers to bloom in the greenhouse right through to late autumn (October). After this time it is advisable to remove any buds that appear, so that the plants can rest and recuperate – unless you are prepared to maintain a constant temperature of about 10–16°C (50–61°F). Buds that look promising in late autumn (October) almost always damp off in winter if there is insufficient heat to dry the atmosphere. The plants require very little water during winter, but demand more the following spring when they begin to flower for their second season. Stop feeding during winter if you are not maintaining a high temperature, except perhaps for an occasional high potash feed, as a kind of tonic.

Propagation from cuttings

Perpetual carnations can be grown on for a third year, but they require so much attention that it is better to start again with new young plants that you can produce from your own cuttings. Take axillary side growths off the plant during early or mid spring (February or March), by pulling them out sideways (as with disbudding). If the cuttings have not broken out cleanly, remove the lowest pair of leaves and trim the stem across, with a razor blade, just below a joint.

Set the cuttings firmly in pots or trays in a half peat, half sharp sand mixture, and spaced about 4cm ($1\frac{1}{2}$ in) apart. Hormone rooting powder is useful to speed up the rooting process, and it is also helpful if you can heat the trays from the bottom with soil-warming cables. The cuttings take three or four weeks to form roots; after this lift them carefully and put them into 8cm (3 in) pots, using J.I. No 1 or a proprietary soilless compost.

Keep young potted plants out of cold draughts and water them sparingly until they begin to make new growth. After a month or so the rooted cuttings should have about ten pairs of leaves – sufficient growth for them to be stopped. Do this when the plants are turgid so that you can make a clean break. Hold the plant firmly in one hand and snap the top of the plant clean out with the other, leaving about six pairs of leaves. Do not be tempted to use the top piece as a cutting as it would make a very poor plant. Provided the stopped plants do not receive any serious checks, they should begin to produce axillary growths or sideshoots that, after a few weeks growth, turn the rooted cutting into a stopped and broken plant, like the ones you bought at the beginning.

Pests and diseases

The most serious pest attacking greenhouse carnations is the red spider mite, a sure killer if it is not dealt with quickly. The pest is a mite, not a spider, but it is so-called because it spins a web to protect its eggs. The mites are not easily seen with the naked eye, but are readily visible through a magnifying glass. They vary in colour from yellow and orange to red, and can usually be found on the underside of the leaf. Here, covered with their web, the hatching mites are protected from contact insecticides. The m
by sucking the sap
multiply so rapidly
occur before you
presence. The sap-s
plants to such an ex
lifeless, brittle, strawy in appearance and eventually ruined.

Azobenzene smokes are useful as a measure against the mites, if your greenhouse can be sealed effectively against loss of smoke. Use the smokes twice in about ten days to catch the in-between hatching period. Organo-phosphorus compound sprays such as demeton-s-methyl and dimethoate are also effective against the mites because of their systemic action.

Other pests that attack carnations are thrips, caterpillars and greenfly. Greenfly are not just a nuisance but a menace. They suck the plants' sap and can transmit viruses from diseased plants to healthy ones. They, and the other pests, can be controlled with standard insecticidal sprays, used according to the manufacturer's instructions.

Some varieties to choose

There are a great many different varieties available today, with new ones continually appearing. Those listed below are of short to medium height unless described otherwise.

Bailey's Masterpiece	crimson self.
Deep Purple	unique purple colour.
Fragrant Ann	white self, the most popular of all.
G. J. Sim	light red with white stripes; tall.
Golden Rain	clear, canary yellow.
Joker	large crimson blooms that are deeply serrated.
Laddie Sim	salmon-pink, does not fade.
Lavender Rose	lavender-pink, with strong stems.
Paris	light salmon self.
Red-edged Skyline	orange-apricot, striped and edged with red.
Rose Splendour	cerise self.
Tangerine Sim	brilliant cerise self.
William Sim	scarlet; the forerunner of all the Sim types.
Yasmina	light purple with a paler edge.
Yellow Dusty	yellow self; tall.
Zanzibar	French grey, suffused cerise and maroon.

PROPAGATING AND STORING CHRYSANTHEMUMS

Chrysanthemums that have been propagated with care and grown on well should produce good quality blooms that will make a fine display in the garden or greenhouse. Here we detail propagation procedures and consider the cultivation of late-flowering types.

Stock selection of chrysanthemums is carried out by retaining for propagation the plants that have produced the best blooms in the previous season. Cuttings for propagation are taken from a 'stool' – the root of an old plant with a portion of the old stem and surrounding young shoots – that has been lifted and stored at the end of the growing season.

HOW TO PROPAGATE

Both early- and late-flowering chrysanthemums are propagated from cuttings of basal shoots taken from stools that have been stored in a cold frame.

Lifting and storing stools

Leave the stools of the early-flowering types of chrysanthemum in the garden until the beginning of early winter (November). This provides a period of time during which the temperature occasionally falls below 4·5°C (40°F) – a cooling period that is necessary before plants can produce flowers.

Cut the main stems down to 15cm (6 in), then lift the stools carefully with a fork and wash off the soil with water that

has had a little disinfectant such as Jeyes fluid added, to remove any pests. Remove all the leaves and cut down all green growth. Box the stools up into clean containers to a level no deeper than the original soil mark, in J.I. No 1 or a mixture of equal parts of loam, peat and grit. Water the stools well in to settle the compost. Make sure they are labelled correctly and try to keep to one cultivar per tray. Place these trays somewhere dry and frost-free, such as a cold frame, where there is plenty of light and air. Probably no more water will be needed until the trays go into the greenhouse in late winter (January). Keep an eye on them until then so that you can deal with any diseases such as mildew or botrytis that may appear; if they do, dust with flowers of sulphur or captan.

During early and mid winter (November and December) the late-flowering chrysanthemums will be coming into full bloom in the greenhouse. As they mature, mark the plants that produce the best blooms and use them for future propagation in the same way.

Lift each stool carefully, label it, then store it in a clean container (above)
Good propagation will result in fine display blooms such as Princess (left)

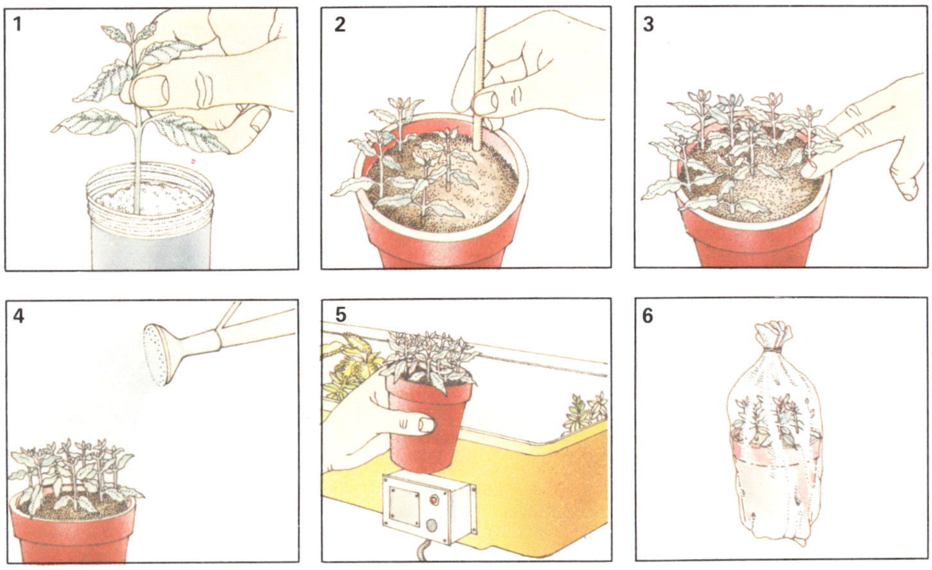

Above: to propagate chrysanthemums from cuttings, dip the stem of each shoot into a proprietary hormone rooting powder, **1,** *insert it into the compost using a small dibber,* **2,** *firm gently round the stem,* **3,** *and water the cutting well in with a fine spray,* **4.** *Place containers in a bottom-heated propagator,* **5,** *or individual polythene bag,* **6,** *until the cuttings have rooted firmly*

Taking cuttings

In late winter (January) start to propagate plants for the new season. The late-flowering types should come first, particularly the large exhibition cultivars and those that require early stopping.

Prepare a rooting compost of J.I. No 1 or a mixture of equal parts of peat, loam and coarse grit, or any soilless compost. Water the stools well the day before you wish to take the cuttings, so that they have time to plump up. Depending on the number to be rooted, insert about six cuttings round the edge of an 8cm (3 in) pot. If you use a standard seed-tray, the compost should be about 5cm (2 in) deep. Firm it with a board, then sprinkle a layer of sharp sand on the surface, and space cuttings 4–5cm (1½–2 in) apart each way.

Snap off a new basal shoot from the stool, just below a leaf joint, to form a cutting about 4–5cm (1½–2 in) long. It is optional whether you remove the two bottom leaves as the cuttings will root well either way. Dip the bottom 13mm (½ in) of the stem into a hormone rooting powder, and make a hole 20mm (¾ in) deep in the compost with a dibber the size of an ordinary pencil. Place the cutting in it and firm gently right up to the stem. Some of the sand sprinkled onto the surface of the compost will fall to the bottom of the hole, creating drainage that helps to prevent decay. Water the cuttings well in using a fine rose.

Keep the cuttings in the greenhouse until they have rooted. The time taken for rooting will depend on the conditions provided. In a propagator with a bottom heat of about 16°C (61°F) and an air temperature above 4·5–7°C (40–45°F) they should root in about two weeks, but on an open bench with a general temperature of 10°C (50°F) they will take a week or so longer. The cuttings can be rooted without heat when the risk of frost is over, but they take longer and the delay also affects the timing of blooms.

You can continue propagating until mid spring (early March); the late-flowering varieties should root during late winter and early spring, and the early-flowering during early and mid spring.

Growing on

As soon as cuttings of both early- and late-flowering chrysanthemums have rooted, remove them from the heat to a cold frame. They need slow and steady growth in a cool place to produce short, sturdy plants with big root systems. Some growers plant cuttings of early-flowering chrysanthemums directly from the rooting tray into a 10–15cm (4–6 in) deep layer of compost on top of a 15cm (6 in) bed of weathered clinker or ashes. Others prefer 10cm (4 in) deep trays or a succession of pots up to 13–15cm (5–6 in). All these methods have proved satisfactory, so each grower should adopt the system that will suit the facilities available to him or her.

Late-flowering plants, however, must be transferred from their rooting quarters into a succession of pots, starting with an 8cm (3 in) pot and moving on as the root system develops to a final pot size of 20, 23 or 25cm (8, 9 or 10 in). Grown in this way, they can easily be transferred back

Yvonne Arnaud (above); Anna Marie (left)

from the open garden into the greenhouse towards the end of mid autumn (September), so that they will come into flower during early and mid winter (November and December).

When you move the rooted cuttings into the cold frame, ensure that they have as much light and air as possible. Leave the frame lights off whenever the weather permits, and when they are on keep them raised a little at all times, unless there is a risk of frost. During early spring (February), frost usually occurs at night, so cover the frame lights with sacks or pieces of old carpet. Water sparingly – just enough to keep the plants going. A strong root-system will develop from plants that have to forage a little for moisture. When the plants are settled in the frame, spray with a good insecticide such as malathion or a systemic insecticide containing gamma HCH (BHC) and menazon, as a control against pest attack – leaf-miner flies and aphides become active as the weather warms up during spring. During late spring (April), give the plants more air; by the end of the month the lights can be removed from the frames permanently. Replace them temporarily if a heavy rainstorm threatens.

LATE-FLOWERING TYPES

Late-flowering chrysanthemums are put out to stand in the open garden after being potted on twice, but they must be brought back into the greenhouse to flower in late autumn and winter.

Potting-on

In mid spring (March), the young plants that have been grown in 8cm (3 in) pots must be moved into larger pots to accommodate the developing root system. A compost containing a stronger mixture of fertilizer is necessary – J.I. No 2 is most suitable, or you can use an equivalent soilless compost. Before potting, decide on the type of compost you intend to use for the final potting. If you choose a soilless mixture, then the second potting should consist of similar material.

Use a 13cm (5 in) pot for the second potting, then return the plants to the cold frame, ensuring that there is a space of 5–8cm (2–3 in) between each pot to allow for leaf development. Leave the frame lights off at all times unless heavy rain, hailstorms or frost threaten – all such hazards are possible in late spring (April). The chrysanthemum is not a tender plant, and it would survive the hazards referred to, but the growing point could be damaged and the timing of growth and flower development affected.

Final potting

The final potting is the most important of all. The plant will remain in this pot from early or mid summer (mid May or early June) until it flowers in mid winter (November), or even later in some cases. You will need a selection of 20–25cm (8–10 in) pots because some plants make more vigorous growth than others and therefore require more space. J.I. No 3 is suitable for most cultivars, but if you are using a soilless compost, follow the recommendations for use given by the manufacturer.

Put some crocks or pebbles at the bottom of the pot to provide drainage, then place a 2–3cm (1 in) layer of peat on top. Partly fill the remainder of the pot with compost and firm gently with a rammer. Finally, put in a handful of loose compost, on which you can rest the plant taken from the 13cm (5 in) pot. Place the plant in the pot, ensuring that you have left about 5cm (2 in) of space down from the rim for future top dressing. Fill in around the plant and firm well, using the rammer. Insert a cane on each side of the plant and secure it with soft string. Stand the pots close together when you have completed potting so that moisture is conserved. If possible, withhold water for 10–14 days after potting, to encourage the roots to move into the new compost. An overhead spray in the evening should prevent undue flagging.

Preparing a standing-out ground

Prepare a level site, in full sun if possible, for the late-flowering chrysanthemums to stand throughout the summer. The aim is to give each plant as much room as possible. Stand them in rows, preferably on an ash base; each pot should also stand on a slate or tile to keep out worms.

Drive strong posts into the ground at the end of each row, and stretch wires between them at 45 and 105cm (18 in and 3½ ft) high. Fasten the wires to the canes, to keep the plants from being blown over. This advice may sound unnecessary on a quiet day in midsummer, when the plants are only 75cm (2½ ft) high, but it is quite another matter in early autumn (August) when they are 1·5m (5 ft) or more tall.

Watering procedure is similar to that recommended for the early-flowering varieties (Week 88). An overhead spray on warm evenings usually suffices, but during dry spells water more heavily, giving a really good soaking. With pot-grown plants, watering should generally be more frequent than with the early varieties that are planted in the ground. Because of this extra watering, a certain amount of food is leached through the pot. About six weeks after the final potting, therefore, it is necessary to feed the plants. Dry and liquid fertilizers both give good results, as does a mixture of both. If you use dry fertilizers, give a pinch every other day. With liquid fertilizers, better results can frequently be obtained by applying little and often rather than a full dose every ten days, so dilute the feed to a quarter strength and use it at alternate waterings.

Top dressing

In late summer (the end of July), roots will appear on the surface of the compost. When this occurs, apply about 13mm (½ in) of top dressing made up of the final potting compost – either soil-based or soilless – that you used before. A further top dressing will be necessary about three weeks later.

As with the early-flowering varieties, decide how many blooms you want to grow and restrict the laterals accordingly.

Pamela – an early-flowering spray chrysanthemum – is ideal for cutting

If you are growing for show purposes, restrict them as follows: large and medium exhibition – one or two laterals; exhibition incurved and decoratives – three laterals; large singles – four or five; and medium singles – five or six. Apart from the large exhibition type, these will all carry a larger crop of smaller blooms when being grown for cut flower uses.

Securing the buds and housing

At the beginning of early autumn (August), the first buds will start to appear on late-flowering chrysanthemums – the large exhibition type first. If possible, these should be comfortably secured towards the end of early autumn (by the third week of August). Buds on the incurved and decorative types will appear from early to mid autumn (the end of August to September). Once the buds are secured and growing well, remove any surplus laterals, always selecting those with the weakest bud. Continue feeding on alternate days until the calyx breaks and the buds begin to show colour. Then gradually reduce the feed over the next few weeks.

Prepare your greenhouse for late-flowering chrysanthemums by washing down the glass and framework and fumigating inside to clear away any pests.

As soon as the buds show colour, and before the frost comes, remove all dead leaves and weeds around the plants, wash the outside of the pots, and spray over and under the leaves with an insecticide such as gamma HCH (BHC) and menazon to kill any pests, and a fungicide such as benomyl to rid the plants of any disease. Then bring the plants into the greenhouse and position them in their winter stations. Leave doors and ventilators fully open for as long as possible to enable the plants to become acclimatized to the change of environment.

After bringing in all the plants it is advisable to fumigate the greenhouse occasionally – this should help to keep your chrysanthemums free from pests and diseases. Always keep a buoyant atmosphere in the greenhouse. High temperatures are not necessary – just enough heat to keep the air moving and to maintain a temperature of 10°C (50°F) is all that is required. A fan-heater is most suitable and will provide both warmth and air movement. Your chrysanthemums should then bloom well throughout the dreary months of early and mid winter (November and December).

MAKING AN ORCHID COLLECTION

Here we introduce some orchids for beginners, and others that are suitable for hot greenhouses, and give hints on buying and starting a collection. We will then be going on to cover aspects of cultivation.

When a potential orchid-grower takes a look round at the range of orchids offered by orchid nurseries it is all too easy to become bewildered by the sheer number of plants available, all with completely different descriptions. It is therefore advisable to visit an orchid nursery and make a first choice with expert assistance. If an orchid nursery is not within easy reach, order direct from one that offers beginners' collections, or visit one or two of the many orchid shows held throughout the country. Chelsea Flower Show is a good place to start as it always has a large section devoted to orchids. In addition there are many reliable books available, with illustrations to help the beginner understand the long lists of names quoted in catalogues.

Orchids for beginners

Hybridization has created easily-grown orchids of great variety and beauty.

Cymbidiums The most widely grown orchid plants are the cymbidium hybrids. The blooms are used extensively for cut flowers, and they can often be seen in florists' shop windows. These are quite large-growing plants, with pseudo-bulbs and long, narrow leaves. Their flowering season extends throughout the winter and spring months. The flower spikes are produced from the base of the leading bulb during the summer, and grow steadily until they reach a height of 90cm–1.2m (3–4 ft). They can carry an average of 12 large, colourful blooms that will last in perfection for a good ten weeks. These long-lasting qualities, together with their ease of flowering, make this group the most popular in cultivation today. The colours found among the cymbidiums range from pure white, through many delicate shades of pink and yellow, to the stronger reds, bronzes and greens, all with contrasting-coloured lips. Where room permits a large collection of these gives a wonderful show of colour for nine months of the year.

Cymbidiums have all been hybridized from a mere handful of original wild species coming mostly from India and Burma. From the earliest days of hybridization, new varieties have always created a good deal of excitement and as generation after generation of hybrids have been bred so the size, shape and colour of the plants has become larger, rounder and more exotic. One specialized line of breeding has produced cymbidiums in miniature form, the plants and flowers being half the size of the standards. These varieties are often more acceptable for the smaller greenhouse. Today the species are seldom seen in collections, the hybrids having surpassed them in every way, and the latest always being the most eagerly sought after.

Odontoglossums Next to the cymbidiums, and second in line for popularity are the beautiful odontoglossums and their allies. Like the cymbidiums, the odontoglossums have been interbred for many generations and will cross-pollinate with several closely-related genera. These crossings have given the odontoglossums added colour and new shapes, and they and their allies now cover a very wide range of different types. Many 'meristem' plants (that is, those propagated by a particular method) are available, in every colour of the rainbow, with an endless array of intricate patterns and markings on the petals and lip.

The odontoglossums are smaller-growing than the cymbidiums and are bulbous, with less foliage. They are continuous-growing, with their flowering season spread throughout the year. The plants will bloom upon completion of their bulbs, that is approximately every nine months, but they do not always produce their flowers at the same time each year. The blooms will last for eight to ten weeks, depending on the time of year: not quite so long during the summer as the winter.

The original odontoglossum species are high altitude plants, growing at great heights in the Andes. In some cases they grow almost on the snow-line, at heights of up to 1800m (6000 ft). At this altitude they are subjected to nightly frosts that do them no harm. Therefore they like very cool conditions under cultivation, and if a greenhouse becomes overheated during the summer, they will do better if placed outdoors in a suitably shady position.

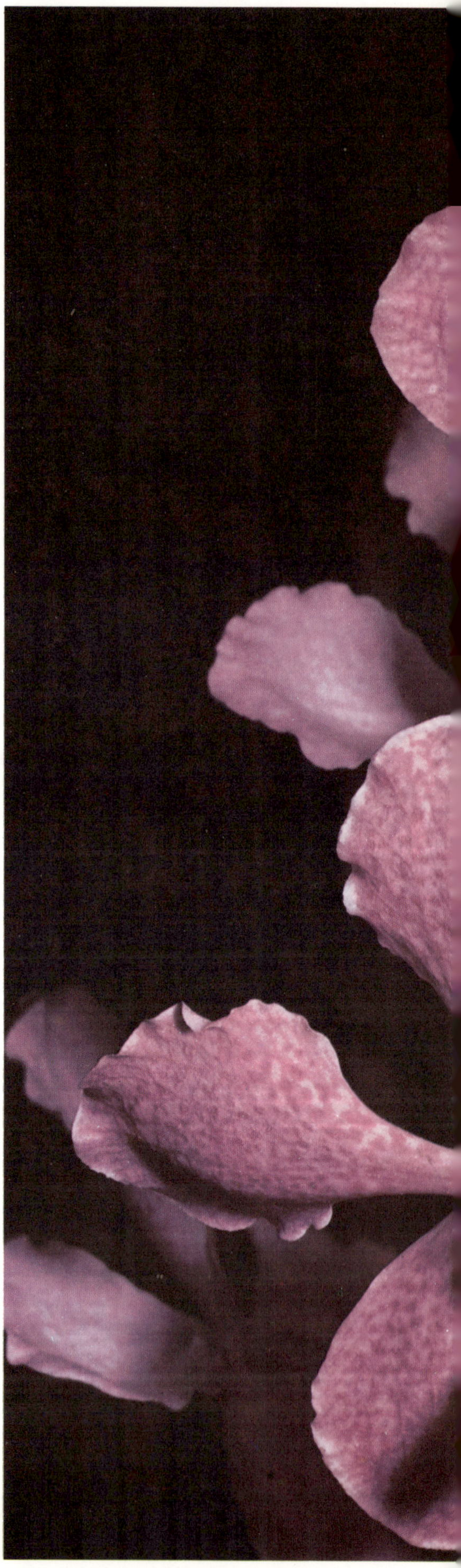

Cattleyas Where slightly warmer conditions are available, you can try the large, glossy 'chocolate box' cattleyas. Here again we have a large group of plants, highly bred and intercrossed with their closest relatives. The largest and most flamboyant are the result of careful, selected breeding. Their huge blooms, up to six at a time, have a colour range from pure white, through many shades of yellow, to pink and rich mauve. Mostly the lip is large, rounded and much frilled around the edges.

Although considered a little too large for today's cut-flower requirements, they are the most exotic of plants to grow for pleasure. The blooms will last approximately two to three weeks and they flower in either spring or autumn. Often, a well-grown plant can be encouraged to bloom twice in one year. The best types available are often meristem plants.

The cattleyas and their allies are bulbous, their bulbs being long and club-

Above: two paphiopedilum or 'slipper' orchids, showing how varied the shape of the petals and 'pouch' can be
Left: vanda hybrids like this brilliantly-coloured specimen can bloom twice in one year and like a hot greenhouse

shaped. One, or sometimes two, thick leaves are carried by each of the bulbs, which flower from their tips. The young buds are protected by a sheath, through which they grow to eventual flowering.

'Slipper' orchids The well-known 'slipper' orchids include yet another large and varied group of orchids that differ from all other forms by their pouch-like lip. These plants are generally modest in size, without pseudo-bulbs, and produce a number of lateral growths. The species is usually found growing on grasslands, or on rocky outcrops with very little soil, the roots keeping just beneath the humus. The foliage can be plain green in colour, or mottled and marbled in attractive patterns. The undersides of the leaves are often a dark purple.

The species are widely grown and have different flowering seasons. The winter varieties are in bloom by mid winter (December), and carry a single bloom on a slender stem. These will last for eight weeks or more on the plant, and the larger the plant the more flower stems it will produce in one season. The spring-flowering varieties quickly follow the winter ones, and these in turn are followed by the summer- and autumn-flowering types. It is possible to grow nothing but the delicate paphiopedilums and have some in flower all the year round. The species vary greatly one from the other, and contain among them many combinations of colour – brown, green, purple, yellow, red, as well as white, all in numerous variations. The white and yellow varieties belong to a group of stemless paphiopedilums that are plants of small stature and have the most delightful of flowers sitting just above the

foliage. Closely related to the paphiopedilums are the phragmipediums, a small genus noted for the few species that have long, trailing, ribbon-like petals. These lateral petals will extend while the flower is opening, growing 2–3cm (1 in) a day until they attain a length of over 45cm (18 in). Taking these petals between finger and thumb and extending them at full length creates a flower 90cm (3 ft) or so across, surely the largest flower in the world!

The paphiopedilums and phragmipediums have steadfastly remained well at the top of the popularity list, and although many fine hybrids are grown today, the true species are still widely grown and admired for their graceful, handsome flowers.

Hot greenhouse orchids

If you have a hot greenhouse, there is a completely different range of orchids that is easy to grow with sufficient heat.

Phalaenopsis This reigns supreme among hothouse orchids. Commonly known as 'moth' orchids because of the spread of their pure white petals, they are monopodial in habit, but do not attain any great height. A standard-sized plant will

Phalaenopsis are expensive plants to raise from seed, mainly owing to the high temperatures they require, but the grower is amply rewarded by long, drooping sprays of delicate and beautiful flowers. The flowers are large and circular and will last for many weeks; when it has finished flowering, a flower spike will often grow again from its length, producing even more flowers. A large, mature plant that has been well grown is almost continuously in bloom. Phalaenopsis hybrids have no set time for flowering and can be in bloom at any time of the year.

Vandas The vandas are a further group of sun-loving, hot-growing orchids that are monopodial in habit, with some varieties growing to a height of 1·2–1·5m (4–5 ft). However, the average flowering size is about 25–30cm (9–12 in) tall. Long aerial roots sometimes accompany the growth of these most attractive plants. Their flowering season is variable, and they are capable of blooming twice in one year. The flower spikes come from the axils of the leaves and carry up to a dozen large, long-lasting blooms.

There are many colourful species to be found among the vandas, and these are grown as much as the plentiful hybrids. This group also produces the beautiful blue colour so rare in orchids, and one species in particular, *Vanda caerulea*, is the parent of the many blue hybrids now available. The best of these is *Vanda Rothschildiana*, that is greatly sought after for its unusual colour. Other colours scattered among the vandas include pink, yellow and brown. The flowers are generally spotted, veined or tessellated. New hybrids are continuously being raised from seed, bringing in other genera closely related to increase the colour variations still further.

Above: Odontoglossum cirrhosum *comes from Ecuador and likes cool conditions*
Left: the unusual Dendrobium stratiotes *is from the tropical forests of Asia*
Right: attractive cymbidium orchid with strongly contrasting lip markings

carry up to six large, broad leaves, that are thick and fleshy, compensating the plant for its lack of pseudo-bulbs. They are often grown on pieces of wood and have a downward habit, at the same time producing the typical orchid aerial roots, flattened and silvery on the outside. Orchids that are grown on wood very soon adhere to it with these strong, clinging roots; within a few months supporting ties can be removed and the plant becomes self-supporting.

The foliage on some of the phalaenopsis species is beautifully marked and mottled with light and dark grey-green spots. The undersides of these leaves may be purple, making a most handsome-looking plant, even when it is not in flower. The colours of phalaenopsis are somewhat restricted to white and pink, but there are a few yellow ones that have been recently introduced, as well as some very fine reds and mauves.

A selection of species

So far we have mentioned most of the popular genera among orchids, dwelling on the types that are being greatly hybridized. There remain many species that are grown for their individual beauty and appeal, and that are ideal for the amateur grower who has only limited space available. The following species have been chosen for their compact habit of growth, ease of culture and free-flowering habit. All are cool-growing and recommended for the beginner, being showy and interesting and are sure to whet the appetite and encourage the new grower to seek further knowledge of these fascinating plants.

Brassia verrucosa The 'spider' orchid. It has large flowers on gracefully-arching sprays. Sepals and petals are long and narrow, green-spotted with brown. From Honduras.

Coelogyne ochracea Sweet-scented sprays of small, delightful flowers. It is snow-white, the lip marked with yellow and orange. Spring-flowering. From India.

Cymbidium devonianum Miniature flowers, reddish-green on long, pendant sprays, with a dull purple lip. Early spring-flowering. From India.

Dendrobium infundibulum Large, pure white flowers, in clusters from the top of the bulb, with a deep yellow stain at the throat. Early summer-flowering. From India.

Dendrobium nobile Attractive rose-pink and white flowers, the length of the cane, with a white lip and a large, deep maroon blotch in the centre. From India.

Encyclia cochleata Upright spray of curious dark-green and dark-purple flowers with lip held uppermost. Common name is 'cockle-shell' orchid. Blooms for long periods during spring and summer. Comes from Honduras and Guatemala.

Laelia anceps Tall flower spikes that average four blooms. Large, showy and delicate mauve with lip richly-coloured and marked yellow in the throat. Autumn-to winter-flowering. From Mexico.

Lycaste cruenta Bright golden-yellow flowers. Three-cornered in appearance. Single, fragrant blooms. Spring-flowering. From Guatemala.

Odontoglossum grande 'Tiger' orchid. Large, richly-coloured flowers in yellow with chestnut-brown bars and a shell-shaped lip in creamy-yellow and brown. Autumn-flowering. From Guatemala.

Paphiopedilum hirsutissimum Large single bloom, very long-lasting. Petals pale green tapering to bold pink, heavily dotted with purple. Pouch, light green. Spring-flowering. From India.

Above: Dendrobium infundibulum *is from India and forms clusters of white flowers*
Left: Lycasta cruenta *is spring-flowering and comes from Guatemala*
Far left: two phalaenopsis orchids, often known as 'moth' orchids because of the spread of their pure white petals
Below: delicately-coloured Cattleya saskelliana *comes from Venezuela*

ORCHID CARE AND CULTIVATION

Here we deal with all aspects of orchid cultivation including indoor culture, and tell you how to make the most of these fascinating and beautiful plants.

Orchids under cultivation can be divided into three groups according to their temperature requirements. These comprise the cool, the intermediate and the hot growing types. The cool house orchids, that are more generally grown and usually recommended for the beginner, require a winter minimum night temperature of 10°C (50°F). This will rise by at least 5°C (10°F) during the daytime. Summer night-time temperatures will be approximately 3°C (5°F) higher, but be sure to keep daytime temperatures down to a maximum of 24°C (75°F).

Intermediate house orchids require temperatures at least 3°C (5°F) higher than the cool, while in the hot house, plants succeed well with a minimum night temperature of 18°C (65°F) winter and summer, and a correspondingly high daytime temperature.

It therefore follows that a cool greenhouse will require artificial heating during the autumn and winter months (end of September to early May), depending on the outside weather conditions. In the intermediate, and especially in the hot section, artificial heating will be required all the year round.

Ventilation and shading

Temperatures inside the greenhouse are controlled by ventilation and shading. Ventilation is most important to orchids, and fresh air, without a draught, should be applied at all times. During the winter, with cold, dull days and little or no sun, it may be possible only to open one ventilator just a crack for an hour or so. This will be sufficient to freshen up the air inside without causing a drop in temperature. During the summer months fresh air can be applied to the cool house almost permanently. It is far better to leave the ventilators open all night during very warm spells of weather than to allow the temperature to rise in the early morning before opening the ventilators. You must be a little more careful, however, in applying fresh air in the hotter houses, where a drop in temperature could be harmful. Small electric fans can work wonders in a small greenhouse, and will keep the air continually on the move without altering the required temperature. They can be used with equal advantage throughout the year, and are an important asset for people who have to be away from home all day. Automatic ventilators can be brought into play whenever required, taking much of the worry out of growing greenhouse orchids.

Orchids enjoy light, but cannot stand the direct burning sun that penetrates the glass during the summer months. However, take advantage of any bright sunny days that occur from mid autumn to early spring (September to February) to give the orchids full light without fear of burning. From mid spring (March) onwards and throughout the summer months, use some form of shading in the greenhouse. The ideal form of shading is roller blinds that can be attached to the outside of the glass, with a 25cm (9 in) gap between the blinds and the glass to allow for a cooling air flow. They can be rolled up and down as required, allowing the plants maximum light on sunless days. Apart from preventing scorching of the plants, the shading also assists in keeping the temperature down in summer. It may also be necessary to shade the glass with white paint that reflects the light.

Humidity and damping down

Humidity is perhaps the most important single factor in orchid culture. Remember that the plants thrive where humidity is naturally high, and they have evolved as epiphytes living more or less on nothing but humidity. The orchid greenhouse must therefore be damped down daily, until the floors, staging, and all parts of the house are thoroughly soaked. In the summer damp down two or three times daily, and spray the plants overhead once a day. Do this towards late afternoon, or when the sun is just passing over the greenhouse. Providing all foliage is dry by nightfall, the plants will enjoy their daily spraying. During the winter months damping down will probably be necessary only once a day, or every two days, depending upon the immediate weather conditions. The aim should always be to balance the temperature with the humidity. When the temperature is low on cold

winter days, the humidity must also be low, and when the temperature is at its maximum on hot summer days, there should be maximum humidity to balance.

Don't spray overhead during the winter as the water is cold and will remain on the foliage too long before drying up, leading to the appearance of damp marks. Soft-leaved plants such as the lycastes and also the paphiopedilums and phalaenopsis should not be sprayed at any time, since they are particularly prone to damp spots on the foliage. They do, however, require a humid atmosphere around them.

Damping down is carried out to create the humid growing conditions that orchids enjoy, but should not be confused with the actual watering of the plants: this is a separate routine procedure. Water with a spouted can, flooding the surface once or twice to wet the compost thoroughly. This should drain away immediately. Watering of orchids is carried out according to their growing cycle. During the summer months the orchids are growing at the maximum, new bulbs are being made and the plants are in their period of peak energy. This means they will consume copious supplies of water. The ideal is to maintain the compost in a constantly moist condition. Allowing the compost to become bone dry for any period will slow growth, while the other extreme of soaking it to the extent that it eventually becomes sodden, will lead to souring and loss of the plant roots.

During this summer growing period the orchids can also take limited amounts of artificial food; this can be in the form of a liquid food diluted and sprayed over the foliage, or given directly through the compost at regular 10-day intervals. Feeding should be gradually lessened towards the autumn and discontinued throughout the winter.

Rest periods

Many orchids rest during the winter months, when little or no activity is going on within the plants. They can be likened in this respect to an animal that hibernates for the winter after spending the summer storing food within itself to carry it safely through the winter sleep. A resting plant is in a similar state, having spent the summer making up bulbs that contain sufficient moisture to carry it through the winter. The roots stop growing and taking in moisture. Many orchids will spend the winter months in

Left: Paphiopedilum insigne *is a 'slipper' orchid. Below left: graceful* Dendrobium nobile *comes from India*

Below: perfectly-shaped specimen of Odontonia amphea *Vanguard, a popular and striking meristem hybrid orchid*

this dormant state, their bulbs remaining hard and plump without the assistance of extra water.

It does not follow, however, that all orchids rest, and this can be clearly seen by observing the plants themselves. By autumn some orchids have completed their pseudo-bulbs, but the bulbless types do not rest, and must therefore be kept moist throughout the winter. The bulbous types may, at this time, shed some or all of their foliage (the first indication of their coming dormant period). Provided there are no signs of new growth, the plant is, to all appearances, commencing its rest. From this time on the plants need no water and can stand in the full light. It may be an advantage to move them from the staging to a shelf close to the glass, where they can enjoy maximum light.

Those orchids that do not rest for the winter usually slow down their growth, but otherwise they require the same attention as during the summer. Continue watering, to keep the plants evenly moist – though at longer intervals as they will take longer to dry out. These continuous-growing plants lose a percentage of their foliage at the beginning of winter, but at the same time new growth will appear from the base of the latest completed bulb, and this will continue to grow throughout the winter. To withhold water from a growing plant will result in a much smaller bulb being made by the end of the season. The bulbs should progress in size until they reach maturity. If they become smaller year by year, it is clear that the conditions provided do not suit them.

The resting plants should retain plump bulbs while they are in their dormant state. If any undue shrivelling takes place, water the plants thoroughly once and the bulbs will plump up again in a very short time. At any time after late winter (January), watch the resting orchids for signs of new growth. Once this happens, it is clear the plants have woken up and are on the move again. When the new growth is about 5–10cm (2–4 in) high (smaller on dwarf plants) the new roots will appear. Begin watering again at this stage; the new roots just being made will need all the moisture they can get, but be careful to avoid over-watering.

Flowering cycles

It has been seen that orchids flower at different times of the year, and therefore at different periods of their growing cycle. Some orchids bloom during their resting period while others produce spikes when in full growth. Therefore the flowering-time need not necessarily be taken into consideration when deciding whether or not to water. A plant that blooms during its resting period has retained sufficient energy in its bulbs to support the growth and flowering of the spike without the assistance of extra water. Plants that flower during their growing season usually do so from the new growth when very young, and only after flowering do the new roots appear, so again the older bulbs support the new growth and flower spike. Watering should be quite straightforward if you watch your plants instead of the calendar, and make sure to water growing plants only.

Orchids should bloom annually quite naturally after a good growing season. If they fail to do so, the culture is at fault. A well-grown, contented plant will bloom without any further assistance from the grower. This, basically, is the art of orchid culture, and every grower strives to bloom every plant in their collection at least once a year.

Potting and repotting

When it comes to potting orchids, bear in mind that the vast majority of those grown in greenhouses are epiphytic by nature. A good basic compost for all orchids is fine bark chippings, either used by itself or mixed with a small percentage of sphagnum peat or sphagnum moss. This provides a good, open, well-drained compost that does not deteriorate quickly and through which the orchids can push their roots with ease. Either plastic or clay pots can be used, but you will find that with such an open compost clay pots will dry the plants out very much quicker. Most growers today use plastic pots.

An orchid plant is in need of repotting when the leading bulb or growth has reached the rim of the pot and there is no room for any further bulbs to be made within it. It also requires repotting if the roots have become so numerous that they have pushed the plant up above the rim.

The showy Vanda sanderiana *originally came from the Philippines and is often considered to be the finest of all orchids.*

In any case, you should repot orchids every year, choosing a pot large enough to allow for a further season's growth. Remove the plant from its old pot, shake the old compost from the roots or clean it out from between the thick rootball. Trim the roots if they are very long, and remove any dead ones.

Orchids are propagated by removing the oldest bulbs from the back portion of the plants. Provided these are firm and not too old, they can be potted up on their own, and will most likely begin new growth within six weeks or so. Any number of leafless back bulbs can be removed from a plant, provided it is left with at least three strong bulbs to maintain its flowering size. The slightly-reduced plant will probably fit back into its original pot. Place the last remaining bulb towards the rim of the pot and leave maximum room for growth to the front of the plant.

Good drainage is important for all orchids, so place a layer of broken crockery at the bottom of the pot. Put the plant into its new position, keeping the base of the new growth level with the pot rim. Fill in the compost all round and push down with the fingertips until the surface is slightly below the rim of the pot. This will allow for future watering and prevent the compost from being washed over the edge.

Indoor culture

The cultivation of orchids in the home is becoming increasingly popular. In spite of certain difficulties over conditions, you can encourage orchids to thrive indoors if you understand what requirements are necessary. Standing a plant over a hot radiator or in the centre of an ill-lit room gives it no incentive to grow and only spells disaster. Much more thought must be given to growing orchids indoors, and you will only be successful if you can maintain the all-important growing environment that they need. If you have a large, south-facing bay window available where house plants thrive, there is a good chance that some orchids will do well there also. The best type of orchids to select are those that can do with less humidity and that generally rest for part of the year. One or two examples are *Odontoglossum grande*, with large, striking flowers of rich yellow and chestnut; *Laelia gouldiana*, with large, brightly-coloured flowers of mauve; *Dendrobium nobile*, with clusters of pink and white flowers; *Coelogyne ochracea*, with small sprays of fragrant white and yellow flowers; and *Paphiopedilum insigne*, with long-lasting bronze and green flowers.

By far the best and most certain way of growing orchids in the home is to put them in a mini indoor greenhouse or orchid case. These are now generally available, including ones that have been designed specially for orchids. They provide heat, light and ventilation, giving a permanently controlled microclimate in which the orchids can thrive, with minimal cost, throughout the year. Ferns and foliage plants can be added to create a good-looking showcase for permanent display.

Propagation by meristem culture

Many seedlings can be grown from a single pod taken from a hybrid. When these finally reach flowering size (a process that takes approximately four years), no two plants ever produce identical blooms, each one being an individual.

Only the best quality plants produced are taken on for meristem culture. This is a method of mass propagation of a single clone or plant. It is a highly-organized technique (mainly practised by commercial growers with cymbidiums) that involves taking the youngest growth from the plant and removing from its centre the nucleus of growing cells that is the meristem tip. No larger than a pinhead, this small embryo is cultured in the same way as the seed; from this minute piece of tissue any number of identical 'carbon copies' can be successfully produced. This process takes a further three to four years before the plants will be of flowering size. These orchids will always be referred to as 'meristems'.

The grower now has two choices. He may prefer to purchase unflowered seedlings of unknown expectancy, with the excitement of flowering them for the first time and hoping for one outstanding variety, or he can obtain proven meristem-cultured plants, knowing exactly what he is buying. This latter choice is preferable when buying for the cut flower market since you can obtain exactly what the florists require.

The orchid seed pod is produced by crossing two selected flowers. It takes up to nine months to ripen on the plant. The pod, heavily laden with literally millions of incredibly small seeds, is ready for sowing when splits begin to appear along the edges. The seed is sown in sterile flasks on a special growing medium (obtainable from a specialist nursery) that includes various salts and sugars for the nourishment of the seed. The young plants thrive in these sterile conditions and after 12 months they are strong enough to be taken from the flasks and potted up. From this stage on they are repotted at regular intervals until they reach flowering size.

Above: meristem culture – seedlings grown on agar under sterile conditions – with temperature and humidity gauges

SCENTED FLOWERS FOR THE GREENHOUSE

Many flowers are famous for their scent, and it is not difficult to fill a greenhouse full of fragrance. We include others here that become more sweet-smelling under greenhouse or conservatory conditions.

When growing flowers for their scent it is important to choose your varieties carefully. Many flowers, usually thought of as sweet-smelling, such as lilies and freesias, also have varieties that are completely scentless.

Above: delicate-flowered freesia may not always be scented. To be sure, buy corms of a named variety
Left: strongly-perfumed Lilium auratum *bears striking bloom up to 30cm (12 in) across in early to mid autumn (August to September)*

Fragrant lilies

Among the easiest plants to grow are the bulbs and other storage organs. Lilies immediately spring to mind, but most of those that make the best pot plants are not particularly scented. But certain lilies can be temperamental outdoors and by growing them indoors under glass you may get more reliable results – and more perfume. Also some of the new hybrid lilies are expensive and you may prefer to give them protection. However, when cultivated this way the plants do tend to grow tall and will need staking.

One of the most powerfully-scented lilies is *L. auratum* (goldband lily). The variety *L. a. platyphyllum* has very large, beautiful flowers and a strong stem. The various forms of *L. speciosum* are also good for the greenhouse. They have charming flowers with reflexed petals in carmine and red shades as well as white. Their height varies from about 90cm–1·5m (3–5 ft). *L. japonicum* (bamboo lily) is of neat habit and makes fine pot plants when grouped in threes in 18cm (7 in) pots. It has fragrant, pinky, trumpet flowers and rarely exceeds 90cm (3 ft) in height.

Tuberose and Peruvian daffodil

Polianthes tuberosa (tuberose) has been an important plant in the manufacture of perfume. For pots a good choice is the variety The Pearl with its attractive spikes of double white flowers. It is, however, an untidy plant and is best grown as three bulbs to each 18cm (7 in) pot. Plant the large, elongated bulbs with their tops well protruding from the surface of the compost. You can force the bulbs in gentle warmth to flower at almost any time of year, but spring is the easiest time to get them to flower. After flowering, expose the bulbs to as much sunlight as possible. This seems to 'ripen' them and they are more likely to flower again the following year.

Provided you buy the largest possible bulbs, *Hymenocallis narcissiflora* (Peruvian daffodil) is easy to grow and very impressive. The variety usually sold is *H. n.* Advance. This has a tall, strong stem that bears several large, spidery, white flowers with a structure similar to the daffodil (they belong to the same family) but sweetly scented. If potted in spring, flowering will continue during summer. Plant one bulb in each 18cm (7 in) pot.

Cyclamen and freesia

At one time the cyclamen also gave its name to many fancy perfumes. Like so many plants where there have been attempts to breed larger flowers, the scent has often become faint or lost altogether. Even so, there are still strongly-scented strains such as Sweet-scented Mixed. The flowers are not so large as the giant-flowered forms, but the scent is strong and the range of colours delightful. The Puppet strain of cyclamen are also strongly fragrant. These are pleasing miniatures that can be grown in very small pots.

The freesia is another plant that may or may not be scented. Flowers grown from seed or from corms of obscure origin may have no fragrance at all. The strain Van Staaveren, however, has a lovely perfume and can be sown in mid winter (late December) for summer flowers and in late spring to mid summer (April to June) for flowers in autumn and winter. About seven seeds to each 13cm (5 in) pot will make a good group of bloom for decoration. They also make fine cut flowers.

Certain freesia varieties available as corms also have a fine fragrance – for example Snow Queen, Blue Banner and Golden Melody. In addition, these all have very large, beautiful flowers.

Scented flowers from seed

Several very fragrant plants can be raised quickly from seed. The lovely *Calonyction aculeatum* (moonflower) is one that is not well known. It opens its large, white, convolvulus-like flowers in the evening and fills the air with scent. Although perennial, it is easy to raise as an annual and it will climb up a few bamboo canes or can be trained on a wall support.

Exacum affine is best grown as several seedlings per 13cm (5 in) pot. The blue flowers are small but have a strong, spicy scent, providing you take care to choose a scented strain of seed.

Several types of stock make good pot plants or can be used for cutting in winter. The strain Giant Brilliant Column produces handsome spikes of exhibition blooms and some of them are excellent for cutting. For exhibition, remove all sideshoots and allow one central spike only to develop. Beauty of Nice is also a favourite with flower arrangers. For winter cut flowers, sow the seed from late summer to early autumn (July to August). For the large double flowers get the Hansens 100 per cent double strains and prick out only those seedlings with light green leaves; these are the ones that give the double flowers.

Sweet-smelling climbers

There are three perennial greenhouse climbers outstanding for both beautiful flowers and perfume. The easiest is *Jasminum polyanthum*, which is happy with a winter minimum temperature of about 4–7°C (40–45°F). It can be kept within bounds by drastic pruning, but it tends to become rampant and is ideal for covering a large expanse of wall, for example in a lean-to. It becomes covered with masses of white flowers from about early spring (February) onwards (depending on temperature) and its scent is very strong. Not difficult, but needing more overall warmth for healthy growth, is *Stephanotis floribunda* (Madagascar jasmine), which has clusters of white tubular flowers during summer, and *Hoya carnosa*, with its umbels of pink-to-white starry flowers from mid summer to mid autumn (June to September).

Carnations and gardenias

Of the specialists' flowers, carnations are probably the most renowned for scent – but again the variety is very important. Consult the catalogue of a specialist grower of perpetual-flowering types; varieties with good scent will be so described.

Gardenias have tended to go out of fashion. This may be because they often need a fairly high level of greenhouse heating, at least during part of their development, and now that fuel is so expensive fewer people want to grow them. Unless you can give a winter minimum of about 13°C (55°F) it is better to avoid them.

Cold greenhouse flowers

For cold greenhouses, roses in pots should not be forgotten for early fragrant blooms, and, of course, many of the favourite spring-flowering bulbs (such as narcissus and hyacinth) are also highly fragrant. In addition, there are scented shrubs like daphne – the best for the greenhouse being *Daphne odora* that has strongly citrus-scented, pale purplish flowers in winter.

Stephanotis floribunda *(Madagascar jasmine) climbs up to 3m (10 ft) high*

SCENTED FOLIAGE PLANTS

Plants with scented foliage are not often noted for their showy flowers, but the leaves are usually attractive. Grown under glass, the fragrance from the leaves is generally even more pronounced, especially when the temperature rises, and the air of the greenhouse can become filled with their scent.

In most cases you can release the fragrant essential oils from the leaves of plants with scented foliage by gently pressing (or sometimes crushing) a leaf between the fingers.

Hardy plants with scented foliage

A number of the plants are almost hardy, some may even be perfectly hardy in sheltered parts of the country. This makes them a good choice for a cold or unheated greenhouse or conservatory. Popular as a house plant in recent years is *Eucalyptus globulus* (Tasmanian blue gum). This will eventually become far too large for pots, but in mild regions it can thrive outdoors. The leaves on young plants up to about three years old are roundish. Mature foliage is elongated. When crushed, the foliage emits the familiar smell of eucalyptus, but the scent is more 'flowery' and pleasant than the oil you buy from the chemist when you have a cold. The plants are easily raised from seed sown in early spring (February).

In mild areas *Choisya ternata*, sometimes called Mexican orange blossom, is hardy. In colder regions it may be successful if given a sheltered spot. It makes a good evergreen for large pots in cold greenhouses (provided you give it room to spread), or it can be grown as a wall shrub. The foliage is a glossy light green, giving out a strong citrus smell when bruised. Clusters of small, attractive and fragrant white flowers are also produced from time to time during the year, often continuing well into winter in a cold greenhouse. Small container-grown plants are usually available from good garden centres.

A few alpine species (such as the alpine species of artemisia) have scented foliage, and there are various reasonably-compact or low-growing aromatic herbs that, with frost protection, may also serve a useful purpose by providing leaves to flavour cooking during the winter.

Above left: erect-growing Myrtus communis. *Left: many pelargoniums have strongly scented leaves*

Above: Eucalyptus globulus *(Tasmanian blue gum) is an excellent choice for unheated greenhouse or conservatory*

Sweet-smelling myrtles

Excellent for a cold greenhouse are the various species and varieties of myrtle. *Myrtus communis* (common myrtle), can be grown but it needs a tub or a large pot and may become too big for a small greenhouse. It is erect in habit and the white blossom is delightfully fragrant; the rarer double form is especially attractive. Where space is lacking the compact variety *M.c.* Tarentina is useful. It bears pink buds that open to creamy-white flowers from early to mid autumn (August to September).

Especially suited to a greenhouse, too, are *M. bullata* and *M. ugni*. Both can be kept to below about 110cm (3½ ft). The former is a splendid foliage plant and is sometimes sold as a house plant. It has bronze-coloured puckered foliage of waxy texture, giving it the common name of puckered-leaf myrtle. Large white flowers are followed by red berries. *M. ugni* is the edible myrtle having pink, bell-shaped flowers and dark red fruit rather like the strawberry in flavour. It is neat and compact in growth.

For a cold conservatory with plenty of height there are two lovely myrtles. *M. apiculata* (Chilean tree myrtle) needs at least 2·5m (8 ft) of height. The form *M. a.* Glanleam Gold is very striking, having dark green foliage with golden-yellow margins.

M. lechleriana also needs plenty of height – at least 1·8m (6 ft) to display itself properly. The white flowers, borne in spring, are deliciously scented and the young growth has a bronze tint.

Lemon-scented leaves

Lippia citriodora, lemon-scented verbena, often called aloysia, can easily be grown in 20–25cm (8–10 in) pots in a cold greenhouse. The leaves emit a powerful lemon scent when crushed, but the shrub is deciduous. Panicles of small, mauve tubular flowers appear in early autumn (August). The shrub is easy to keep 'within bounds' and will withstand quite drastic pruning – best done in late spring (April).

Another plant giving a powerful lemon scent when the foliage is crushed or gently pressed between the fingers is *Eucalyptus citriodora* (lemon-scented gum). However, this species is suited only to reasonably warm conditions. Raise it from seed sown in spring in a warm propagating case and it will grow on slowly during the summer. In autumn you must put it in a warm greenhouse or on a warm windowsill in the home. The leaves are a pleasing olive green and slightly hairy. The minimum winter temperature it needs is about 10°C (50°F), preferably higher, and you should be sure to maintain a fair humidity. It can be kept for several years quite happily in a 13cm (5 in) pot before you will need to repot it, or replace the plant altogether.

Fragrant-leaved pelargoniums

The most popular of all scented-leaved plants are the pelargoniums. There are numerous pungent-smelling varieties and species and others that have a specific scent such as rose, lemon, mint or a fruity smell. The shape of the foliage is very variable and they often make good house plants although the flowers are rarely showy. *P. crispum* Catford Belle and *P.c.* Mabel Cirey have lemon-scented leaves and good flowers. *P. crispum minor* (finger bowl geranium) has very tiny leaves and a scent that is fragrant and lemony, rather like citronella. *P. citriodorum* Prince of Orange grows to be a fairly large plant with white flowers. *P. quercifolium* has an unusual scent – a mixture of pine and lime. It has 'oak-leaf' foliage and a somewhat creeping habit.

Pelargonium capitatum (attar of roses) has attractive foliage that is strongly rose-scented. The variety *P. denticulatum* (fern leaf) is so named because of its ferny leaf-shape. It has a fairly strong rose scent and also very small white flowers.

P. denticulatum tomentosum has a powerful mint scent and *P. tomentosum* a peppermint-like perfume. Both have rather hairy foliage.

Among the fruit-scented types, *P. fragrans* has a pleasing, piney-nutmeg smell and *P. odoratissimum* resembles apples. *P. grossularoides* has an apricot-rose perfume, while *P.g.* Lady Plymouth has attractive variegated foliage and a peppery lemon scent.

GREENHOUSE CLIMBERS

A few climbers in the greenhouse will greatly enhance its appearance. Choose from plants that are small and compact and can be fitted into the tiniest space, or from others that will cover a large area. Some will grow quickly from seed, some are annuals, and some become steadily more beautiful as the years pass.

The description 'climber' is often loosely used to include plants that could more properly be called wall shrubs – plants that are unable to support themselves by tendrils or by twining. Special provision has to be made for supporting them and training them into the required shape. Nearly all climbers, however, will need some support; very few can be left to ramble without some artificial means to hold them in position.

Root restriction

A common characteristic of climbers is that they tend to be rampant and rather too vigorous. Left to themselves (and perhaps given too much food and water) they may become a tangle of stems and foliage, producing little in the way of flowers. This is especially true of perennials that are planted in a border of ground soil in the greenhouse or given excessively large pots.

The first cultural hint, therefore, is to use relatively small pots or containers, or restrict root spread in the ground by planting in a plunged clay pot or placing slates, tiles, bricks or asbestos sheeting around the sides of the planting hole when it is made. For most annuals an ordinary flowerpot 13–25cm (5–10 in) in diameter is satisfactory – depending on the expected (or required) ultimate size of the plant.

Selecting the support

When it comes to supporting, training and displaying the plants there are a number of points to be considered. Often the nature of the plant will suggest the best method, while in other cases there may already be a support in existence for which you need to choose a suitable climber; for example you may wish to cover a lean-to greenhouse wall or a roof-supporting column, pillar or post.

If you intend to plant permanent wall

Vigorous Ipomoea tricolor *Heavenly Blue (left, above) and* Cobaea scandens *(left) will both flower in the year of planting*

Training greenhouse climbers

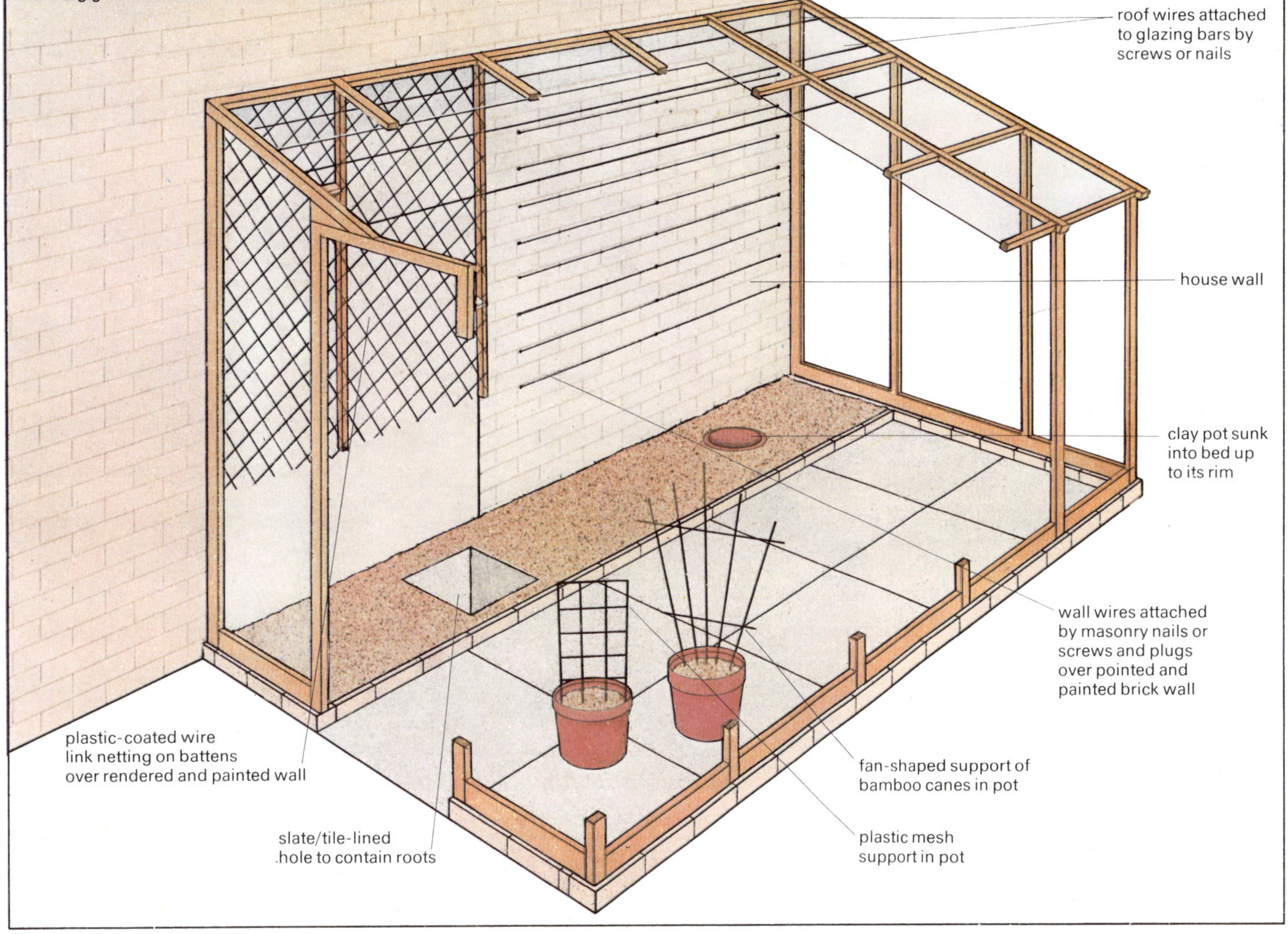

shrubs or climbers, then first pay some attention to the wall itself. A brick wall, or similar rough surface, is best rendered to give a smooth finish, filling in all holes so that there are no crevices where pests or diseases may accumulate. A coat of white vinyl emulsion or exterior paint will give a background that is both hygienic and pleasing.

To give wall support, attach wires to masonry nails driven into the wall or to screws fixed with plugs. Or you can use plastic-coated wire netting or mesh (obtainable in white for white walls) fastened to a wall or other part of the greenhouse structure. Plastic mesh without wire reinforcement is also sold for the support of climbers, but is less advisable for long-term use, as some plastics become brittle with age (especially in a sunny greenhouse) and may then collapse under the increasing weight of a growing climber. For a similar reason perishable materials like string or canes should be avoided for perennial climbers.

If you want your climber to grow up into the greenhouse roof, train it along wires stretched from end to end of the building, fastened to the glazing bars. For very small climbers, and particularly annuals, bamboo canes are suitable. You can usually insert several in the pot and arrange them like the spines of a fan. Small plastic mesh supports, intended for inserting in the flowerpots of house plants, are also convenient. For fastening stems to supports, a number of 'patent' plant ties are sold in garden shops. These are neat and secure and most can easily be moved from place to place.

Quick-flowering climbers

Several delightful climbers will flower in the first year of sowing and planting. *Ipomoea tricolor (rubro-caerulea)*, better known as morning glory, has long been prized for its glorious, large, blue, convolvulus-like blooms borne freely each morning but fading by early afternoon. In recent years varieties with new colours have been introduced, such as the blue and white striped Flying Saucers, the mauve Wedding Bells and the deep, rose-coloured Early Call that also has very long-lasting flowers. Sow seed in a warm propagator in mid spring (March) and transfer single seedlings to 13cm (5 in) pots or several to larger pots. Well-grown plants will reach about 1·8m (6 ft) high in one year and become smothered with bloom.

Similar in height and vigour is *Cobaea scandens* (cup and saucer plant) – so called because of the flower shape. The flowers are deep violet, but a rare white form is said to exist. Another fast-grower is *Eccremocarpus scaber* (Chilean glory flower). Provided it is sown early it will flower the same year, and it is hardy in sheltered places in mild areas although not often a long-lived perennial. It bears masses of showy, vivid orange flowers.

Some people like to grow sweet peas under glass especially for cutting, but not all varieties are suitable. Choose types that flower in late autumn to early winter (October–November) and Cuthbertson varieties. With care the large-flowered Spencer varieties can flower well, but rarely before late spring (April). In all cases there is a tendency for buds to drop and a greenhouse with good light is vital to success. All plants must be stopped at the seedling stage.

Extremely easy (even for children) to grow, is the lovely little climber *Thunbergia alata* (black-eyed Susan). Even the small seedlings are impatient to flower and at this stage the best bright orange colours with jet black eyes can be selected for growing on. Inferior colours can be discarded if desired. Growth will only reach 1m (3 ft) or so and there is usually room for this climber in the smallest greenhouse.

Exotic climbers

Striking and exotic, and much easier to grow than most gardening books imply, is *Gloriosa rothschildiana* (glory lily). This is grown from a long tuber that can be planted late on in spring (April) when the warmer weather keeps up the greenhouse temperature. Pot so that the blunt, roundish end is at the centre of an 18cm (7 in) pot. It is from here that the roots and shoots will grow. Just cover the tuber with potting compost; it does not matter if the pointed end protrudes above after placing the tuber longways. The plant will support itself by tendrils formed at the end of the leaves but will nearly always need further assistance from the grower. The flowers are like reflexed lilies, with bright crimson and yellow flowers from summer to autumn. Over winter store them, completely dry, with the pots on their sides. Usually at least two new tubers will be formed and can be separated when replanting at the appropriate time the following year.

Some climbers are best bought as small plants (usually rooted cuttings) from a garden centre, nursery or gardening shop. Being perennial they may take several years to reach full flowering size but, like most climbers and wall shrubs, are a wonderful sight when in bloom. Bougainvillea is among the most showy and colourful. In this case it is the bracts and not the flowers that make the long-lasting display. There are a number of named hybrids of *Bougainvillea* × *buttiana*, and *B. glabra* is also popular. The colours range from orange to mauve shades and even young plants will cover themselves with bracts. Bougainvilleas can be trained as wall shrubs or the stems led up along wires in the greenhouse roof when the plants have reached sufficient height. A winter minimum of about 10°C (50°F) is advisable for best results. Pruning should be done in early spring (February) by cutting out all weak growth and cutting back to keep the desired shape.

Scented climbers

A very vigorous but popular jasmine for the greenhouse is *Jasminum polyanthum*.

Left: Bougainvillea glabra, *covered with long-lasting bracts; below left: fragrant-flowered* Hoya carnosa; *below: bell-shaped flowers of* Abutilon megapotamicum *Right: the beautiful* Lapageria rosea

It has creamy-white flowers during late winter (January) and is extremely powerfully scented. To prevent rampant growth the roots are best restricted by growing in 25cm (10 in) pots. Do not be afraid to prune or cut back at almost any time, otherwise this climber can smother everything. It is ideal if you have a large area to cover but when strictly controlled is also suitable for a small greenhouse. A winter minimum temperature of about 7°C (45°F) is adequate.

A superb fragrant climber is *Stephanotis floribunda*, sometimes sold as a house plant trained around a wire hoop. In the greenhouse it will grow up into the roof and the waxy white tubular flowers, delightful because of their scent, will hang down in clusters. This climber likes a rather humid atmosphere and a winter minimum of about 10°C (50°F). It will survive lower temperatures if kept on the dry side during the cold months. *Hoya carnosa* also likes a fair degree of humidity. It is sweetly scented and has umbels of pinkish, starry flowers. The foliage is evergreen and there is a form with cream-margined leaves, greatly enhancing its beauty. Although surviving winter at about 7°F (45°F), best results are obtained if 10–13°C (50–55°F) can be maintained. It does well in shade and little pruning is required. Both stephanotis and hoya greatly benefit if you spray them with tepid water from time to time during summer.

Other popular climbers

A very beautiful evergreen climber for a greenhouse just kept free from frost is *Lapageria rosea* (Chilean bell-flower). Large, red tubular flowers of waxy texture are borne during autumn. It is a good choice for a shady greenhouse, even a north-facing conservatory or lean-to. The plants need little pruning and are happy in 25cm (10 in) pots. Pink and white forms are sometimes available but are not common.

An easy wall shrub for a frost-free conservatory is *Plumbago capensis*. This has either blue or white phlox-like flowers from spring to autumn. Pruned sparingly it will reach a height of at least 3.5m (12 ft) and looks most impressive if a blue and a white form are grown together and allowed to intermingle. When flowering is over, prune back all growth by about two-thirds.

Abutilon megapotamicum is a quaint, almost hardy climber with dainty red and yellow lantern-like flowers borne from spring to autumn. It is a good choice for a pillar or roof-supporting column, and demands little attention. Popular, but not a very wise selection for the greenhouse is *Passiflora caerulea*, the common passion flower – which is, in any case, perfectly hardy. Far better for under glass is the species *P. quadrangularis* (granadilla), with much larger, exotic flowers, and other warmth-loving species when available. These need 10°C (50°F) in winter and moderate humidity. They are best trained along wires and if you don't let the shoots become too long, then the flowers can be kept reasonably low.

HOW TO USE A SHADY GREENHOUSE

There is no doubt that the ideal site for a greenhouse is one in full sun. You can shade easily enough, but it is not so simple to provide light of solar intensity. The sun is also an important source of free heat in winter. Nevertheless, you can still put a shady greenhouse site to excellent use.

Town dwellers, in particular, often have little choice but to put their greenhouses in the shade. Small town gardens are frequently overshadowed by walls or other buildings. But don't let this discourage you; it merely means you will have to choose your plants with care and common sense.

There is a wide range of greenhouse plants for which shade can be a great advantage (if not vital), at least during their flowering period. And if you already have a sunny-sited greenhouse and are contemplating erecting an extra one, you may consider deliberately putting it in a shady place. For example, a north-facing conservatory built as a lean-to against your house may not be ideal as a suntrap but it will be excellent for displaying most of your favourite pot plants for a large part of the year.

If you wish to put a shady greenhouse to use in winter, remember that it will cost more to heat than one that traps the sun's warmth. If you cannot provide artificial heat, choose hardy (or almost hardy) shade-tolerant plants.

Enough warmth to keep out frost will greatly extend your range. Although a little extra warmth does not necessarily mean more scope in terms of colourful and decorative plants, it does mean that you can grow some less common and more exotic species.

Exotic hardy plants
Where there is no heat at all, create an impression of tropical warmth with foliage plants like *Fatsia japonica* and the various hardy palms. These will thrive in

There is a wide range of flowering plants suitable for shady greenhouses. Above right: evergreen climber Lapageria rosea albiflora *and (right)* Cyclamen persicum *Far right, above: spring-flowering* Primula × kewensis*; far right:* Fuchsia cordifolia

semi-shade, but not in extreme gloom. Most of the hardy ferns, however, positively enjoy having very little light.

For both attractive evergreen foliage and glorious flowers, the camellias are very important where light is limited.

They will usually flower well as quite young plants in pots as small as 13mm (5 in). When they eventually become too large for the cold greenhouse you can put them out in the garden. Another evergreen (and an indispensible climber for the rear wall of a cold, shady lean-to) is *Lapageria rosea* (Chilean bell-flower). This has shiny foliage and large, tubular, waxy flowers that are usually carmine in colour – less commonly pink. They are borne in early autumn to early winter (August to November).

Most of the hedera (ivies) will tolerate a good deal of shade and there are now many decorative variegated forms that can be used as small pot plants or to cover an expanse of wall. *Hedera canariensis* is particularly pleasing and in cool conditions develops a reddish tint to the green and cream variegated foliage. This ivy is almost hardy, if not entirely so in sheltered places, and so it will grow especially vigorously in a warm greenhouse or room.

Hardy border plants

A number of hardy border plants make good pot subjects for an unheated shady house. Especially suitable are the hardy cyclamen, bergenia (the handsome flowers tend to get damaged outdoors in winter), primulas of various kinds, a number of lilies, trillium (which should be given a leafy compost and will even enjoy deep shade), the long-spurred aquilegias (columbine), Excelsior hybrid digitalis (foxglove) – if there's height for them to grow to about 1·5m (5 ft) – and hostas (plantain lily) that bear delightful flowers as well as having beautiful foliage. All the hardy spring-flowering bulbs should ideally be given a cold, shady greenhouse for them to display their flowers which will then last much longer, but good light is essential in mid and late winter (December and January) to keep their foliage short and green.

Pot plant displays

A shady, frost-free greenhouse makes an ideal conservatory for the display of nearly all the popular pot plants that are grown to give a mass of colour from mid winter to early summer (December to May). These include cineraria, calceolaria, primulas such as *P. malacoides*, *P. obconica*, *P. sinensis* and *P.* × *kewensis*, autumn-sown schizanthus (butterfly flower), salpiglossis and other annuals, and cyclamen.

If the house is not too shady most of these can also be grown in it from the earliest stages – from seed or storage organs. Where the amount of shade is considerable, however, it is better to use frames warmed with soil-warming cables. Place them where there is good light for the earlier stages of growing, so that strong, compact plants will develop. Ideally, of course, this is where another greenhouse with an open, sunny position can help enormously.

Flowers for summer and autumn

For summer- and autumn-flowering plants shade is usually vital, and as most of those grown in the home greenhouse will need no extra heat during the summer, a shady greenhouse is the ideal home for them. The 'top' group of shade lovers is the family GESNERIACEAE. This includes saintpaulia (African violet), streptocarpus (Cape primrose), gloxinia, *Rechsteineria leucotricha* (silver song), now commonly grown from seed, the gesneria varieties (that are now classed with the genus rechsteineria), achimenes and smithianthas.

Nearly all the popular foliage plants, with the exception of coleus, also like a fair degree of shade. Shade in summer is particularly essential to most of those now known as house plants, such as foliage begonias, peperomia, pilea, maranta (prayer plant) and calathea. Most of these will be happy under the staging.

Fuchsias will generally do better with some summer shade, more especially to prevent high temperatures that cause the flowers to fall or be short-lived, but the shade must not be too heavy. Regal pelargoniums also benefit from slight shade; it makes the flowers last longer.

Bulbs and vegetables

Many of the summer-to-autumn-flowering bulbs or other storage organs may have to be fairly heavily shaded, both to keep the temperature down and to prevent sun scorching flowers or foliage. The giant-flowered begonias can be severely damaged by excessive light, the flower petals becoming bleached or scorched at the edges. Hippeastrums and lilies may suffer similarly.

Few vegetables will enjoy a shady greenhouse, but if there is warmth it can be used for blanching plants like endive, and for forcing and blanching seakale, chicory and rhubarb. One exception, however, is the mushroom. This does not need light – but darkness is not essential either, as many people suppose.

SALAD CROPS FOR GROWING UNDER GLASS

Anyone with a greenhouse, frame or a few cloches should give serious thought to growing salad crops. They are rich in vitamins and minerals, low in fat content and, usually, in carbohydrates. With weather protection a wide range of these vegetables can be cropped almost all year round

To make the best use of the type of protection you have, and to employ it economically (especially important where heating is employed), give proper consideration to its height. A greenhouse has plenty of headroom and you can use this to advantage by growing tall crops like tomato and cucumber, while low-growing crops can often be grown as catch crops (quick crops grown alongside a main crop) in the remaining space.

You can also adopt the catch-crop technique with frames and cloches; for example, along with lettuce grow even smaller vegetables like radishes, so that no space is wasted.

Tomatoes

Undoubtedly the tomato is the most popular of all salad crops. It does, however, have its fair share of problems. Many of these arise from the practice of growing plants in the ground soil and using crude animal manures or garden compost that has not been properly fermented. These methods introduce innumerable pests and diseases to which tomatoes are very susceptible. Like most crops they also succumb to 'soil sickness' if grown in the same ground year after year. For this reason it is wise for the home grower, with the average-sized greenhouse, to grow the plants in good soil compost in pots at least 25cm (10 in) in diameter, or in a trough made from a frame of timber boards draped with polythene with slits cut for drainage. Growing bags, filled with special tomato compost are now also available. These are placed flat on the floor and holes are then cut in them to take the plants. You can, however, make your own simple and inexpensive compost. Mix three parts of peat with one part of washed grit and add (according to instructions) a proprietary, balanced, complete fertilizer containing magnesium, iron and trace elements.

Erratic watering of tomatoes and extremes of feeding lead to cracked and split fruit, and often to premature falling of flowers and young fruits. Ring-culture was designed to even out water uptake, but the method is still much misunderstood. The plants are grown in bottomless pots, and you can buy inexpensive fibre cylinders for the purpose. Set the ring on an aggregate consisting of 'ballast'. This is a mixture of coarse, stony pieces (that help support the rings of compost) and fine particles that convey moisture to the rings by capillary action. Keep the aggregate thoroughly moist, but not waterlogged. Apply liquid feeds to the compost in the rings. Alternatively, instead of this aggregate, you can use peat. Discard it at the end of the year (dig it into the outdoor garden) and use fresh peat for the next tomato crop. This way you don't have to dispose of heavy aggregate, nor do you have to clean and sterilize it for future use. You also avoid the risk of carrying over pests and diseases from one crop to the next.

It is important to put the aggregate down on plastic sheeting so as to prevent the tomato roots entering the ground soil. Do not, in place of aggregate, use ashes or other materials that may contain harmful chemicals, and do not overwater as this can cause root rot.

Although tomatoes can be cropped all the year round, this is an uneconomical practice for most people, owing to the fairly high degree of warmth needed for winter fruiting. The usual method is to sow from early spring (February) onwards, depending on the warmth available (a minimum of 10°C 50°F). If your greenhouse is sited in a sunny position, and warmth can be maintained, you can start sowing in early winter (November). Tomatoes need shading only when the

weather is at its hottes[t] temperatures below 27°C ripening – otherwise there ... ing troubles.

Cucumbers

Similar advice applies to cucumber, which most people find convenient to sow in late spring (April). This is another crop apt to be frequently overwatered; remember, cucumbers are not bog plants! If the roots get too wet they decay, and the young fruits rot and fall. Growing methods can be much the same as for tomatoes, but the plants must be properly trained for the best results. For a small greenhouse, stretch about five wires along the roof some 15–20cm (6–8 in) apart and stand the pots on the staging so that the plants can be grown up underneath the wires. Stop the plants (by taking out the growing tip) when they reach the top wires; then train any lateral shoots along the wires and tie them in. When a flower bearing a little fruit has formed stop (by cutting off) the shoot two leaves further on. Remove all flowers not bearing fruits. These are male flowers and if they are allowed to pollinate the females, they will cause the fruits to become seedy, club-shaped and often bitter. Varieties bearing only female flowers are now obtainable and well worth consideration. Cucumbers need more shade than tomatoes, and this is ideally provided by a coating of white Coolglass on the exterior of the greenhouse.

Sweet Peppers

These peppers, which you may also encounter under their Spanish name of pimiento or generic name of capsicum, are an excellent crop to grow with tomatoes, and they take up less height. You can eat the fruits when green, yellow or red, and you can cook them or use them raw. Modern hybrids are easy to grow and give splendid yields. If possible, sow early – at the same time as your tomatoes, in a similar compost and in 18–20cm (7–8 in) pots. Again, if there is sufficient warmth, sowing can be done in early winter (November) to give pickings by late the

A fine crop of ripe tomatoes (above left) and cucumbers (right) raised under glass

following spring (April). Well-grown plants produce as many as 30 fruits on each, but thinning is usually necessary to prevent overcrowding and distortion of the fruit that may press together when swelling. Otherwise they need little attention apart from watering and feeding as required. Green fruits will ripen to a full red colour after picking if put in a warm place indoors. You can also grow plants outside, keeping them under cloches until summer. Do not uncover them before all danger of frost is past.

Lettuce

Lettuce is most conveniently grown in frames or under cloches, but greenhouses are often devoted to this valuable year-round crop. A cold greenhouse or, for out-of-season production, a frost-free greenhouse, is all that is necessary. Frames can be equipped with electric soil-warming cables or special outdoor cables can be run in the soil under rows of cloches. These are operated from a transformer (that lowers the voltage) so there is no danger if the cables are accidentally cut when working the soil with tools.

It is vital when growing lettuce to choose your varieties with care. Not all are suited to winter culture, and winter types may bolt in summer. Examine the seedsmen's catalogues carefully. The descriptions of the various types explain which are suited to which seasons.

Like tomatoes (and for similar reasons) lettuce are prone to pests and diseases if grown in the ground soil. The most deadly enemy is grey mould (botrytis) a common fungus that attacks most plants living or dead. It is especially serious for lettuce and can wipe out the contents of frames or greenhouses in a few days unless promptly checked. Poor ventilation, allowing an excessive humidity, encourages the fungus that forms a greying, furry covering over the plants and causes them to rot. If you have added decaying manure or vegetable matter to the soil, this will certainly encourage an outbreak. So as a wise precaution, fumigate with TCNB smokes or spray with a fungicide such as Benlate, according to maker's instructions. In winter, when conditions in the greenhouse are best kept drier, it is not advisable to use a spray, so use TCNB smokes. It is not practical to fumigate frames as it is difficult to measure the correct dosage and to disperse the smoke evenly.

You can produce fine crops of lettuce by growing them in pots or troughs of a prepared sterile compost as described for tomatoes. You can also use this compost in frames, taking care to line them first with polythene to avoid contact with the ground soil. Under cloches it is usually convenient to sow lettuce directly into the soil and thin out, but you can, if preferred, raise the plants in seed trays in the greenhouse and transplant them.

Radish and Beetroot

There are several different varieties of radish that are easy to grow as catch crops. Study the catalogues carefully to select suitable types. Some force more easily than others. Radishes are remarkably free from pests and disease, but active surface pests like slugs and cutworms will eat them however 'hot' they may be to our taste. The variety Red Forcing is particularly good for under cover cultivation. Always thin out radish as soon as possible, otherwise the roots never get a chance to grow to their proper size, and their flavour never fully develops.

Globe beetroot make a useful frame crop, and there will usually be room for radish, too, while the beetroot is developing. Sowing can be made in a heated frame from early to mid spring (February to March). Thin to one plant at each sowing point, since the 'seeds' sown are really capsules containing several seeds.

Spring Onions and Carrots

Spring onions, either sown in spring or summer, need only cloche protection. White Lisbon is still a favourite variety.

Carrots are often overlooked as salad vegetables, but young, raw carrots are delicious when grated and seasoned, and are extremely nutritious. Choose the stump-rooted types for frames and cloches; read the catalogue descriptions carefully since not all varieties are happy under cover. Sow in a warmed frame in mid autumn (September) and late winter (January); in a cold frame sow from early spring (February) onwards.

Other Vegetables

Mustard and cress and several other sprouting vegetables like fenugreek, alfalfa, Mung bean and Adzuki bean can be fitted in as catch crops to most heated greenhouses and frames all the year round. They are easy to grow and need no elaborate preparations or compost making, and they are probably the quickest-yielding of all crops. It is only recently that their important food value has been appreciated, and they are a valuable source of protein.

GROWING FRUIT IN THE GREENHOUSE

To make it worthwhile growing most types of dessert fruit under glass, you really need a large greenhouse. However, it need not necessarily be expensive to run, as in many cases little or no artificial heat is required. You may be lucky enough to have an old property whose garden already contains a derelict greenhouse that could be renovated and adapted for the purpose. If you are thinking of installing one specially, a lean-to greenhouse against a south-facing wall is particularly good for fruit-growing.

Among the fruits that can be grown successfully in an unheated or cool greenhouse are peaches, apricots, nectarines, grapes, figs and melons.

Grapes

Interest in grape-growing is developing alongside the increasing popularity of wine-making. A lean-to greenhouse is an excellent home for a vine, though you may have difficulty finding room in it for much else.

Usually the roots of the vines are planted outside in a border alongside the front of the greenhouse. The rods (vine stems) are then passed through a little arch made in the greenhouse base and trained up the side and over the roof. Plant in late winter (January), spacing 1·2m (4 ft) between plants, and cut back the rods if necessary to 45cm (18 in). For a single plant allow two shoots to grow freely during the first year; if you are growing several vines, allow only one shoot on each. With a solitary vine the shoots can be trained horizontally in opposite directions.

Top laterals that form can then be led vertically and all others removed. Side growth from verticals should be kept to 60cm (24 in), by pinching off the tips, and removed completely in winter. Also in winter cut back the main leading shoot (or shoots from a solitary vine) to hard wood.

In the second year wires will be needed to support the lateral shoots, and in winter cut back all these laterals to one or two buds. By the third year, you should have a good crop.

In all cases only one bunch of grapes should be allowed to each lateral, and the berries should be thinned to permit those remaining to swell and have room to develop and ripen. No winter heat is necessary, but a minimum of about 10–13°C (50–55°F) during flowering is an advantage. Ventilation must be given freely when possible to avoid trouble with powdery mildew. Consult nurseries for varieties to recommend as suitable for growing under glass.

Peaches, nectarines and apricots

These are ideally suited to a lean-to, and are generally best grown in a border at the foot of the wall and trained against it (preferably as fans), using securely-fastened support wires.

It is essential to obtain varieties suited to indoor culture and on suitable root-stocks. Since the availability of varieties tends to vary from place to place in the country, it is important that a specialist grower should be consulted before you buy; nurseries are usually pleased to advise. Dwarf peaches suitable for pots are sometimes advertised in the horticultural press. Apricots are slightly more difficult to crop well than peaches or nectarines.

Preparation of the soil border and training the vine can be carried out as for plants that are grown out of doors. However, under glass it is more important to keep the plants low-growing and to induce as many base branches as possible. Also pollination under glass may be poor if left to insects that find their way in. To be certain of good pollination it is better to tie a generous tuft of cotton wool to a stick, fluffing it up loosely as much as possible, and then lightly brushing it over the flowers – preferably about midday.

Good ventilation is vital to avoid

You should have a good crop of Black Hamburg grapes three years after planting

excessive temperatures, and damping-down is necessary to keep up the humidity level. Keep all water off the blossoms and off the fruit in the ripening stage, but at other times the foliage will benefit from a spray with water.

Figs

Although often thought of as exotic, good crops of figs are easily possible. The fig is usually best grown in pots since, if given an unrestricted root-run, it can smother everything else in the greenhouse. If planted in a border, the roots should be cased in with sheets of asbestos or slates or similar material. Some varieties can be placed outdoors for the summer if grown in large pots or small tubs. Always keep the plants free from weak or untidy straggly wood. Also, for best quality figs, restrict the fruit to about three per shoot. However, in the greenhouse both the current and the previous year's shoots will yield fruit. During active growth give the plants plenty of water and moderate feeding, preferably using a balanced, soluble feed. Since the roots are restricted this feeding must not be neglected, but neither should it be excessive as this will encourage rampant growth. Avoid high nitrogen feeds as these encourage lush, leafy growth.

Above: good-quality Brown Turkey figs,
Left above: fan-train Moorpark apricots against the greenhouse wall
Below left: melon Blenheim Orange

Melons

For the greenhouse it is best to grow casaba melons – those usually described in the catalogues as indoor melons. The smaller cantaloupes will grow just as well in frames.

Raise them from seed in a warm propagator in mid spring (March). The plants are best grown in large pots on greenhouse staging, using any good potting compost. Supporting wires should be fastened to the side and roof of the house, from end to end, spaced 30cm (12 in) apart. From then on culture is very similar to cucumber regarding training. There is, however, a vital difference and this is that the flowers must be pollinated. To do this first identify the female flowers by the tiny fruit behind them and pollinate by picking a male flower (that has a straight stem and no swelling) and brushing off some of its pollen onto the female flowers.

After pollination you will see the melons soon begin to swell and when it is certain that they are healthy and are continuing to grow, thin them to allow only three or four to mature on each plant. You can buy special nets to support the large, heavy fruits.

The finest flavour and aroma only comes from properly ripe fruit. The end farthest from the stalk should then be slightly soft to the touch if gently pressed with the finger. During ripening it is best to reduce watering and increase ventilation. Slight shading should be given during exceptionally bright, hot weather.

RECOMMENDED VARIETIES

PEACHES

Duke of York White-fleshed; ripens in late summer (mid July).

Hale's Early White-fleshed; ripens at the end of summer (late July).

NECTARINES

Early Rivers White-fleshed; ripens at the end of summer (late July).

Lord Napier White-fleshed; ripens in early autumn (early August).

APRICOTS

Moorpark Large, fine-flavoured fruit; deep yellow skins flushed with red; ripens in late summer to early autumn (mid July to early August).

GRAPES

Black Hamburg For cold or heated greenhouses; produces large bunches of large, fine-flavoured, black fruit.

Royal Muscadine For cold or heated greenhouses; amber-coloured, muscat-flavoured grapes.

FIGS

Brown Turkey Hardy variety, fruiting in mid autumn (early September); large, sweet, brownish-purple fruit.

MELONS

Superlative Succulent, medium-sized fruit.

Hero of Lockinge White flesh; fine flavour.

King George Richly-flavoured with orange flesh.

Emerald Gem Thick green succulent flesh with excellent flavour.

WATERING AND FEEDING GREENHOUSE PLANTS

Even today, when modern scientific knowledge should be making the issues clear, greenhouse gardeners find themselves frustrated by numerous incorrect and illogical recommendations on the subject of feeding and watering plants. Some of these are nothing more than primitive customs that have not yet been abandoned in favour of common sense.

Most pot plant failures are caused by overwatering and, to a lesser extent, by overfeeding.

WATERING

Your first important step is to learn the difference between dry, moist and waterlogged soil or compost. Moist conditions should be your aim. If the soil or compost feels moist to the touch, adheres slightly to the fingers but does not ooze free water when pressed, then it is moist. However, do not press hard when testing as this can lead to the soil becoming compacted.

How much water?

The water requirements of a plant vary – often from one day to the next. For instance when the weather is cool or dull (and also in winter when growth slows down) they need far less water – sometimes hardly any if they are dormant. When, as during summer, they have warmth and lots of light, they drink enormous quantities by comparison.

The needs of a plant are also governed by its size and vigour, and whether it is flowering, fruiting or growing vigorously. For these reasons you cannot give fixed doses of water to a plant all year round. The question 'how much water should I give my plant?' cannot be answered by a simple sentence. You must take into account the time of year, the nature of the plant and the prevailing conditions, and then decide.

When in doubt err on the side of less rather than more water. Most plants are able to survive drought to some degree and the symptoms of slight wilting are not serious; they will soon recover when watered. Excess water has a far more serious and insidious effect. The main symptoms are usually slow, sickly growth, yellowing foliage and wilting. But by this time the roots may be in an advanced state of rot, and it may be too late to save the plant by reducing watering. Note that wilting can be a symptom of both overwatering and underwatering, so test the compost.

Desert and water-loving plants

You must, of course, consider the nature of each plant and its natural habitat. But, strangely enough, this is not always a reliable guide for providing the best artificial conditions, for in the wild plants often have to struggle to survive. Many cacti and other succulents, for example, will grow vigorously if given far more water than they would get growing naturally.

On the other hand, aquatic plants need an abundance of water all year round. Not many of these are cultivated as pot plants, but if you are growing them they must be kept standing in water so that the potting compost is always wet.

Previous page: colourful staging displays result from correct care of plants
Below: symptoms of overwatering – brown edges on the leaves of a pot primula

Waterlogged soils

A waterlogged soil or compost is usually badly aerated. This encourages species of bacteria and fungi that cause rotting of plant roots. Plants with fleshy roots (like bulbs and tubers) are prone to rot if kept wet during their period of dormancy. But modern potting composts are usually based on peat; this means they will hold plenty of water without actually becoming waterlogged, and can still maintain excellent aeration. For some greenhouse plants (like columneas, orchids, bromeliads and certain palms) plenty of air with moisture is vital. You can help aeration by adding sphagnum moss, charcoal or polystyrene granules to the compost.

Insert moisture-measuring device so that the tip is completely covered by soil

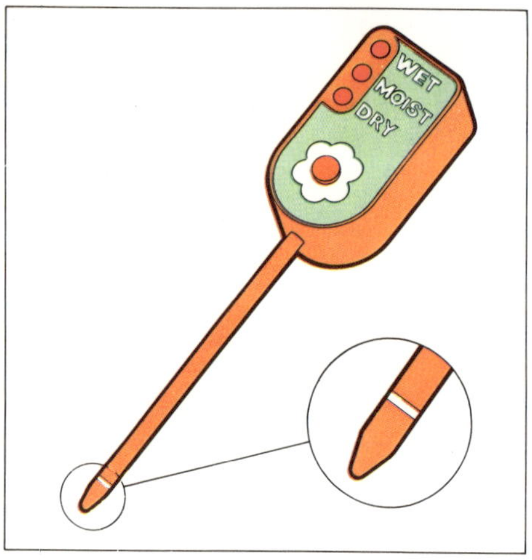

Testing for moisture

Nowadays plastic pots have become very popular. They are convenient and hygienic, being easy to clean. They check evaporation of water, so that plants growing in them need less than in clay pots. The time-honoured method of assessing whether a clay pot needs watering is to tap it with a cotton reel fixed to the end of a cane. If the compost is moist, the pot will emit a dull thud; the sound will be a higher-pitched note if the soil is dry.

Unfortunately this does not work very well with plastic pots, and a better way is to assess the moisture content by feeling the weight of the pot.

Recently, electronic devices have become available that give a rough idea of the water content of compost. They usually consist of a probe which is inserted into the compost, and a meter (or arrangement of tiny neon lights) that indicates the moisture content. With one design the scale is numbered and a booklet is supplied with the meter so that the numbers can be related to the

Rotted roots caused by excessive watering

moisture requirements of different classes of plant. As you gain experience you will find that the 'dry', 'moist' and 'wet' indications on a scale are a perfectly adequate guide.

In spite of these aids, practical experience is the best way to become confident about watering. You will eventually be able to tell all you need to know by feeling the compost with your fingers and by letting the appearance of your plants tell you what they require.

How to water

A common recommendation is to water freely, when you do water, and then leave the plant alone until the pot is almost dry again. This is a helpful guide for some plants – but not all. For example, erratic watering of this kind will not do for tomatoes as it will certainly lead to blossom end rot or cracked fruit; and many ornamental plants (such as fuchsias and begonias) may react by dropping buds or flowers.

Never give so much water that large quantities run from the drainage holes of pots or trays. This will soon carry away any soluble fertilizers in the compost. (A good way to water seed trays or pots is to use a fine-mist sprayer. This will thoroughly penetrate the compost without washing away any nutrients or loosening the seedlings.

During warm weather many plants enjoy an overhead spray. This cleans the foliage and aids plant respiration. Once again you must use your common sense as to how much water to apply. Do not spray open blooms because the tender petals can easily be damaged and brown rot or grey mould may occur. Also, in very sunny greenhouses, avoid getting water on the foliage. The droplets act like lenses to focus the sun's rays on the leaves and may cause burning.

The importance of clean water

Be careful what sort of water you use on your plants. Some people advocate rainwater; if the rainwater is clean, all well and good. Unfortunately it is often collected from roofs and stored in open tanks or butts, which rapidly become stagnant pools of pests, diseases and weed seeds. As you are probably using sterilized potting composts in your greenhouse, it is obviously foolish to water these with dirty rainwater. Mains drinking water is safer – even if it tends to be hard and limey. There are numerous greenhouse plants that object to lime, but they will suffer much more from the dangers inherent in dirty water.

Uneven watering gives split tomato fruits

If you do need soft water for special lime-hating plants, put out clean bowls just after it starts to rain, and store the rainwater in clean, closed vessels. Water that has been boiled for some time and then allowed to cool and settle will also be softer than tap water.

FEEDING

Avoid using animal manures in the greenhouse or for potting composts – unless they are a modern, sterilized, proprietary type. Crude manures can introduce many pests and diseases that can be dangerous to humans as well as to plants. Moreover, they often have few of the nutrients that plants require.

One of the main advantages of manures is that they improve soil texture, but modern seed and potting composts have body built in, usually by the addition of peat. Most pot plants need a higher ratio of nitrogen than plants grown in the soil outdoors; all proprietar posts take this into acco these products, no feedin the plants are well advanced.

The need for feeding is assessed in much the same way as watering – taking into account the vigour of the plants and the time of year. None is necessary when plants are dormant. But when plants are producing buds, flowers and fruits, some extra feeding is essential. Use a proprietary balanced fertilizer according to the maker's directions. Never give more than is suggested. 'Little and often' is a good feeding rule.

Modern feeding now takes into account the preference of some plants for acid or alkaline soils. In alkaline soils (or composts) iron, magnesium and trace elements essential to plants become 'locked in' and therefore unavailable to the plants.

These nutrients can now be restored in a special form (known as sequestered or chelated) which is easily absorbed. Avoid using hit or miss mixtures or additions of what are known as 'straight' fertilizers that supply only one or two of the basic nutrients (such as sulphate of ammonia or sulphate of potash). Properly formulated feeds for plants like tomatoes, carnations and chrysanthemums that need special nutrient ratios can be bought in proprietary form.

Foliar feeding

You can apply the basic plant nutrients (nitrogen, potassium and phosphorus) as foliar feeds – in specially formulated mixtures. A very recent product of this type includes vitamins and trace elements as well. It is particularly useful for plants that have not yet made an extensive root system, and can also be used as a general plant tonic. Seedlings, newly potted plants and cuttings often react dramatically to such feeds.

Soluble feeds

Plants can only use liquid solutions of nutrients. The quickest-acting are soluble feeds that dissolve readily in water; use these for all short-term, fast-growing plants, such as annuals and biennials. Greenhouse perennials will also benefit from liquid feeds when they are making active growth.

You can also top-dress perennials by mixing a little of a balanced, slow-acting, solid feed (such as John Innes base fertilizer or Growmore) with the top layers of the soil or compost. These will dissolve a little at each watering. Specially formulated proprietary feeds in tablet form are also obtainable.

USING THE SUB-STAGE AREA IN THE GREENHOUSE

The area under the greenhouse staging can be a very useful place for growing plants – provided it is not already being used to house garden oddments. Just how useful depends largely on the greenhouse design, but with a little planning most of these often-neglected areas can be made very productive.

Never be tempted to use the space under the staging in your greenhouse as a gardening 'glory hole'. Keep some clean bins, bags of compost, clean pots or boxes there by all means, but remember that dirty rubbish will harbour pests and diseases and make cleaning the greenhouse a tedious business.

Plants grown under the staging should not be set directly on the greenhouse floor. Cover the ground with plastic sheeting covered, in turn, with a layer of gravel or coarse sand; alternatively, place the pots on a slatted or mesh stage raised a few centimetres above the ground. This will prevent the plant roots from entering the soil, and also keep soil pests or worms from getting into the drainage holes.

Use common sense when positioning your plants; put those needing most light at the back in the case of a glass-to-ground house, and at the front when the greenhouse has a base wall.

Light areas

Undoubtedly the area under the staging is most versatile in a glass-to-ground greenhouse since it will receive plenty of light. The more light that penetrates the better, since a wider range of plants can then be accommodated. In the Dutch-light type of house, with slightly sloping sides, there is specially good illumination and plants set well back will get almost as much light as plants on the staging top. In all cases light can be increased by using slatted or mesh-topped staging. Some overhead light then usually finds its way through.

Try to prevent plant debris like dead leaves, faded flowers and drips from watering from falling off the plants on the staging onto the plants below; water or organic material left lying on plant foliage for any length of time can cause brown markings or instigate rot and fungoid growth. One way of avoiding this is to stand potted plants in plastic trays that have a layer of coarse gravel in the bottom; space the trays apart to let light through.

Dark areas

In the case of the base wall type of house the under-stage area will probably be very gloomy. This means you will have to be more selective in what you put there, but for some plants shade can be an advantage – even vital. In a few cases no light at all is wanted, for instance when blanching and forcing vegetables like chicory, rhubarb and endive. For these the area will have to be deliberately blacked out with black polythene. Where there is little light and not enough space to make the area useful for more ordinary plants, you can always grow mushrooms. These do not need light (though there is no need to black out completely) and they are easy to grow in containers filled with special compost that has been spawned by the supplier. Full growing instructions are issued with the containers.

Above: mushrooms like these Agaricus hortensis *are very easy to grow under the staging, because they do not need light. Right: sub-tropical* Calathea mackoyana *is a colourful shade-lover*

Where light is extremely poor, very many ferns will thrive and can be used simply to give decoration to what would otherwise be an uninteresting spot, or to supply cut fronds for floral decoration, or as pot ferns for the house. What type of ferns you can grow depends on the temperature of the greenhouse. It is possible to buy spores of selected varieties of hardy, half-hardy and tender ferns in separate packets, to get initial stock.

Warm greenhouses

If the greenhouse is a warm one or, at least, has a congenial temperature in winter, many exceedingly beautiful and colourful foliage plants of a sub-tropical nature will live happily under the staging

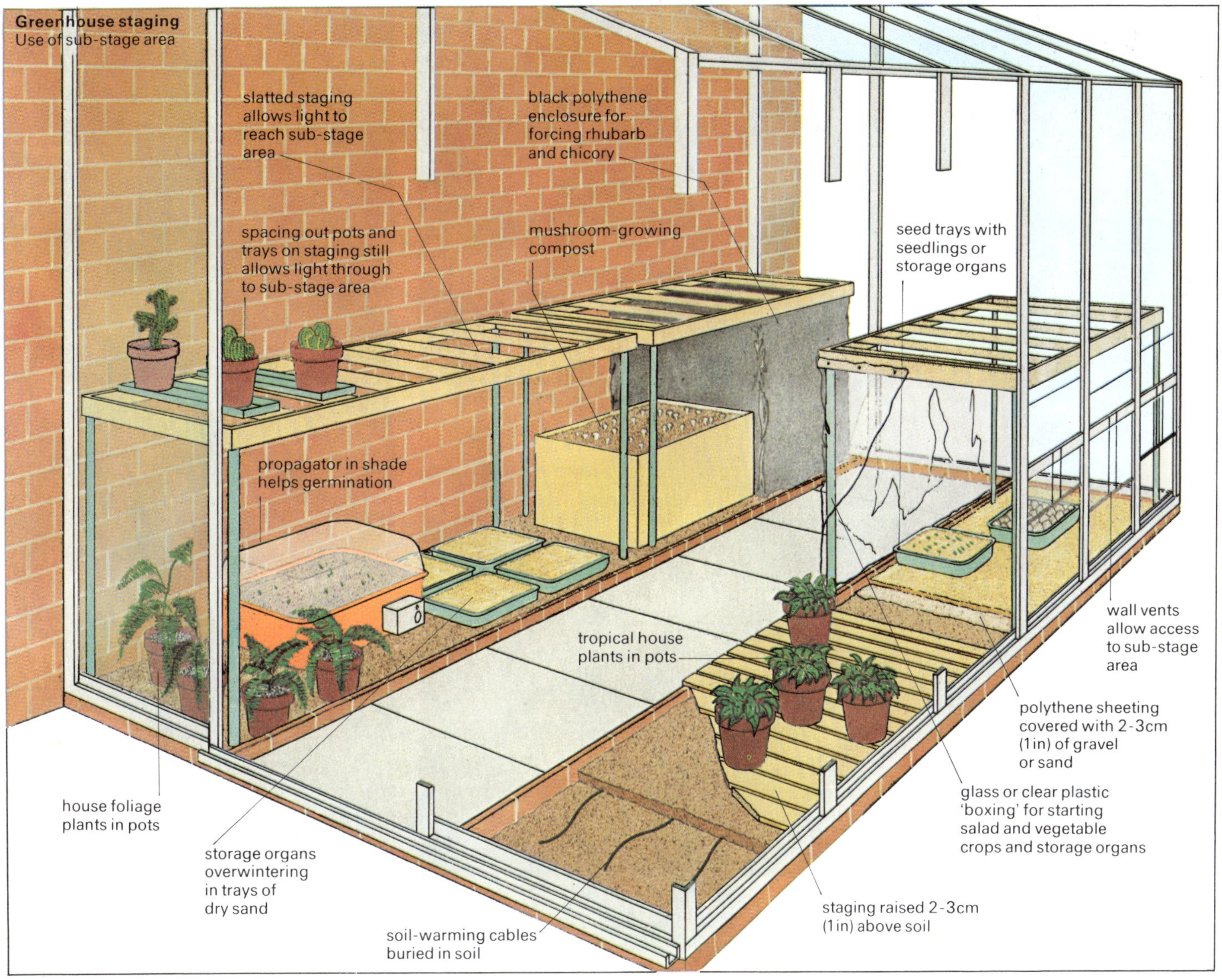

– in their natural jungle habitat they would enjoy considerable shade. Suitable plants include maranta (prayer plant), calathea, ctenanthe, foliage begonias, peperomia, *Fittonia argyroneura* and *Dieffenbachia picta* all have exotically marked and coloured leaves. Plants of the GESNERIACEAE family enjoy shade, and most of them have charming foliage and delightful flowers. These include streptocarpus (Cape primrose), sinningia (gloxinia), saintpaulia (African violet), smithiantha (temple bells), achimenes and *Rechsteineria leucotricha*.

Raising the temperature

You can raise the temperature of the area under the staging easily and cheaply, especially when the greenhouse has a base wall that will help retain warmth. In some cases the space can be 'boxed' or 'cased' with glass or plastic so that temperatures can be elevated quite considerably. The simplest method of heating is to use soil-warming cables.

In a glass-to-ground house useful early salad crops can be raised in soil-warmed beds under the staging – lettuce, beet, radish, carrot and numerous sprouting vegetables including mustard and cress. Later in the year these warmed beds can be used for starting tubers – like dahlias, begonias, sinningia (gloxinia), canna and the like – into growth and also for seed germination. Propagators can be sited under the staging where the shade will be an advantage for most forms of seed germination and for establishing cuttings.

Cold greenhouses

Where there is little or no warmth, the area can be employed for storing dormant plants over the winter and for keeping overwintering storage organs or roots such as dahlias, summer-flowering greenhouse bulbs, chrysanthemum stools and the roots of tender garden plants. Most storage organs are best kept in boxes of clean sand or peat, but many roots have to be prevented from drying out completely during winter and you should make sure you have easy access to them for regular inspection. Some designs of greenhouse have ground-level vents

Above: three sub-stage beauties, (left) Ctenanthe oppenheimiana tricolor, *(centre) smithiantha and (right)* Aeschynanthus nanus

allowing the under-stage area to be reached from the outside. This can be useful for cultivating salad crops.

Growing-on pot plants

Much of the general growing-on of pot plants can be done under the staging. Popular pot plants like cineraria, calceolaria, primula, polyanthus, cyclamen, coleus and ornamental capsicum can be housed there from the seedling stage to the size when they can be put into their final pots. For many of these plants the diffused light of the under-stage area is a great advantage and even when you move them to the top of the staging for display the glass will need to be shaded. The under-stage area is particularly useful to these plants when they are being grown on during the summer months. Most house plants, too, do not demand full light and can be raised from seed or cuttings under the staging for later removal to the house. Established house

plants can also be given a holiday under the staging from time to time – they will appreciate the humidity.

Raising bedding plants

In the glass-to-ground house the under-stage area is invaluable in late winter to mid spring (January to March) when it is time to raise bedding plants and your greenhouse tends to become very overcrowded. As well as the initial germination of bedding plants, the trays and boxes can be kept under the staging for a time until the seedlings are well established. Take care, however, that the area is not too gloomy or the seedlings may become weak and spindly. The idea is to protect the seedlings from sunlight rather than to cast them into deep shade.

Left: exotic green and white foliage of Dieffenbachia picta, *a lover of jungle-like habitat*
Right: Sinningia speciosa, *whose tubers can be started in sub-stage warmed beds*

RESTING PLANTS FOR THE WINTER

For very many plants a winter rest is essential for their continued development and success but, in the greenhouse, some plants that would naturally be growing almost all year round can also be kept dormant over the winter to economize on heating and lighting. How you treat plants as they approach their winter rest is extremely important. So, too, is the way you treat them over the winter, and how you care for storage organs like bulbs, corms, tubers and rhizomes.

Many tender plants can survive cold winters in an unheated greenhouse. For instance, many of the summer-flowering bulbs use this cool period to develop embryo flowers and leaves while appearing dormant externally. Others (like tender herbaceous plants and exotic greenhouse perennials), if kept in a dry environment, slow their growth rate right down until they are ready to flourish again in the spring.

Plants with storage organs

Plants that overwinter in the form of storage organs include all the summer-flowering bulbs, tubers such as gloxinia, begonia, and gloriosa, and rhizomes like achimenes, smithiantha (temple bells) and canna. A critical time for these comes after the flowers fade; they then begin to store the foods needed for strong growth in the following year.

In the case of bulbs the entire flower in embryo form is developed inside the bulb, starting after flowering and continuing to form until the foliage begins to wither. So at this time, care with regard to feeding and watering will reward you with a good performance after the plant is started into growth again the following year. Do not chop the foliage off bulbs or tie the leaves in knots as soon as the flowers have faded. Do all you can to keep growth luxuriant and healthy; give frequent liquid feeds, foliar feeds and pesticide sprays to keep the foliage free from pests and to build up the storage organ so that it will grow well the following year. Only when the foliage begins to die down naturally should you gradually reduce watering and feeding. In most cases you can allow the soil in the pots to dry out slowly. Then turn the pots on their sides and store the plants (dry) in this manner in a frost-free place for the winter period.

With some plants (such as tuberous-rooted begonia and gloxinia) it is better to remove the storage organs and store them in clean, dry sand after removing any adhering potting compost, dead roots and foliage. Drying out as a winter rest, however, is not a general rule. There are cases where storage organs are better kept slowly growing. A typical example is hippeastrum (often wrongly called amaryllis). This is an evergreen bulbous plant that will produce far better blooms if you give it just enough warmth and moisture to maintain the foliage; 5–7°C (40–45°F) is an adequate temperature. Leave plants with brittle tubers or rhizomes (like gloriosa and achimenes) undisturbed, and store them in pots of dry soil on their sides. These plants will have multiplied considerably during the growing season. Wait until it is time to restart them into growth in the spring before splitting or dividing them. If you damage them then they are much more likely to heal quickly, but if the organs are damaged just before the winter rest period there is a greater risk of rot setting in.

Protecting with fungicides

To help reduce the likelihood of rot or fungal attack, it often helps to dip the storage organs in a solution of benomyl and allow them to dry thoroughly before storing. Fungicidal dusts (used according to maker's instructions) can also be beneficial and there are several suitable proprietary products on the market.

Ripening before storing

Some plants, particularly those with bulbs or corms, may not flower well unless they undergo a short ripening process before storage for the winter. Typical of these is polianthes (tuberose); it likes to be given a 'sun bath' so expose it to as much sunshine as the late summer and early autumn (July and August) will provide before immersing it in dry sand for the winter.

Place dahlia tubers in the greenhouse (with their stems pointing downwards) for a few weeks, to allow all sap to drain before storing in dry peat or sand. Cut back chrysanthemum growth, lift the plants, free the roots from soil and then store them in trays of sterilized potting compost until it is time to restart them in late spring or early summer (April–May).

Herbaceous and pot plants

When herbaceous plants and perennial pot plants in the greenhouse begin to slow down or reach dormancy in autumn, you can prune them back – not too severely – so that they will not take up so much storage room. Most plants with ordinary roots should not be allowed to go completely dry over the winter but, on the other hand, never let them get too moist. Much also depends on winter temperature, and where this is very low – perhaps approaching freezing – keep the plants almost dry. Wet, cold conditions are certain to cause root rot. Tender plants like greenhouse fuchsia, pelargonium and even the more exotic subjects like strelitzia, *Nerium oleander*, maranta (prayer plant) and aphelandra, will usually survive a very cold winter if kept on the dry side. Some, like maranta and other foliage plants, may come through the cold of winter looking the worse for wear, but

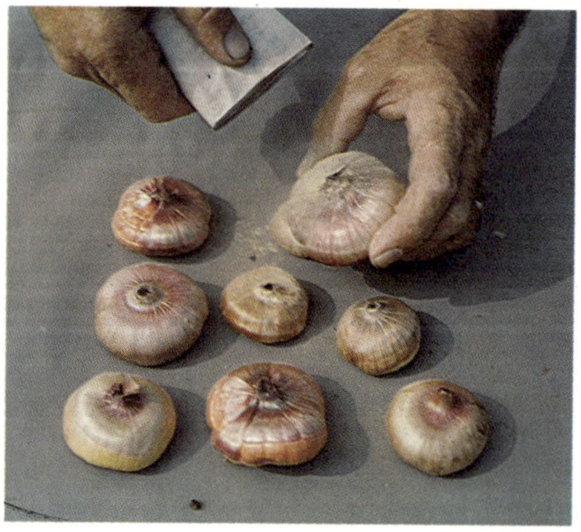

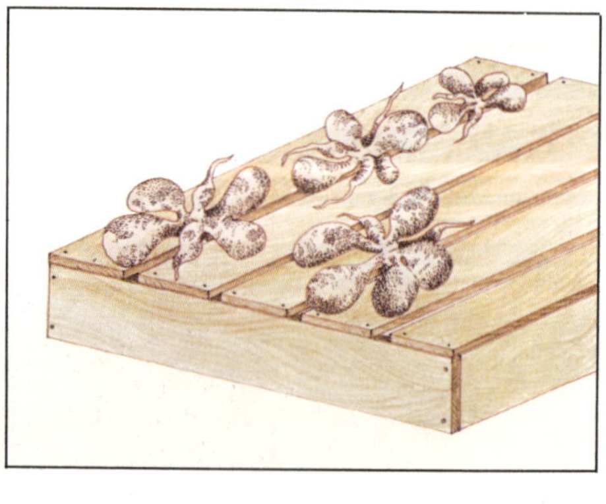

Above right: a dusting with fungicide is an aid against rot; right: drain sap from dahlias before storing

new growth rapidly occurs in spring when you recommence watering. Shabby growth can then be removed.

If you grow standard fuchsias, take great care not to rest them to the extent that they die back. Although growth will resume in spring the head could fail and new shoots come from the lower stem.

When whips (the supporting stems of standards) are being grown on from rooted cuttings, they must not be allowed to rest too much. Keep them growing slowly by maintaining adequate temperature and moisture. This applies to all plants grown as standards including abutilon, pelargonium and chrysanthemum (marguerite).

Greenhouse atmosphere in winter

The greenhouse atmosphere is also important to the well-being of resting and overwintering plants. It is vital to avoid excessive humidity, so provide plenty of ventilation whenever weather permits. Home greenhouse owners tend to be afraid to ventilate. Winters in Britain are rarely freezing for long periods and often there are very mild spells. Since most people grow plants needing little more than frost-free conditions there is no reason why ventilation is not possible much of the time.

Special care is needed if you heat the greenhouse with paraffin heaters. Oil produces about its own volume of water on combustion. This leads to much condensation and a very wet atmosphere unless there is adequate ventilation. In such conditions dormant plants are very prone to fungal troubles. The main enemy is grey mould (botrytis) that attacks both dead and living vegetable matter. It forms a greyish-brown furry mould that, when disturbed, distributes clouds of dust-like spores and so spread the fungus to other plants.

If your paraffin heater is fitted with a humidity trough, do not fill it with water in winter and, of course, never damp down the greenhouse. To help protect resting plants from grey mould in winter a wise routine measure is to fumigate (on a still day) with TCNB smokes. In winter this is better than the use of wet sprays, since it avoids raising humidity.

If you have an automatic watering system, allow it to go dry, or shut it off, for the winter months and water by hand. This will lessen the danger of plants – and air – becoming too moist.

Fumigation protects against grey mould, a common infection in winter

COMMON PESTS AND DISEASES IN THE GREENHOUSE

Although pests and diseases are generally easier to control under glass than in the open, they will multiply and spread more freely unless you make routine checks and take prompt action. In addition, whereas winter in the outdoor garden is a fairly trouble-free time, many common pests and diseases can be troublesome all year round in the greenhouse.

A clean and tidy greenhouse will often deter many pests and diseases. By *not* storing rubbish and garden oddments there, you deprive pests of excellent hiding places, and by throwing away dead foliage and flowers you can discourage fungus diseases such as moulds, mildews and rusts. Make a daily inspection of the underside of the foliage; many pests and diseases make their first appearance here. Discard plants that are sickly for unknown reasons; they can endanger others.

Plants with pale or distorted flowers or foliage (sometimes stunted or mottled, or with striped blooms that fail to open properly) may be suffering from one or other of a number of virus diseases. These diseases can be spread by sap-sucking insects (like greenfly), by knives or scissors, or by your fingers. There is no cure for virus diseases and affected plants are best burned. Tomatoes are especially vulnerable, and ideally grown alone.

Flying pests

Many familiar garden pests invade the greenhouse. Those that fly can enter through the vents. As a good preventive measure, fit screens of muslin to greenhouse vents in summer. This will stop butterflies and moths getting in; the eggs they lay may turn overnight into caterpillars that can do enormous damage before you spot them. Birds can also enter through the vents and may do much damage to plants, besides injuring themselves while trying to escape.

Crawling pests

'Creepy crawlies' may be brought indoors on the bottom of pots that have been standing in the garden. Slugs and snails are easily controlled by the usual baits used outdoors. These pests will often

may not realize that earwigs are the culprits, and the cause of the damage will remain a mystery. Chrysanthemums need special protection so use BHC dusts liberally. Ant bait is also often effective against earwigs, and can be put in possible hiding places.

Aphides and whitefly

Aphides (or plant lice) are a group of insects that include greenfly and blackfly as well as numerous other closely-related pests that suck plant sap. Few plants are safe from attack, so take routine preventive measures. Systemic pesticides give long-term protection under glass, and there are numerous quick-acting products now sold. Those containing malathion act very quickly, but the old-fashioned liquid derris pesticides are still efficient and very safe.

Above left: earwigs hide during the day in cracks and crevices in the greenhouse, emerging at night to seek out their prey
Left: the aftermath of an earwig attack on the flower petals of a chrysanthemum
Top: aphides clustered on a rose bud
Above right: the common garden snail, unless controlled, will climb up glass walls of a greenhouse and eat seedlings
Above: whitefly sucking sap from a leaf

climb up the glass sides and gain access to pots and trays on the staging. Just one slug or snail can eat a whole tray of small seedlings during the night.

Never stand pots directly on the ground soil of the greenhouse (or outdoors). Stand them on sharp shingle, tile, stone or plastic. This prevents worms entering through the drainage holes. If they do get in, the constant disturbance to the roots will make plants wilt.

Ants have a similar effect, but can be eradicated with a proprietary ant bait; there are several kinds (all very effective) on the market. Woodlice are not, as many believe, harmless to plants and they are especially damaging to seedlings. You will find these pests hiding among greenhouse rubbish. Dusts containing BHC will control them.

Earwigs can hide in the smallest cracks and crevices of the greenhouse structure. There they stay unseen during the day. At night they fly out (it is often not known that they can fly) and eat plants – flowers particularly – leaving the petals holed and ragged. Because they operate at night you

Whitefly has become a serious greenhouse pest. It often infests outdoor weeds, like nettles, and will then be a source of trouble to any nearby greenhouse in summer, and overwinter in greenhouses that are free from frost. In appearance, the fly is minute, with pale grey wings. Like aphides, it sucks sap and also causes leaves and surfaces below them to become sticky with honeydew secretion. This often encourages a growth of black mould which, though not harmful, makes the plants look most unsightly.

Fortunately, a recently-introduced pesticide called resmethrin is particularly effective for whitefly control, and generally useful for other similar pests. Apply it by spraying. Alternatively, malathion and BHC smokes can be used.

Thrips and red spider mite

The tiny thrips cause foliage to become marked with whitish patches that are often encircled by dark specks. To check for their presence, put white paper below the foliage and then shake the leaves. The thrips fall off and you will be able to see them squirming against the white background. Most general pesticides will control thrips; systemics will be absorbed into the plant tissues and remain effective for a long time.

If, during summer, foliage becomes yellow and mottled and tends to fall, suspect a pest called red spider mite. If you look at the undersides of the leaves with a powerful magnifying glass, what you will see (if the pest is present) is a very tiny, mite-like creature and minute round, whitish eggs. In large and severe infestations the mites will show up as many thousands of pale-reddish 'spiders' spinning fine webbing. Since they enjoy hot, dry conditions, you can discourage them by keeping up humidity. Fumigation with azobenzene is very effective, but

Right: the red spider mite will attack foliage, turning it yellow and mouldy
Below: thrips, too, attack foliage but can be controlled by a general pesticide
Below right: the tiny sciarid fly, whose maggot will infest compost unless killed
Bottom: tomato plant, showing the damage caused by sciarid fly maggots

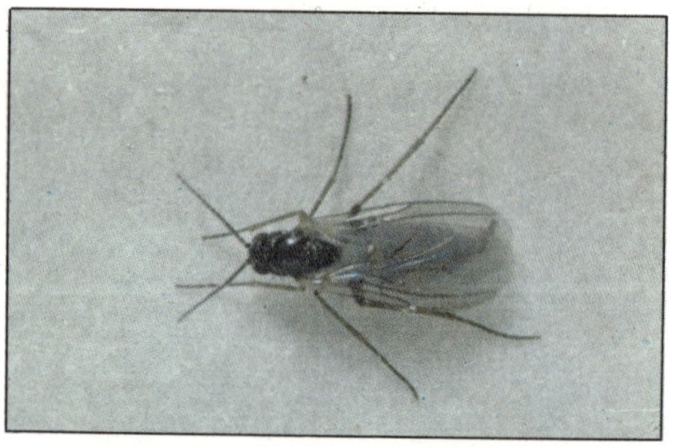

numerous greenhouse plants may be slightly damaged by this treatment, so be sure to check with the maker's label. Liquid extract of derris (not dusts) is a good general control if applied thoroughly.

Sciarid fly
With the now widespread use of peat composts, sciarid fly maggots are becoming increasingly common. These are tiny, whitish, wriggling worms infesting the composts, or the peat spread over staging. There will also be tiny flies about – the 'worms' being their maggots. These maggots can do enormous harm to plant roots, especially seedlings, and may also eat lower parts of stems. Moist conditions encourage them. Water with a malathion insecticide, but try to keep moistûre lower subsequently. The flies must be killed since they are the source of the trouble. Most general insecticides will do this.

Fungus diseases
Two very common diseases caused by fungi are damping-off of seedlings and grey mould. If pricked-out seedlings topple over, it is a sure sign of damping-off. Always water in with Cheshunt compound as a precaution. Damping-off is less prevalent now that modern sterilized composts are used. Grey mould (or botrytis) will attack both living and dead plant tissue. It is usually seen as a brownish-grey, furry mould which, if disturbed, distributes a cloud of fine 'dust' – the spores that spread the disease. On tomatoes the mould will cause flowers and fruit to drop, and fruit may be marked with small whitish rings with a black speck at the centre. Lettuce and chrysanthemums are especially prone to attack. To check the disease, increase ventilation and, at night, lower the humidity. Benlate sprays and TCNB fumigation are excellent controls and preventives of grey mould.

Using pesticides
Whenever possible, buy pesticides especially designed for greenhouse use. Read the labels carefully because some plants can be damaged by certain pesticides. In certain cases you can simply remove these plants from the greenhouse, or cover them with plastic bags, while other plants are being treated. Follow all safety precautions exactly (especially where edible crops are concerned) and, in the enclosed atmosphere of your greenhouse, take care that you do not inhale any pesticides yourself.

THE MODERN CONSERVATORY

STYLES OF CONSERVATORY

Here we look at some other types of conservatory structures and how you can link them with both house and garden. The following examples illustrate both the traditional and the new in a range of styles that can be suitably adapted to a contemporary setting.

A feature such as a conservatory is something of a hybrid, being neither a free-standing greenhouse nor an integral part of the building. It fulfills both functions in part, acting as an informal living room that can be richly furnished with vegetation.

Long ago conservatories were invariably ornate and usually large, needing a corresponding budget to maintain them in peak condition. Today our style of living has changed and houses are smaller and more intimate. It makes sense therefore to build a conservatory that will not only preserve the form of its parent building but remain within your financial limits as well.

Once you have budgeted you can think about the style and possible position of

Left and previous page: this custom-built conservatory room was designed as a straightforward addition for an owner who wanted a room to use more as a living room-sun lounge than a plant conservatory with the latter's implications of humidity. The simple timber structure follows the lines of the house to provide continuity. Walls are brick-based with bricks carefully selected to match those of the original house wall – now part of the interior

the new feature. The latter will be determined to some extent by the direction of the sun and by the point of access from the house. In general terms however a conservatory will look more at home in a situation where it extends the visual line of a roof, fitting snugly into the angle formed by a projecting wall. This technique has been well exploited in the example shown at left.

White is the traditional colour for interior and exterior painting, but remember to use common sense and respect existing colour schemes when making your choice.

Planting is just as important outside the conservatory as inside and provides the ideal link between house and garden. Notice how foliage softens virtually all the examples shown, the walls becoming incidental and the view synonymous with the garden.

We have already emphasized the importance of a well-paved, non-slip floor and it is worth bearing in mind that the choice of a surface does much to influence the mood of the overall composition. Natural materials such as slate or stone tend to look and feel cool; they are traditional, as many of the fine historical conservatories bear witness, but on the debit side they tend to become slippery unless regularly scrubbed down.

As with any variety of floor paving, make sure that the joints are carefully grouted in the case of tiles, and neatly pointed for brickwork. The stable-type paviors are attractive, but rarely used these days. They are dark blue and the size of bricks, the surface being divided into cubes to give a finished effect not unlike bars of chocolate laid side by side.

Below and right: architect Stephen Gardiner's glass-walled structure acts as a total contrast to the owner's more conventional red brick house. The informal arrangement of pot plants, climbers and uncut grass softens the dramatic tent-like framework. Although it appears free-standing, the conservatory is in fact connected to the house by a glass-walled walk-through, a solid wood slat ceiling emphasizing its light, open atmosphere

Whatever the flooring, make sure that levels are true; with a slight fall there should be a gully available for drainage.

So far we have suggested primarily traditional materials and methods of construction. Since the 1920s there have been striking advances in building technology and this has certainly been echoed in the design of the conservatory's close relation – the greenhouse. It is surprising therefore that so few conservatories take full advantage of such obvious developments as lightweight alloys, geodetic (dome-shaped) construction, and improved glazing techniques. Where conventional ideas are set aside, the results can be not only striking but eminently practical, as shown on the previous page, where the self-contained outside conservatory room is linked to the house by a glass-walled walk-through.

There is no rule that says a conservatory should be at ground level. Many flat-dwellers have no direct access to a garden and here there is obviously scope for a planned conversion that can fulfill a variety of functions.

In the final analysis, should you feel that a modern approach is out of keeping with your own environment, and should you also be able to afford a substantial budget, it might be worth considering a conservatory designed and built by a specialist firm. Here the expertise of craftsmen is brought into play and a superb finished result may be achieved.

Traditional designs can be recreated using up-to-date techniques, thus providing a visually-appropriate structure according to the style of the setting.

If you are lucky enough to own such a conservatory, it is important to handle the situation with sympathy. In other words, the whole setting must be considered as a design exercise. There is nothing worse than a superb building that sits in a poorly-planned area of crazy paving and dwarf walling.

Far left, below: a traditional design that would blend well with most settings, by the conservatory specialists Richardsons of Darlington. It serves equally well as an extra living room or plant conservatory-cum-sun room.

Far left, bottom: built out and at a lower level, this conservatory interior provides plenty of room for a dining or work table area. The 3-tier jardinière with trellised back gives scope for extra plants without taking up valuable floor space

Left, below: there is nothing harsh about this conservatory; its delicate glazing bars and fanlight blend well with the period-style house. Brick paviors and age-old York stone combine with climbers and plants to produce a charming atmosphere

Below: the contemporary approach at its best in a two-tone colour scheme with elegant furniture and dramatic plants. This above-ground conservatory room with its view of sky and chimney pots provides a feeling of space rare in the city

THE CONSERVATORY ROOM

You may have an old conservatory in need of renovation or a spare room that you can adapt to the benefit of plants and people alike. Here we present our ideas to show you how to make a charming conservatory room and cultivate plants within.

Little can be done to prevent the disappearance of the larger houses and their accompanying conservatories that are often vast and separate from the main building. They were expensive to keep up in their heyday and the expense of running such places in modern times is formidable.

But the other types of conservatory – annexes to the house and of more modest proportions – are still in evidence and need not share the same fate as their larger counterparts. These smaller buildings, originally conceived in Victorian times, vary greatly both in shape and style. Some still date back to that era and are easily recognized by their highly ornate design, domed roofs, moulded iron gantries and pillars. But with the passage of time styles have changed.

A true conservatory should be more than simply a home for plants, it should also provide an extra living room, a pleasant place for tea, for dinner, for friends, for relaxation – an oasis. So if you have such a spot, why not rescue it from the clutter of old toys, lawn-mowers and bric-à-brac? As long as it's not in such a

state of disrepair that it really defies restoration, there is no excuse for not refurbishing what has become little more than a storage area.

Providing heat

Nowadays heating should not be a problem as long as your conservatory is a half-brick structure, as most of the older types are, and it is built onto the house wall so that frost is unlikely to creep in. Anyhow, efficient paraffin heaters are available today that are very cheap to run and will prevent this.

If you can go to the expense of providing extra warmth, the plant world is at your command, and you will have an enviable display of plants during winter. However, being practical and with your bank balance in mind, we will describe a simple frost-free conservatory.

The basic requirements

Naturally, you could lavish money on the interior design of your conservatory, but all you really need is a water tap and a central paved or non-slip floor on which to arrange your furniture. Tiled floors are expensive and beautiful but may be treacherous when wet.

Open beds around the interior perimeter of the conservatory should be left and are best edged with kerbings or bricks; railway sleepers are a good alternative – all will prevent soil spillage. Include greenhouse staging along one side but do keep the house wall free so that climbing plants can be shown off to full advantage. The borders need to be wide enough – say 90cm (3 ft) – to accommodate a reasonable range of plants for year-round flowering. Always remember that in an ordinary greenhouse the plants are the sole occupants and you the caretaker. In the true conservatory you and your plants share a home.

Problems of space

If space is limited, you may have to forget about borders altogether and grow plants in tubs, but don't be discouraged. Get the largest tubs you can and try to keep to one size. If you're going to paint them, stick to one colour such as plain white; nothing looks worse than a motley assortment of pots, urns and planters in all the colours of the rainbow. Do not compete artificially with the brilliant, natural colour of your plants.

If, on the other hand, you have plenty of room, a small pool built in the centre of the conservatory, with perhaps a fountain playing merrily away, would give a superb focal point. But, as a word of warning, border the pool with a low, wide wall, say 45cm (18 in) high and 23cm (9 in) wide. This should stop children in particular from taking an unexpected bath and save any fish with which you may have stocked your pool from undue alarm. A pool is not advisable if you have small children.

Types of furnishings

Your next adventure will be to choose furniture for the conservatory. The choice is wide and really a matter for your own taste. Upholstered styles, however, must be excluded. Conservatories are of necessity humid and with all the water you're going to be dispensing, stuffed settees or chairs will soon be reduced to little more than culture media for a host of moulds. But you can make a free choice from metal, wood and cane, or plastics.

Tubs and urns come in a vast range of styles, colours and materials. Try to match your tubs with your furniture to get the best effect. Empty wooden tubs and concrete urns are light enough to lift about but filled with 25kg (56 lb) of compost this is no fun. Fibreglass ones, modern or classical reproductions, are light and extremely tough.

Planted-out conservatory room with space for relaxation and entertainment

The positioning of your furniture must depend on how you have laid out your beds and pots. If you have made a central focal point by using a free-standing tree or pool, don't clutter the conservatory. Try placing a bench or settee with its back to one of the borders or putting a low coffee table in front with two chairs on either side. This will enable you to view and enjoy the greater part of the room from one position.

Plants for the conservatory

Having organized your basic structure, don't spend all your money on furnishings before stocking up with plants. When entertaining in your conservatory room you can always import furniture from other rooms for the occasion.

Wall shrubs and climbers

You should now mount the house wall with wires or a trellis since most of the plants for this wall will cling by tendrils, or via twine, or be low-growing shrub types. The border next to the wall can be narrow – 60cm (24 in) in width is ample. But it is best to dig it out to a depth of 45–60cm (18–24 in) and, along with the other borders, fill it with compost such as J.I. No 3. Try to use evergreen climbers as bare stems are out of place in a conservatory where the last thing you want is a feeling of bleakness.

Key to planting plan

1 *Jasminum polyanthum*
2 *Trachycarpus fortunei*
3 Jacaranda
4 *Prostranthera rotundifolia*
5 *Gerbera jamesonii*
6 *Hibiscus rosa-sinensis*
7 *Tibouchina semidecandra*
8 Protea
9 *Clivia miniata*
10 *Strelitzia reginae*
11 *Grevillea rosmarinifolia*
12 *Bletilla striata*
13 *Nerium oleander*
14 *Grevillea robusta*
15 *Salvia leucantha*
16 *Phoenix canariensis*
17 *Nerium oleander*
18 *Rhodochiton atrosanguineum*
19 *Hibiscus rosa-sinensis*
20 Bougainvillea
21 *Agave americana*

Conservatories in corner areas can be laid out with an adaptation of this plan simply by following the diagonal **A–B**.

Conservatory
Plan

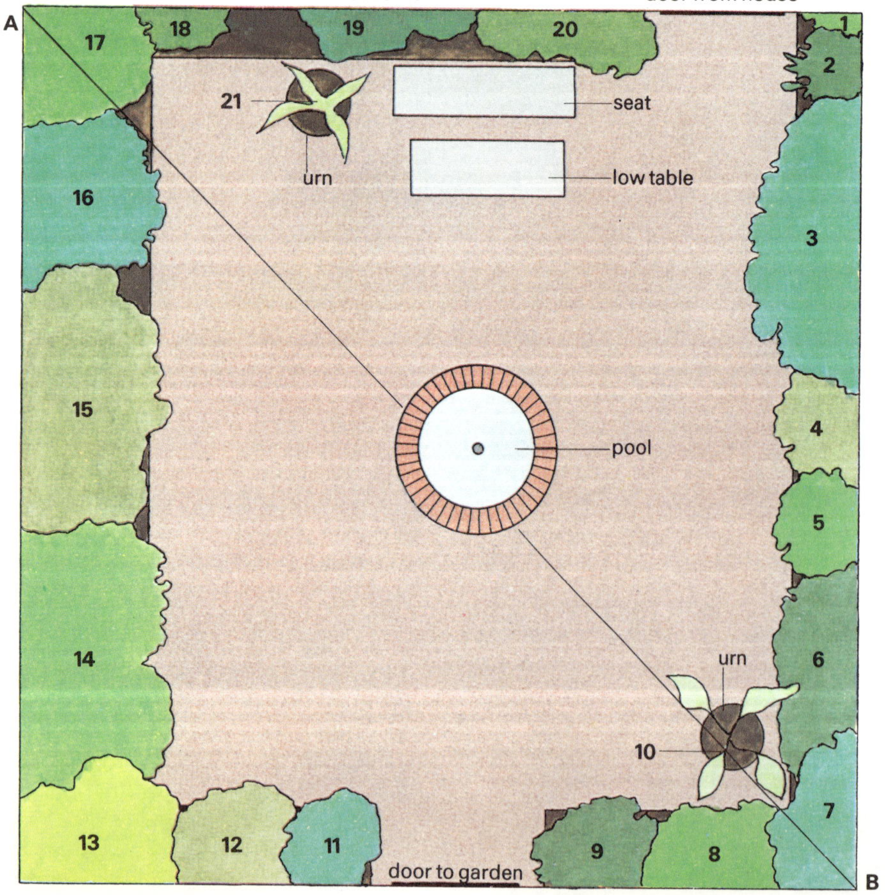

The winter-flowering jasmine *Jasminum polyanthum* is easy, reliable and astonishingly vigorous too. The clusters of starry, heavily banana-scented white flowers will fill the whole place with an exotic perfume from early to mid spring (February to late March). You will rarely see it flower as you will if you grow it like this. It needs plenty of water so don't let it dry out. You should also cut it back severely after flowering, otherwise the whole wall will be taken over.

Left: Plumbago capensis *remains in bloom throughout the summer*
Below: the showy Bougainvillea glabra
Below right: Gloriosa glabra

Albizia lophantha (sometimes known as the pink siris, or Nemu tree) is a lovely shrub when grown against a wall. The finely-divided leaves are attractive in themselves but when the pale lemon, fluffy flowers appear in winter (borne in profusion from December onwards), it is a truly magnificent sight. When seen in the half light or dusk, these flowers possess an almost luminous, ethereal quality. It will grow fast and if you need to prune it remove only the previous year's wood immediately after flowering. Albizia is closely related to acacia and so hates hard pruning and may die back as a result.

Streptosolen jamesonii is a loose-growing shrub that needs support. Orange flowers appear in large clusters from early to late summer (May to July) after which you can prune it. It's a forgiving plant and copes with pruning surgery quite well. Watch out for greenfly though. They seem to be very fond of this plant, and whitefly have been known to cause problems as well. Sprayings of malathion at five-day intervals over a couple of weeks will soon put paid to them.

Plumbago capensis (Cape leadwort) is superb for clothing walls. Its showy heads of light-blue flowers appear throughout most of the summer. *P.c.* Alba is a white form that some people prefer.

Eccremocarpus scaber (Chilean glory flower), a type of climbing plant that becomes woody, is to be recommended. It is a vigorous plant and produces scarlet and yellow flowers throughout the British summer. Do not be afraid to cut it back hard each year. It can become untidy if left to its own devices. A rare yellow form, *E.s.* Lutea, can sometimes be found.

Rhodochiton atrosanguineum (purple bells) is a curious though unspectacular climber that is well worth trying. This quaint plant with slender stems bears drooping, blackish-purple flowers in summer and makes an unusual display.

Passiflora caerulea, the common blue passion flower, should in no circumstances be planted under glass because it is far too vigorous. It grows well on a sunny wall out of doors unless you live in a particularly cold area. It is better to make room for *P. antioquiensis* (or *Tacsonia van-volxemii*), one of the red passion flowers. It will grow and flower well when established and is best trained up the walls and across the roof so that the hanging red flowers can be seen to their best advantage. *P. racemosa*, that has scarlet and purple flowers, is worth establishing. Both require a lot of room, though, and do take a while to settle in before producing flowers.

Another climber that can be shy about coming into flower when young is, surprisingly, one of the honeysuckles, *Lonicera hildebrandiana*. It is far too tender for all but the warmest areas but, where space allows, this giant honey-

suckle should be grown. Huge, leathery leaves, 15–18cm (6–7 in) long, make the plant seem uncharacteristic of the family. But when you see the 10–15cm (4–6 in) long, creamy-white flowers changing to yellow and occasionally flushed with orange, there is no mistaking it or its truly delightful perfume.

Two climbers you might like to bear in mind that do better out of pots are the *Bougainvillea glabra* and *Gloriosa rothschildiana*. The bougainvillea and its many hybrids with showy bracts of pink, salmon-pink, orange, purple and white, is spectacular in summer. *G. rothschildiana* is a climbing lily that dies back to a tuber each autumn. The reflexed orange and yellow sepals and petals live up to their name of 'glorious'.

Border shrubs and perennials

The borders along the sides of the conservatory can be planted with numerous shrubs and herbaceous plants. Always treat this part of the conservatory as though you were planting a shrub border in the garden, and plan beforehand. The following suggestions will help you to make your choice.

Nerium oleander (oleander) is a large leafy shrub bearing pink, rose-red or white flowers that can be single, semi-double or double. There are also variegated forms that are worth searching for. Always choose a scented variety: some plants offered for sale are unscented and the loss of that heavy, vanilla-like odour is a great pity.

Hibiscus rosa-sinensis comes in such a wide range of colours nowadays that a choice is difficult. Large flowers, both double and single, can be had in deep rose, scarlet, orange, maroon and even yellow. They'll grow into sturdy bushes in

Above left: long-flowering Tibouchina urvilleana *need pruning back in spring*
Above: Clivia miniata, *the Kaffir lily*
Right: Protea nerifolia, *upright in habit, likes full sunlight under glass*
Below right: daisy-like Gerbera jamesonii
Far right: Agave americana *Variegata may take 50 years to reach maturity*

the border and these, together with the oleanders, will probably need pruning after a while. However, do not worry if you prune in mid spring (March) as they will come to no harm.

One shrub you should not be without is *Tibouchina urvilleana* (Brazilian spider flower). It has large, velvety, deep purple flowers right up till early winter (November) and the soft, hairy leaves develop orange tints before falling. Cut it back hard in mid spring (March) to prevent it from dominating a whole border.

You will probably be familiar with that fast-growing plant *Grevillea robusta* (silk bark oak). Where space allows it should certainly be allowed to develop. Apart from its silky, lacinate leaves it can, when old and large enough, produce clusters of bright orange flowers.

The smaller *G. rosmarinifolia* is a cousin that bears no resemblance in size or leaf. It grows to 1·8m (6 ft) and looks almost gorse-like from a distance. The flowers are freely produced even on a young plant and are bright red.

Palms, despite what some people would have us believe, love to have a free root run and you should try *Trachycarpus fortunei* (fan palm) that grows slowly up to 3m (10 ft) or so, *Neanthe bella* (dwarf parlour palm) that rarely exceeds 90cm (3 ft) and the feathery *Phoenix canariensis*. The last will eventually become very large so you will either have

to take an axe to it or have the roof raised. There is, however, a dwarf form, *P. roebelinii*, that grows slowly to 1·8m (6 ft).

Other shrubs that will do well in your border are proteas, with their huge quilled flowers and stiff, upright growth. They require full sunlight to do well and their root systems are much happier in a border than in a pot. Jacarandas are primarily foliage plants with soft, ferny leaves, but given time they will produce clusters of lovely blue flowers.

Prostantheras are not only valuable for their aromatic foliage but also for the freedom with which they produce their lovely flowers. *P. rotundifolia*, a neat, little shrub that grows to 90cm (3 ft), bears masses of light heliotrope flowers in mid spring (March). *Salvia leucantha* is a far cry from its edible cousin *S. officinalis* (common sage). The stems and undersides of the leaves are thickly white-felted, so too are the flower spikes, but it is the intense magenta flowers seen through this white felt that make the plant unique.

There are other plants besides shrubby ones that will enhance your conservatory. *Gerbera jamesonii* (Barberton daisy) with daisy-like flowers produced almost throughout the year is essential. Modern strains will give many shades of yellow, orange and red. *Clivia miniata*, one of the Kaffir lilies, is a joy in spring. It has umbels of orange and yellow flowers amid its leathery foliage. Orchids are hard to ignore and one in particular – ideal for conservatory borders – is *Bletilla striata*, the Japanese Geisha orchid. Its small, 4cm ($1\frac{1}{2}$ in), flowers are glistening purple and, when given a free undisturbed root run, the plants can produce up to 15 flowers per growth on 60cm (24 in) stems.

In shadier spots all manner of ferns will grow to sizes never possible in pots. *Adiantum cuneatum* Fragrantissimum (maidenhair fern), *Asplenium bulbiferum* (spleenwort) and *Cyrtomium falcatum* (holly fern) are best.

Plants for staging, tubs or urns

If staging is incorporated in the conservatory, you can use this for temporary displays of annuals or plants such as begonia, charm and cascade chrysanthemums, cyclamen, gloxinia and primulas. These, together with forced bulbs, will help to increase the floral display throughout the year.

Some plants are of such architectural value they look better singled out in tubs or urns. *Strelitzia reginae*, the fabulous bird of paradise flower with spikes of blue and orange, is particularly fine. *Agave americana* Variegata, the variegated century plant, is a beauty when large but beware of its vicious spine-tipped leaves.

Zantedeschia (arum lilies) always outgrow their welcome when given freedom so restrict them to a tub where their handsome leaves can best be appreciated. There are yellow and pink forms too.

These are the ones to buy: *Zantedeschia aethiopica*, *Z. albo-maculata* (both white but the latter has spotted leaves), *Z. elliottiana* (yellow with white-spotted leaves) and *Z. rehmannii* (pink arum).

Outdoor planting

Having looked at plants within the conservatory, you must not neglect the world outside. Your new 'room' should not just be part of the house but part of the garden too. Blend them together by training slightly tender shrubs along the outside walls of the conservatory where they will flourish in the protection of the walls. Plant *Callistemon linearis* and *C. citrinus* in a dry, sunny position. These scarlet bottle brushes will provide a riot of colour in summer and their flexuous stems lend themselves admirably to training along a wall.

Acacia verticillata (prickly Moses) is a wonderful plant that hates severe cold but, if trained along a sunny wall, it will astonish you with a show of canary-yellow miniature brushes in late spring (April) and early summer (May).

A single garland of the purple-leaved *Vitis vinifera* Purpurea (Teinturier grape), trained along the guttering on a wire, is very effective. Cut it back hard to prevent light being shut out.

Maintenance and protection

All plants, whether in pots or in the border, will be all the happier for a liquid feed at 10-day intervals in spring and summer. But if your borders are so large as to make this impractical, then a top dressing with a standard fertilizer will do. Make sure none of your plants become dry at the roots and if you can spray overhead daily so much the better.

The more common pests you will encounter and have to deal with include aphides, red spider mites and whitefly. They are all sap-sucking pests that if allowed to multiply will cause serious damage. Red spider only thrives in a dry atmosphere so overhead mistings of water are the best means of protection.

Aphides and whitefly appear at any time and the best way to control them is to use one of the many insecticides available. Always make sure you follow the instructions carefully, otherwise more harm can be caused by pesticide than pest.

So, at its best, the conservatory is an indoor garden, a real link between the house and the outdoor garden, and a living room that can give lasting pleasure, comfort and enjoyment.

Above right: Chamaedorea elegans, *dwarf mountain palm. Right:* Callistemon citrinus

BIBLIOGRAPHY

Bartrum, Douglas *Exotic Plants* (John Gifford Ltd, London 1970)

Eigeldinger, O. and Murphy, L. S. *Orchids* (John Gifford Ltd, London 1971)

Flawn, Louis N. *Gardening with Cloches* (John Gifford Ltd, London 1972)

Menage, R. H. *Greenhouse Gardening* (Penguin, London 1977)

Menage, R. H. *Growing Indoor Plants* (Ward Lock, London 1977)

Menage, R. H. *The Unheated Greenhouse* (Thorsons Publishers Ltd, Wellingborough 1978)

Mossman, Keith *Indoor Light Gardening* (William Luscombe, London 1977)

Oldale, Adrienne and Peter *Growing Food Under Glass* (David and Charles, Newton Abbott 1978)

Price, Bob *Today's Guide to Greenhouse Gardening* (William Luscombe, London 1975)

Puttock, A. G. *Lovely Fuchsias* (John Gifford Ltd, London 1971)

Rochford, Thomas *The Rochford Book of House Plants* (Faber & Faber, London 1973)

Schonfelder, Bruno and Fischer, W. J. *Cacti and Indoor Plants* (Harold Starke Ltd, London 1972)

Shewell-Cooper, W. E. *The Beginners Guide to Pot Plants* (John Gifford Ltd, London 1971)

Sitch, Peter *Carnations* (John Gifford Ltd, London 1975)

Walls, Ian G. *The Complete Book of the Greenhouse* (Ward Lock, London 1973)

Witham Fogg, H. G. *Geraniums and Pelargoniums* (John Gifford Ltd, London 1975)

Woolman, John *Chrysanthemum Culture* (H. Woolman Ltd, 1977)

Wright, Michael (Ed.) *The Complete Indoor Gardener* (Pan Books, London 1974)

INDEX

Page numbers in italic refer to illustrations